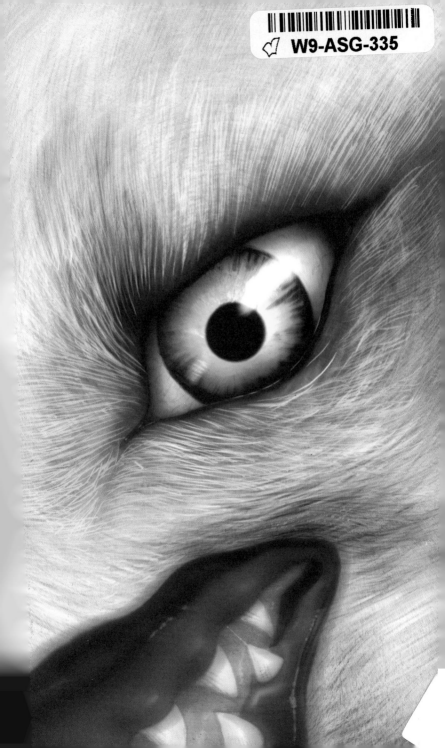

W9-ASG-335

JINX ON THE
DIVIDE

JINX ON THE
DIVIDE

Elizabeth Kay
Illustrated by Ted Dewan

Chicken The House

SCHOLASTIC INC.
New York

For Dorothy

Text copyright © 2005 by Elizabeth Kay
www.elizabeth-kay.co.uk
Illustrations copyright © 2005 by Ted Dewan

First published in the United Kingdom in 2005 by The Chicken House,
2 Palmer Street, Frome, Somerset BA11 1DS.
www.doublecluck.com

All rights reserved. Published by Scholastic Inc., *Publishers since 1920*, by arrangement
with The Chicken House. SCHOLASTIC and associated logos are trademarks and/or
registered trademarks of Scholastic Inc. THE CHICKEN HOUSE is a trademark of
The Chicken House.

No part of this publication may be reproduced in whole or in part, stored in a retrieval
system, or transmitted in any form or by any means, electronic, mechanical,
photocopying, recording, or otherwise, without prior written permission of the
publisher. For information regarding permission, write to Scholastic Inc.,
Attention: Permissions Department, 557 Broadway, New York, NY 10012.

Library of Congress Cataloging-in-Publication data available

ISBN 0-439-72455-4
10   9   8   7   6   5   4   3   2   1   05   06   07   08   09

Printed in Singapore
First American edition, September 2005

The text type was set in 12.5-pt. Garamond 3.
The display type was set in LTCompendio Regular.
Book design by Leyah Jensen

Also available by Elizabeth Kay

THE DIVIDE

BACK TO THE DIVIDE

"I thought that Betony coming to this world for the holidays would be a dream come true.

How wrong I was!

If only I'd been able to see this copy of THE ANDRIAN ECHO before that fateful day, things might have turned out SO differently. . . ."

THE ANDRIAN ECHO

THE K'FADDLE MAGIC LAMP—

MAY YOUR WISHES BE GRANTED! PURCHASE YOUR K'FADDLE MAGIC LAMP TODAY!

New brandee. Now easier to summon! It's so easy — anyone can do it! Commands cannot be over-ruled! **THREE WISHES AT ANY ONE SUMMONS.**

No upkeep needed! Your brandee needs neither food nor water, and will function for several centuries.

NEW! Advanced functions! MAGIC: Your brandee can perform simple illusion spells and hexes. **MEDICINE:** Your brandee can do basic surgery. **VIOLENCE:** Your brandee is capable of killing most beings.

DISCLAIMER

K'Faddle & Offspring are not responsible for any murder or mayhem perpetrated by the brandee in this or any other world. The owner is legally answerable for the brandee's behavior.

WARNING FOR OWNERS!

Because your brandee is a magical being, he can be infected by a powerword from another dimension. If he shows any signs of developing free will, return the lamp to our Service Department immediately for fumigation.

Come to Andria. Visit the world-famous library and the palace, have your ears waxed on the beach, or wriggle the night away to the very latest squawk bands!

THE K'FADDLE JINX BOX IS A MUST!

AMAZE YOUR FRIENDS, ENTERTAIN YOUR OFFSPRING, HUMILIATE YOUR TEACHERS....

Manufactured to the very highest standards and bewitched by a **CERTIFIED SORCERER.**

Use the K'FADDLE JINX BOX to store all sorts of information, but remember, what comes out won't be quite the same as what went in!!!

"I used my K'FADDLE JINX BOX to collect recipes. That was how I got my Rotten Toadstool Soufflé. It made my name as a chef."
—*Flourface, chief lickit in the palace kitchen*

RECALL OF DANGEROUS GOODS

WARNING! Old jinx boxes made before the Common Language was adopted can be extremely malicious. They are capable of tricking people into saying and doing things they later regret.

We believe that all such boxes have now been destroyed, but if you know of one still in existence, please contact our magical hotline by crystal ball, as a matter of urgency.

- MALICE NOW REMOVED! -
NEW, IMPROVED JINX BOXES ARE JUST FOR FUN!

JINX ON THE
DIVIDE

I

It was a dark and drizzly December, and the first lesson was art. Drawing wasn't Felix's favorite subject, and especially not still life — which was why he'd left the subject matter up to his mother. He wondered idly what she'd put in his bag for him to draw. She'd seemed quite pleased with herself that morning. No, science was what he liked best, and what he was best *at*. As he turned the corner, he saw Stephen Rheinhart, otherwise known as Rhino, lounging against the radiator. With his mass of flaming red hair, he was hard to miss.

Rhino noticed Felix looking at him. "Carry your bag, *Professor?*" he sneered, snatching it and dropping it onto the floor. It burst open, and pens and pencils rolled everywhere. When Felix made no attempt to retrieve any of his belongings, Rhino snickered, "What's up, prof? Seen a ghost?"

In a way, thought Felix, staring in horror at a brass lamp that lay there, mute and accusing, on the stone floor.

"What's that?" asked Rhino. "Your tacky little prop for

the art lesson?" When Felix didn't reply, he booted the lamp across the deserted corridor. It landed with a loud clunk against the opposite wall, and rocked back and forth a couple of times before coming to rest.

"Don't," said Felix.

"*Don't*," mimicked Rhino.

"You don't understand," said Felix. He felt a bit dizzy — the way he used to feel in the old days, when he'd been very ill. Coming across the lamp like this had been a shock, because he'd forgotten all about it. His mother must have thought it would be perfect for the art class.

Rhino picked it up, grinned, peered down the spout, and recited in a silly voice, "I command you, djinn, now appear . . ."

"No!" cried Felix, appalled. "You mustn't!"

Rhino's smile widened — then it froze on his face. Something golden and gaseous had started to seep out of the lamp's spout. A moment later, it was streaming out, like steam from a boiling kettle, glittering as it swirled. He dropped the lamp as though it were red-hot.

The golden gas changed shape until it became a man, dressed in a full-length garment that billowed out like washing on a windy day. He had pointed ears and raven-black hair, and he was wearing a curved dagger in his belt. He surveyed Rhino for a moment — the red hair seemed to surprise him — then his expression darkened. He bowed from the waist and said, "Greetings."

"You're an illusionist, aren't you?" said Rhino. "I think I've seen you on TV."

"He's a djinn," said Felix miserably. "Although he calls himself a brandee."

"Give me a break!" scoffed Rhino. "This isn't an Arabian night, it's daytime England."

"England," mused the brandee. He looked appraisingly at Rhino. "I suppose you want either wealth beyond your wildest dreams or the most beautiful woman in the world?"

"Just the wealth, thanks," said Rhino.

"I'm not quite sure how things work in this world," said
the brandee. "This is the first time I've been out of my lamp
on this side of the Divide, you see . . ." He cast a venomous
glance at Felix. "And being out of my lamp is even more
welcome than hailstones the size of pomegranates." His eyes
suddenly turned as glittery-sharp and piercing as the dagger
in his belt. "You have not kept your word, Felix Sanders," he
hissed. "You promised me you would look for a scientific
way to turn me into a proper being. Spending most of your
life as a cloud of gas is as disappointing as liver without
onions."

Before he could elaborate on this, a man in a gray suit
rounded the corner. The brandee turned to look, and Felix
took the opportunity to kick the lamp a little farther away.
The man in the gray suit turned out to be the principal.
"What's going on here?" he asked.

"Nothing, Mr. Goodbody," said Felix hastily.

The brandee burst out laughing. "Goodbody? I'd like a
good body. This one's no fun at all."

"And just who, exactly, are you?" asked the principal,
who'd heard every joke ever made about his name and was
consequently unmoved.

"He's from the local drama group," said Felix quickly.
"He's helping out with the pantomime."

"Oh, yes," said the principal, who liked to appear as
though he always remembered every tiny detail about both

4

the school and its pupils. He treated them all to one of his sarcastic smiles, and walked away. Once he had turned the corner, they were on their own again.

"Now you see him, now you don't," Rhino said with a smirk. "*Abracadabra.*"

An expression of sheer disbelief came over the brandee's face. He grabbed Rhino by the throat, slammed him back against the wall, and said, "*What* did you say?"

Rhino's eyes bulged, and he croaked, "*Abracadabra.*"

The brandee looked as though he really couldn't quite believe what he'd just heard. "That is a word of great power," he said. "*Incredible* power. It is a pity that you did not utter it in my world, for the result would have been even more spectacular. Understand this: You have released me from my obligations to you. *I do not have to grant you any wishes at all.*" He let go of Rhino, who took a deep, shuddering breath. Then he turned to Felix, tight-lipped. "I see now that your promise to find me a scientist was a lie. This time, I shall compel you." He grabbed Rhino by the ear and twisted it, hard.

Rhino yelped and struggled for a moment — then the brandee drew his dagger, pushed the point against Rhino's spine, and forced him over to the lamp. "Pick it up," he ordered, without letting go of the ear.

Rhino picked it up.

"Now rub it."

Rhino rubbed it.

Then, as Felix watched, horror-struck, both the brandee and Rhino turned to gas and streamed back into the lamp.

The lamp clattered to the floor. Felix picked it up and peered down the spout. He could see nothing, but he could hear voices.

"What's going on?" Rhino was yelling, although his voice was tinny and distant. "Where am I?"

"You're my hostage," replied the brandee.

"In your dreams," snorted Rhino.

There was a scrabbling sound followed by a slither, as Rhino presumably tried to climb back up the spout and failed.

Felix put his mouth to the nozzle and called, "Let him go!"

"No way!" the brandee called back. "Not until you get me a real scientist!"

Felix put the lamp into his bag and stood there, thinking. He'd brought it back with him, from the magical world on the other side of the Divide, wrapped in some clothing and forgotten at the bottom of his backpack. His mom must have unpacked it and put it somewhere. She'd remembered it when the art class was mentioned, and dropped it into his schoolbag. Good thing she hadn't polished it first.

It was doubtful that Rhino's disappearance would cause a nationwide manhunt, for he'd disappeared too many times before. The flaming red hair wasn't at school all that often, because Rhino liked playing hooky. He'd been known to disappear for days, when even his mother didn't know where he was — and she didn't care much, either, if her shouting match with the principal a few days earlier had been anything to go by.

"I'm not his jailer!" she'd yelled at Mr. Goodbody. "And you can't blame him for goofing off when he wasn't given no careers advice!"

"He said he wanted to be in rocket science, Mrs. Rheinhart," the principal had icily replied. "We didn't think it was very funny, not after the storage shed incident."

Rhino's mother thought it was hilarious. "He always has a firework or two in his pocket, bless him. And that old shed needed knocking down. Saved you the cost, didn't it?"

Half the school must have heard her. Felix couldn't imagine what it would be like to have a mother like that — but meeting Rhino in the school corridor had been a very bad way to start the day.

In his heart of hearts, Felix knew there was only one thing he could do — take the lamp back across the Divide to the other world, where it belonged. His elf friend Betony was flying over in a couple of days for Christmas, by magic carpet — something he was looking forward to even more than Christmas itself. He could ask her to release the brandee in her own world, and bring Rhino back home again. It sounded like a tall order, though, and not the way to greet an old friend.

The art class was miserable. Felix was given detention for forgetting his still-life object, but there was no way he was going to take the lamp out of his bag. He sat there, drawing someone else's teapot and fantasizing about dropping the lamp down a well or burying it in quick-setting concrete. But each time, his mind's eye watched it resurrect itself, like a mummy from a horror film, and he imagined the brandee searching for him, dagger drawn, bent on vengeance.

Right when he got home, he put the lamp at the bottom of his closet. He didn't want any awkward questions just before Betony's arrival. His mom knew nothing about the other world; she thought Betony was a friend he'd made in Cornwall. As long as Betony kept her elfin ears covered, she could pass for human.

Dad's the problem, thought Felix. *He knows everything. He'd go mental if he suspected there was a djinn on the loose. He's forbidden me to visit Betony's world again, because he thinks it's too dangerous. Like he's the expert? He may have had a ride on a magic carpet last summer — in* this *world — but what does* he *know about heavy-duty wands, or traveling by dragon, or out-riddling sphinxes?*

And then he thought: *I hope Rhino hasn't got any of his fire-crackers with him. Letting one of those off inside a magic lamp is just the kind of stupid thing he might do — but nothing would be as bad as taking an unexploded one to the other world. If it got into the wrong hands, it would be a recipe for disaster.*

"Kidnapping's a criminal offense," said Rhino, once he'd decided there was no way back up the spout. *This is not happening*, he told himself firmly. *I must have fallen down the school garbage chute and knocked myself out for a moment.*

The brandee laughed.

Rhino glanced around. He was standing in the middle of a small dome-shaped room furnished with cushions, a low table, and a Turkish carpet. Light came from a number of lanterns, placed in little alcoves. Presumably, they were in some kind of cellar inside the school. There were two doors set into the brass walls. Before the brandee could stop him, Rhino darted across to one and opened it. For a moment, he thought he'd found himself in a flower shop — then he noticed the vine and the compost heap and the wooden box full of seedlings and realized it was a greenhouse. Bizarre. Was there a grating in the ceiling somewhere that let in the light?

"The other door leads to my study," said the brandee helpfully.

"How long are you going to keep me here?" asked Rhino.

"A century or two ought to do it," replied the brandee.

Since the brandee was obviously as crazy as a loon, Rhino decided to explore the study on his own. It wasn't very big. It smelled of old books and furniture polish, and it didn't lead anywhere at all. He returned to the main chamber. The brandee was sitting on one of the cushions, reading. Rhino sat down on another cushion and decided to sulk.

After a couple of hours of sulking produced no reaction,

Rhino got hungry, so he broke the silence by saying, "What's for lunch?"

The brandee looked up from his book. "Lunch?" he said. "I don't eat, human child. I'm a magical being."

"You're round the twist," said Rhino, with feeling.

"Absolutely," agreed the brandee. "I didn't think you knew anything about magic, though."

"What?" Rhino felt the conversation slipping away from him.

"It would be more accurate to say I was around the half-twist," explained the brandee patiently, "like a sinistrom."

"What?" said Rhino again.

"A sinistrom. A devil-hyena."

Rhino couldn't think of a single thing to say, but fortunately his stomach rumbled loudly instead.

"That is a sign of hunger, isn't it?" said the brandee. "What happens if you don't get anything to eat?"

"I die," said Rhino spitefully. "And you lose your hostage."

The brandee closed his book. "In that case," he said, "I'd better grant you three wishes. What would you like to eat?"

"An endless supply of hamburgers," said Rhino immediately.

The brandee clapped his hands, and a plate appeared on the table. The delicate porcelain was rose-pink on one side and pure gold on the other. The hamburger that materialized on it looked out of place even to Rhino, but it was filled with

11

all his favorite things — charcoal-grilled beef, slices of blue cheese, pickled gherkins, tomatoes, mayonnaise, onions . . . Even so, he hesitated before biting into it. *How* had it appeared there? Had he shut his eyes for a moment? He lifted the lid of the sesame-seed bun, and a wisp of fragrant steam drifted upward. The smell was too much — he picked up the whole thing and crammed as much as he could into his mouth. The hamburger was just as delicious as it looked, and when he'd finished it, another one appeared on the plate.

"What would you like to drink?" inquired the brandee.

"Cola."

A tall blue glass appeared next to the plate and gradually filled with sparkling liquid. Rhino drank deeply. It was the nicest fizzy drink he'd ever tasted — not quite cola, and not quite cream soda. Things were looking up. "There's just one other thing . . ." he said. "Where's the bathroom?"

"I don't need one of those, either," said the brandee. "I suggest you go behind a bush in the greenhouse. Or you could use your third wish to install some bathroom furniture, in the color of your choice."

"Waste a wish on a toilet?" said Rhino. "Get real," and he told the brandee what he really wanted. It was only afterward that it occurred to him he could have asked to go home instead.

That night, Rhino had another couple of hamburgers for supper. Then he curled up on the cushions and slept like a hibernating bear that was particularly good at hibernating.

In the morning, he had yet another hamburger for breakfast, and complained bitterly about the lack of a television to entertain him while he ate. He usually watched cartoons, but he told the brandee he watched the news. After that, they ran out of things to talk about fairly quickly — once the brandee realized that Rhino knew very little about science, he seemed to lose interest — and since Rhino refused to believe in magic, they rapidly reached a stalemate. Rhino tried to impress him with his cigarette lighter, but setting fire to things was obviously not very high on the brandee's agenda — he seemed to be able to light the lanterns with a wave of his hand. The only entertainment was books, and Rhino was not a great reader.

The following day, when he went into the greenhouse again to pee, the layout seemed to have changed. There were a lot of dwarf trees where the compost heap had been, and their branches were laden with luscious purple fruit. He picked one and sniffed it. Then he broke it open, and the most delicious smell of custard wafted out. The inside was creamy white and fluffy and smelled so good that he tasted it. After he'd eaten five of the things, he decided to explore — the greenhouse seemed a lot bigger today. He must have missed part of it last time. He strolled along the little paths that wound between the trees and bushes, surprised at how much more of it there seemed to be. Unrecognizable insects flitted to and fro, and once he could have sworn he heard a couple of them giggling.

13

He ducked beneath an overhanging branch of white blossoms, and cracked his knee on an ornamental marble pedestal. Annoyed, he aimed a kick at it but stopped just in time. It wasn't a marble pedestal at all; it was a cardboard box. And *what* a cardboard box! He instantly recognized the midnight blue of the background and the gold lettering — it was an X303/D49 Battle-Monger, the games console to end all games consoles. There was a picture of it on the outside. It had more knobs than a space capsule. It also had a note pinned to it: PRIVATE PROPERTY, KEEP OUT.

Yeah, right, thought Rhino, hooking his thumbs inside the lid and forcing it open. To his intense disappointment, the box appeared to be empty — and then it spoke.

"Hello," it said. "Who are you?"

Rhino swore in surprise.

"Pardon me?" said the box. "Could you repeat that?"

Rhino swore again.

"I think you're making a joke," said the box. "That's not a real name."

"No, it's Stephen Rheinhart," said Rhino faintly. "Rhino for short."

"Now, that's style," said the box admiringly. "Being named after a mythical beast."

"A rhinoceros isn't a mythical beast."

"I think you'll find that it is. Over here, anyway."

Rhino decided to ignore this, and said, "Where's the way out?"

"There isn't one. Unless . . ."

"Unless what?"

The box hesitated.

"Unless *what?*" repeated Rhino, deciding to disregard the fact that he was talking to reconstituted wood pulp.

"Unless you annoyed the brandee so much that he decided to get rid of you."

Why hadn't Rhino thought of that one himself? "How?"

"What have you got in your pockets?"

Rhino went through them. A few coins, a handkerchief, his remaining firecrackers, a penknife, a cigarette lighter, a candy bar, his cell phone . . . His phone! He'd forgotten about it. Feverishly, he turned it on. There was no signal whatsoever. The suspicion that he was underground returned.

"Well?" said the box.

Rhino listed the contents of his pockets.

"What's a firecracker?" asked the box.

Rhino explained.

"It's scientific?"

"Well . . . yes," said Rhino. "We make things like that in chemistry class." He grinned. "When the teacher's not looking."

"How *excellent*," said the box. "And it makes a very, very loud noise indeed?"

"Yes."

"And in a confined space . . . You'll need to make yourself some earplugs."

15

Rhino looked blank.

"Vamolin seeds," said the box. "You ate several of the fruits, I believe?"

How nuts is that? thought Rhino. *Seeds as earplugs?* But he collected a couple of them as instructed and went back to the brandee, who didn't even look up.

"I want out," said Rhino.

The brandee took no notice.

"And I want out *now*."

The brandee continued to read.

"All right, then," said Rhino, who hated being ignored. He had enough of that at home. He stuffed the vamolin seeds in his ears, lit the fuse with the cigarette lighter, and threw the firecracker across the room. The bang was deafening, even with the earplugs.

The brandee didn't seem upset by the noise at all — he must have had eardrums made of leather.

Rhino removed his earplugs, and wondered how to irritate him next. The solution wasn't that obvious.

The brandee smiled, nonchalantly picked up the empty firecracker case, and read the writing on the side of it. Then something seemed suddenly to occur to him because, for some unaccountable reason, he leaped to his feet and rushed off into his greenhouse. He returned grim-faced, muttering something about no one knowing precisely what effect explosives have on a jinx box.

"Splinters?" suggested Rhino, assuming he was referring to the wooden crate full of seedlings.

The brandee turned to him in a fury. "Magic and science, you fool! They don't mix. They're worse than oil and water."

Magic again. Rhino curled his lip into a sneer, and went back to the greenhouse to see if he could discover some other fruits that were as nice as his earplugs.

"Wow! That's what I call a bang," said the Battle-Monger box appreciatively as soon as Rhino came within range.

"Oh, hello," said Rhino. What on earth was he doing, talking to a box? Had *he* gone bonkers as well? Or was it simply some ingenious little electronic device with artificial intelligence?

"Do you have any more of those scientific firecracker things?" asked the box.

"Yes."

"Lots?"

"A few."

"Terrific," said the box enthusiastically. "I've just remembered something. Well, lots of things, actually. But most important — for you, anyway — I have remembered a way for you to get out of the lamp. And once you're out *there*, those firecrackers will be . . . oh, invaluable. . . ."

Rhino decided not to argue about whether he was inside a lamp or a cellar. "How?" he asked.

"All you need to do is say *abracadabra*."

17

Rhino remembered how overexcited the brandee had become when he'd said the word before: He'd grabbed Rhino by the throat and slammed him up against the wall. Rhino didn't want *that* to happen again. And just why was that box thing being so helpful, anyway? What did it have to gain? He decided to do nothing for a while, and doing nothing on a stone wall with a talking box for company was less attractive than doing nothing on a silk cushion next to something vaguely human. But as he went back into the main room, a wisp of golden gas was disappearing up the spout, and the brandee was nowhere to be seen.

The day after school closed for the Christmas holidays, Felix was on the lookout through the kitchen window for Betony — and every so often he ducked outside and scanned the skies. The first snowflake fell mid-afternoon, big and white and wet, and it melted as soon as it touched the ground. A lot more followed. Visibility wasn't very good, and Felix wondered how Nimby — Betony's magic carpet — would cope. With his blue-and-cream design and cherry-red trim, he wouldn't be hard to spot.

"You can't go out bird-watching in this weather," said Felix's mother, as he headed for the back door again.

Bird-watching? Felix looked stupidly at the binoculars in his hand, his mind elsewhere.

"I'll put some seed in the bird feeder, and you can watch from the window."

Felix edged another couple of steps toward the door. "I'll be perfectly all right. Don't worry."

Felix's mother folded her arms, pursed her lips, and looked determined. Her back was toward the kitchen window.

Something strange was going on outside, in the garden. A shadow of no fixed shape was moving behind the veil of snowflakes, undulating as it descended. Felix blinked, and looked again. This time he caught a glimpse of a face — a girl's face, with slanting eyes and a turned-up nose.

Betony. At last.

A gust of wind cleared the snowflakes for a few seconds — just long enough for Felix to watch the carpet land rather elegantly on the lawn. "I'll go and play on my computer instead," he said, heading for the hallway.

Once out of the kitchen, he broke into a run, opened the front door, and dashed out into the snow. He sprinted around the side of the house and into the back garden, where Betony was rolling up Nimby.

"Hi," she said, looking up and smiling through the wisps of blond hair that had escaped her hood.

"Hi." He was grinning like a lunatic; it was so good to see her. She got to her feet and they hugged, hard. He had grown more than she had, yet again — his body had been making up for lost time. "You'd better come around to the front," he said, "so it looks as though you've arrived in a taxi."

"What's a taxi?"

"A scientific self-propelled vehicle. Listen, Betony, I've got a problem. Remember the brandee? Nearly throttled me in an alleyway last summer? He's kidnapped a boy from my school at knifepoint, and he's holding him prisoner inside his lamp. Come on, before my mom realizes I'm in the backyard."

"Give me time to catch my breath." Betony laughed, but Felix had rushed on ahead. Betony followed him around to the front door. Once inside, he ushered her upstairs to the spare room and hid Nimby under the bed. Then he hurried Betony downstairs again, and into the kitchen.

"Goodness!" said Felix's mother. "I didn't hear you arrive, Betony. Did your parents bring you?"

"Um . . ." said Betony, glancing at Felix. It wouldn't be a good idea to explain that her parents had been temporarily turned to stone by a spell that had misfired, and were currently garden statues in the yard below the family treehouse.

"She came in a taxi," said Felix. "From the station."

"I imagine a hot drink is in order," said Felix's mother. "What would you like?"

Betony looked at Felix. What did they drink in this world? She glanced around the kitchen and spotted a bottle of something by the stove. "Sherry," she said.

Felix's mother laughed, clearly thinking Betony had made a joke.

"Hot chocolate," said Felix quickly. "For both of us."

It was only after they'd taken their drinks upstairs that they were really able to talk.

"You want me to *what*?" Betony gulped. "*Blazing feathers*, Felix, I just got here!"

"It won't take long. Remember last time there was a magical invasion from your world? It could have been the end of all life on Earth."

"That was Snakeweed's doing. It was deliberate."

"How do we know what the brandee might be prepared to do?" said Felix. "Magic and science don't mix, and accidents happen. He's *got* to go back to where he came from."

"Let me get this straight," said Betony. "You want me to take a magic lamp containing an enraged brandee *and* a human back to my world. Then you want me to find a way of leaving the brandee behind and bringing the boy back here?"

Felix nodded. "I could come, too, and help."

"Big of you," said Betony huffily.

"Please?" said Felix. "You're so good at this kind of thing."

Betony wavered.

"Remember that alleyway in Kaflabad, when the brandee nearly strangled me? You talked him into letting me go. You were brilliant."

Betony grinned. "Yeah, I *was* pretty good, wasn't I? What's this boy's name?"

"Rhino."

"*Rhino?* Like a river-fatty — er — rhinoceros?"

"A river-fatty is a *hippo*potamus."

Betony looked annoyed. She was especially proud of her ability to remember Felix's names for the mythical creatures of her own world.

"Rhino's his nickname," said Felix. "His real name's Stephen Rheinhart."

"What's he like?"

"Horrible."

"Oh, terrific. This was going to be my chance to see *your* world, Felix — cities and movies and subways."

"We'll come right back."

"Won't your parents miss you?"

"My dad's going to Edinburgh tomorrow, on business," said Felix. "He won't be back until Christmas Eve. So he's out of the way — just Mom to deal with. I know. I'll tell her we've been invited to a sleepover." He turned to the carpet. "Nimby," he said, "how fast can you fly?"

"Well, I'm not a racer as *such*," said the carpet. "But I do like to think I'm a cut above average."

But it wasn't quite as easy as that.

"What time do you need to be there?" asked Felix's mom. "I'll drive you."

"It's not far. We can walk."

"You can't be too careful, Felix. Don't forget, your school friend Rhino's disappeared."

"Rhinos are always disappearing," said Felix, his heart beating faster. "There are hardly any left in Africa now."

Felix's mother gave him a sharp look.

"Oh, come on. It's not the first time Rhino's disappeared, Mom. He's always doing it."

Betony elbowed Felix in the ribs, and they went into the hall. "I'll do an illusion spell," she said. "It worked on her before — she's a good subject."

"Tell her we're away for several days," said Felix. "Just in case. And make sure she doesn't try to contact us. And that she doesn't worry — she should think we're having a great time, going to theme parks and stuff."

"Anything else?" asked Betony sarcastically. "You don't want me to eradicate all known shadow-beasts and invent a new dance while I'm at it?"

Felix grinned. "How about wealth beyond my wildest dreams?"

Betony laughed. "You'll just have to make do with the most beautiful tangle-girl in the world."

The illusion spell worked perfectly, although Mrs. Sanders insisted on baking a cake for them to take with them. It was one of her best — a walnut sponge cake with chocolate butter-cream sandwiched in the middle. She put it in a plastic container and snapped the lid shut so that it was airtight. Then she gave them both a hug and warned them not to eat it just before going on the roller coaster.

They left conventionally by the front door, and then they ran around to the backyard. Nimby was lying rolled up on the grass, where they'd thrown him out of the bedroom window. "That was the most undignified descent I've ever done," said the carpet. "Why did I have to stay rolled up?"

"In case someone saw you," said Felix. "OK. Back to the Pennine Divide. You know the way."

It was nearly dark by the time they reached the Divide, and they would never have known where it was if they hadn't been there before. Felix read out the spell, and there was that curious little jump sideways as the magic positioned him with mathematical precision, and froze him into place. Then everything went black as the second half of Ironclaw's ingenious spell failed to split Felix's indivisible self in two, and, as intended, shot him off to the other world instead.

The library in Andria, where Betony was studying to be a historian, was the biggest center of learning in her world. It was an ancient wooden building, housing thousands — if not millions — of handwritten volumes, and even a few of the newfangled printed books as well. Betony was Thornbeak's apprentice. Thornbeak had recently become famous for her *History of Flintfeather* and now had her own office. It was situated in the new history section, with a little picture of a brazzle on the door, painted in gold. It was a rather nice painting. It caught the sheen of Thornbeak's plumage perfectly, as well as the gleam of her claws and the soft velvet curve of her hindquarters.

Soft velvet wasn't the best description of Thornbeak's mood as she slammed the door shut with her wing, lashed her tail, fixed her daughter with an acid yellow stare and said, "You're not going, Fuzzy, and that's that."

"*Mom.*" Fuzzy lowered her feathery brows and glowered. "I've flown farther than that on my own before."

"Yergud's a japegrin town. You're a brazzle."

Fuzzy clenched her talons in annoyance. "You're living in the past."

"That's what I'm paid to do," snapped Thornbeak. "I'm a historian. Which you're not, not until you've passed your exams."

"I don't want to be a stupid historian, anyway," said Fuzzy.

Thornbeak's eyes narrowed. "So I've heard."

"Who told you?"

"Never you mind."

Fuzzy unsheathed her claws, and then sheathed them again. Naked claws were the height of bad manners, and a well-bred brazzle never exposed them indoors. She had been expecting a more extreme reaction from her mother — either a full-scale squawking session or a sharp peck where it hurt. "You don't *need* two assistants," she grumbled, "because you never think anyone else can do anything right. You give Betony all the interesting stuff. I want to travel. I want to see snow. We never get any snow in Andria. I could be a courier."

"A *courier?*" Thornbeak lashed her tail so hard this time that the tassel knocked a twig off the antique perching branch fixed to the wall. "With your education? Are you out of your mind? Cock brazzles are mathematicians. Hens are historians. That's the way it is."

"Why?" returned Fuzzy, who liked math very much.

"You're little more than a fledgling, Fuzzy," said Thornbeak icily. "Wait until you've been around for a couple of centuries like me, and you'll see that a sinistrom doesn't change its spots."

"Except when it's disguised as a lickit," said Fuzzy, with a superior lift of her beak as she notched up the best points she'd scored over her mother in a long time.

Thornbeak's eyes narrowed even more.

"It's not fair," complained Fuzzy. "You let Betony go off to *another world.*"

"Betony's different," said Thornbeak. "Just look at you, with your feathers sticking out all over the place. The library isn't some kind of fashion opportunity, Fuzzy, it's a place of serious study. I want to see those feathers properly preened, and I want you back at the perching rocks by sunset."

"*Sunset?*"

"Sunset," repeated Thornbeak. She tucked a few more volumes under her wing, opened the door, and strode off toward the entrance hall.

Well, fishguts to that, thought Fuzzy. *I bet she made up all that stuff about brazzles being unpopular in Yergud. I could sneak off during my lunch break: She'd never notice; she'll have her beak stuck in some boring old manuscript.*

Sure enough, by lunchtime, Thornbeak was hunched in a corner of the library, reading something about peck patterns on pottery. She didn't even look up as Fuzzy hurried past. Fuzzy was doubly glad: She didn't want Thornbeak to ask her where she was going — nor did she want her mother to see that she'd had some of her spikiest golden feathers dyed black, and her talons painted with pink and orange polish.

As soon as she was outside, Fuzzy took off and headed for

the mountains, which lay between Andria and Yergud. The air was crisp and clear, and it felt good to be alive. She settled down to a nice regular wing beat, and started to sing a disgracefully rude raptorial song her father had taught her, which was used to cheer on the local math team. She felt very grown-up. There would be herds of nobble-heads and packs of snagglefangs up north. Rumor even had it that wild fire-breathers lived in the craters of spitfire mountains, but it probably was just a rumor. No one had seen one for decades.

She did a couple of backflip swoops and a tricky little triple-twist tumble. She was one smooth brazzle; Yergud would be a piece of fish.

Felix was aware that he was shivering before he was aware of anything else. He opened his eyes and sat up. He realized he was sitting on snow, so he got to his feet. Everything was pearly gray and misty, as though he'd found himself in the middle of a cloud. Presumably, they were on the Andrian Divide, somewhere above the snow line, but it was impossible to see any detail and therefore impossible to recognize any landmarks.

It was getting dark — and it was bitterly, achingly, lung-crushingly cold. He hugged himself to keep warm, and blew into his hands. His breath swirled out like puffs of dragon smoke, dense and white. He had put on his warmest parka, but it was about as effective as a plastic bag.

Betony stood up, stamped her feet, and gave him a thumbs-up. She was wearing a thick green cloak she'd brought with her, and fur-lined leather boots. She took a pair of woolen mittens out of her pocket and put them on.

"This feels like the Arctic," said Felix. It took him longer than usual to get the words out, because his teeth were chattering like castanets. He'd probably caught a cold already; he'd have to spend Christmas in bed and make do with turkey soup. Just at that moment, the idea had a certain appeal.

"Let's get on with it," said Nimby, hovering so that his warp didn't freeze up. "I think this is a spitfire mountain. There are lots of them around here."

Standing on it didn't particularly bother Felix — he'd visited both Arenal and Irazu, in Costa Rica. The chances of it choosing that moment to erupt were minuscule. "I thought we were going to find someone who would do the summons safely," he said.

"That means going to Andria," said Betony. "It'll take ages. I think we should risk it."

Felix took the lamp out of his backpack. It all seemed a little hit-or-miss. "Suppose the brandee won't release Rhino until I produce a scientist?" he said.

"Lie," said Betony. "Tell him we're still in *your* world and we've come here to meet some famous egghead who knows all about gases and solids and stuff like that."

Felix glanced around at the white expanse that stretched as far as the eye could see — which wasn't very far at all, due to the mist. "That's not very likely, is it?" he said.

"*Fangs and talons*, stop dithering and get on with it."

"I'm not dithering, I'm just trying to cover all the possibilities in advance."

"Give it here, and *I'll* do it."

Betony made a lunge for the lamp, and for a moment they tussled with it. The tussle produced enough friction to summon the brandee, and glittery golden gas started to stream out of the spout.

"Greetings," said the brandee, when he was solid once more. "I wondered when you would summon me again. My hostage is becoming impatient."

"I command you to release him," said Felix, with as much authority as he could muster. It was worth a try.

The brandee's teeth flashed white in the gathering gloom. "Not until I meet the scientist you have found for me. You see, I may have to appear when you rub my lamp, but I don't have to obey your command. *Abracadabra.* The word fairly crackles with the most vibrant of magic."

Felix glanced down the mountainside. For just a moment, the low cloud cleared, and he could see a village nestled in a little valley. Here and there a light twinkled, and smoke was curling from some of the chimneys. "He lives down there," he lied. He really couldn't think of anything else to do.

"Let us depart, then," said the brandee. "We'll use your carpet."

Nimby bristled in the way that only a carpet can bristle.

Betony nudged Felix. "Try rubbing the lamp again," she whispered, "and maybe it'll summon Rhino."

31

Felix ran his fingers over the icy metal, but nothing happened — except that the brandee noticed and drew his knife. "Mine, I think," he said, snatching back the lamp. "Shall we get going?"

"I fly only for my mistress," said Nimby haughtily.

"In that case," said the brandee, grabbing Betony's arm and twisting it behind her back, "you might be better off without a mistress at all." He placed the point of the dagger against her neck.

Nimby immediately laid himself at the brandee's feet, his fringe curling with distaste. The brandee let go of Betony, and the three of them sat down cross-legged on the carpet, which then took off.

By the time they reached the village, Felix was so cold he was numb, and his fingers were an interesting shade of blue. Betony had bundled herself up so thoroughly in her cloak that only her eyes and nose were visible. The brandee didn't seem to feel the cold at all.

"This is awful," whispered Betony. "What are we going to do?"

"Try to get the lamp back. What else *can* we do?"

"I meant, what are we going to do about producing a *scientist*, not what are we going to do about rescuing your stupid friend Rhino."

"He's *not* my friend."

They landed in the market square, which was deserted.

The brandee rolled Nimby into a sausage and stuck him under his arm. "Where is the scientist's dwelling?" he asked.

Felix was finding the lie harder and harder to sustain. "This way," he said, hoping something would turn up. They started to walk away from the square, but although they saw lamplight in the windows and heard the occasional low buzz of voices, they saw no one. Night was falling fast; the clouds were gone, and the sky was spangled with stars. It was colder than ever.

The houses in the village (WELCOME TO VATTAN, SUPPLIER OF FISH TO THE ARISTOCRACY) were made of logs, and they had steeply sloping roofs that were iced with snow. All the window frames and the balcony rails were carved and painted, and glittery with frost. There were sleighs parked outside the houses, the way cars would have been in Felix's world, and some of them had lanterns fixed to the handrails. It wasn't a big village. Felix could see that the houses were petering out — before long, the road would be winding between fields and woods, and his lie would become evident.

He was just wondering what to do next when he heard the jingling of bells. A sleigh rounded the corner, pulled by two cuddyaks. They were unmistakable, with their shaggy brown coats, their painted hooves, and the horns on their noses. The driver was almost completely submerged beneath layers of fur, although his ginger hair was just visible beneath his hat, and his green eyes were on the squinty side. A japegrin, then. Oh, dear.

33

The brandee turned on Felix, his face contorted with fury. "We are back in *my* world!" he screamed. "That driver is a japegrin! You have tricked me!" He dropped Nimby, drew his dagger, and lunged at Felix.

Then a lot of things seemed to happen at once. The japegrin reined in his cuddyaks, and Nimby unrolled himself with the speed of a whiplash. Betony launched herself at the brandee, her bravery as automatic and selfless as ever, her blond hair streaming out behind her as her hood fell back. The japegrin leaped out of his sleigh and landed with a soft thump in the snow. The brandee was a creature of the desert, however, and he wasn't used to ice. His feet slipped out from under him and he crashed to the ground, losing his grip on both the dagger and the lamp. The lamp skidded across the steeply sloping road, rolled downhill, and tumbled into a ditch.

The japegrin retrieved the dagger with a deft swoop of his hand, but the brandee was up and away before there was time to use it. Felix took a deep, shuddering breath. He'd forgotten what life in Betony's world was like. His own world was dull and boring and uneventful by comparison — he was out of practice as far as adventures were concerned.

The japegrin fingered the dagger thoughtfully, and then he looked at Felix. "Blue eyes. What are you doing in Vattan, freak, with a brandee of all things?"

"Sightseeing," interposed Betony quickly.

The japegrin laughed. "I don't think so. People only come

34

here for the fish. But if you're looking for somewhere to spend the night, there's only one inn. The Pink Harpoon. It's pretty empty at this time of year. They *might* rent you a room."

"Why *might*?"

"This is japegrin country, this is. If you were a ragamucky or a diggeluck, you wouldn't have a hope. Tangle-folk are just barely acceptable."

"OK," said Betony, but both the tone of her voice and her stance made it clear that the conversation had gone as far as she wanted. She held out her hand for the brandee's dagger. The japegrin hesitated, but he gave it back to her. After that, he climbed back onto his sleigh and drove off.

Felix walked across the road and started to look for the lamp. He spent a few nerve-racking minutes before he eventually retrieved it from its snowy bed in the ditch, a good fifty yards from where he'd thought it should have been. He was lucky to have found it at all; a tree had shed a branchful of snow over it, so it was half buried. There were some little footprints nearby.

"What made those?" asked Felix.

"Nut-nibbler," said Betony. "Rub the lamp and get it over with. If it brings the brandee back to us, we're no worse off than we were before."

"Hang on," said Felix. "He tried to kill me!"

"You know what he's like," said Betony. "*So* emotional. He won't try it again, not if he remembers that you might be able to get him what he wants. And if rubbing the lamp summons Rhino, so much the better. We can simply leave the lamp here and head back to the Divide on Nimby."

Felix ran his fingers lightly over the icy metal, undecided. To his dismay — and before he'd even started to rub it for real — the brandee reappeared beside him from among the pine trees. He didn't speak. He just glared balefully at Felix, relieved Betony of his knife, sheathed it, turned to gas, and streamed back into the lamp.

"That's a nuisance," said Betony.

"Just a *nuisance*?" snapped Felix. "How about a complete and utter disaster?"

"Oh, don't be so melodramatic."

Felix turned the spout toward him and listened. The brandee was shouting, his voice thin and distant and tinny. Felix put the spout right up against his ear.

"Call yourself a hostage?" The brandee was yelling. "You're not allowed to just *vanish*, it's against the rules! Where *are* you?"

"Complete and utter disaster was right, as it happens," said Felix, lowering the lamp. "Rhino's disappeared."

3

Fuzzy's first sight of Yergud was a surprise. It was a *hodgepodge* of a town — strips and wedges of closely packed wooden buildings painted in pastel colors and laced with a network of frosted roads beneath a brilliantly blue winter sky. It was very cold. There were patches of open snow-covered ground, across which drifted shape-shifting clouds of steam from geothermal springs. She swooped lower, looking for somewhere to land. There was a quarry on the outskirts of the settlement. A triple-head was moving big blocks of stone from one place to another, and diggelucks were breaking them up with sledgehammers. A couple of japegrins shaded their eyes and looked up at her. A third one picked up a stone and threw it at her.

Fuzzy was shocked to the hollows of her bones. Nothing like that had ever happened to her before. Throwing stones at an intelligent being in flight was unthinkable. Perhaps Thornbeak hadn't been exaggerating about brazzles being unwelcome after all. She gained height again as quickly as she could and headed away from the town, looking for the perching rocks. The Andrian rocks, back home, were considered by all to be very fine — they were located in a sheltered hollow and placed in a large isometric grid, fifty flaps apart, for a nice secluded roost.

The Yergud perching rocks turned out to be very downmarket. They hadn't been mathematically positioned by a trained rock designer; they were simply a natural feature of the landscape. They hadn't been cleaned for a while, either, and they were far too close together. Every single perch was vacant.

Fuzzy circled down and selected a roost. A ragamucky came bustling out of a ramshackle little hut and demanded a week's rent in advance. Fuzzy handed over a silver coin, wondering if she'd brought sufficient funds with her.

"And you can't perch there," snapped the ragamucky. "That rock's out of order. Go to number thirteen."

"Why? They're all empty."

"Because you're a brazzle," said the ragamucky. "Carrionwings get the pick of the perching rocks." She stomped off and disappeared back into her shack.

Carrionwings? Fuzzy could hardly believe her ears. Carrionwings disposed of magical garbage. They were probably smelly, and they spent a lot of time shrieking. Brazzles commanded far more respect. "*Gizzards to you*, you crazy old ragbag," she muttered. Then she flew over to the nearest patch of snow and made patterns in it with her feet. After that, she found an icy slope she could slide down, and then she found a really deep snowdrift she could plummet into. Snow was squawking good fun, the smoothest thing ever.

"What's a magic lamp like on the inside?" Felix asked Betony, as they stood in the middle of the main road out of town, which was completely deserted (YOU ARE NOW LEAVING VATTAN, PURVEYOR OF FISH TO THE MONARCHY). The cuddyak hoofprints and the runner ruts from the japegrin's sleigh were already filling up with snow.

"I've no idea," said Betony. "Try lifting the lid."

"It won't budge. Do you think Rhino really *has* disappeared?"

"The brandee wouldn't make it up. What's the point? He's lost his hostage — I bet he's sorry he shouted out the news for everyone to hear. He's got no bargaining power left. The question is, did Rhino vanish *inside* the lamp or *outside* it? The only thing we can do is summon the brandee again and ask him what happened."

Felix groaned. He was so cold now that he couldn't even think straight. "You've turned blue," said Betony. "I think we ought to find that inn, thaw out next to the fire, and get something hot to eat."

"No money," said Felix, his teeth chattering again.

"I've got some, silly," said Betony. "Come on, let's try the Pink Harpoon."

The inn was easy to find. A couple of lanterns illuminated a garish painting of a cross-eyed fish with a harpoon through it. The sign swung from a balcony, creaking in the wind like something from a horror movie, although the coral-pink clapboard was pure PlaySkool. A veranda ran around the outside, although it was hard to imagine the weather ever being good enough to sit out on it. A path to the door had been dug through the snow, and once inside, Felix felt a lot better. The room was filled with rough wooden tables and benches, and there was a huge roaring fire at one end. Betony left Nimby rolled up in a corner, and they found themselves a secluded little alcove where they could watch the goings-on without being conspicuous. The clientele consisted almost entirely of japegrins, although the cook was clearly a lickit. He took a long time to come over with the menu.

"Fish, fish, or fish," mused Betony. "What a decision. I think I'll have fish."

She ordered the blubber sole with squirtled pondweed. Felix didn't fancy the fluorescent-green sauce, so he had river pudding. It took a long time to arrive.

"If you summon the brandee, we could buy *him* a drink," said Betony. "Maybe that'll make him a bit more friendly."

"Isn't that kind of risky? He doesn't have to obey us any longer, does he?"

"Remind him you're his only hope of ever finding a real scientist," said Betony. "You see, he can never actually *refuse* to come out of his lamp or go back into it — it's in his

40

nature, as automatic as breathing. It's just what he does while he's out of the lamp that's the problem. Even then . . . if you had the instruction booklet and knew the right words . . ." She trailed off, wishing she'd paid more attention to the subject at school.

Felix sighed and rubbed the lamp. The brandee streamed out of the spout as usual, looking solemn, and sat down next to them in the alcove. Although no longer murderous, he was clearly sulking. Felix decided to leave the subject of science alone for now.

"Have some squirtled pondweed," said Betony.

The brandee's eyes flashed with annoyance. "I *can't* eat, can I? I'm a magical being, not a real one."

"How come you say things like 'as disappointing as liver without onions,' then?" asked Felix.

"You don't have to go to a desert to know it's hot," snapped the brandee. "And you don't have to eat a dessert to know it's sweet. I read a lot. But I can't eat, can't drink, can't do a lot of things. I want to be a human being so that I can *really* enjoy myself. Immortality's not much fun when you can't even savor a fricassee of fish guts. Rhino thought I was joking when I asked him if he'd tried it. He's no gourmet, is he?"

Betony took a sip of her drink. "So where *is* Rhino?"

"I don't know."

"Could he have gotten lost *inside* the lamp somewhere?" asked Felix.

"It's possible. There are two doors. One leads to my office,

41

another to the greenhouse, which is as mysterious as a sand dune."

"You didn't try looking in there?"

"Of course. But some days the greenhouse is like a forest, and other days it's no bigger than a vegetable patch."

"Suppose," said Felix, "that you took *me* into your lamp. I could go and look for him."

Betony sat bolt upright and tried to say so many things at once that she ended up not saying anything and choking on a piece of pondweed instead. Felix thumped her on the back. The japegrins at a neighboring table got to their feet and asked to be moved somewhere else.

"Why should I do that?" asked the brandee.

"Because I *have* to find Rhino and take him back to my world," replied Felix. "For all I know, he's promising the japegrins chain saws and machine guns — scientific things, which shouldn't *be* here. *I* did enough damage, introducing printing. Supposing I trade you a visit inside your lamp for some books from my world?"

The brandee looked interested, and considered this for a moment. "I'd like some science books," he said eventually. "The stuff about solids and liquids and gases."

"No problem," said Felix. "We've got loads of those."

"How are you going to get them from your world to mine?"

"Betony can bring them," said Felix. "When she comes back from her vacation."

Betony was incensed. "Do you know what you're doing?" she demanded. "Going inside a magic lamp?"

"Of course not," said Felix. "But it has to be done."

"It's a deal," said the brandee. "The little tangle-girl can rub the lamp for us."

Betony's green eyes flashed with indignation. No one had called her a little tangle-girl for a long time. "If Felix goes into the lamp, then so do I," she said.

Felix wanted to hug her; he hadn't been looking forward to doing it on his own, despite pretending not to mind. He and Betony had been through a lot together, and not once had she ever left him in the lurch.

The brandee looked at her with distaste. "You'll have to hold my hand when you rub the lamp, then," he said.

"We'll do it under the table," said Betony. "First, we don't want anyone to see what we're doing. And, second, we need the lamp to stay out of sight while we're away."

"Hang on," said Felix. "If there's no one left outside to rub the lamp, how do we get back?"

"I grant the little tangle-girl the appropriate wish, of course. She's allowed three. At my discretion, naturally, after the *abracadabra* business."

"Not entirely at your discretion," said Betony, remembering something from a magical objects lesson. "You have to grant wishes in trios, don't you? Once I've got the first one, you *have* to give me the next two."

The brandee looked annoyed, but he nodded.

Felix wondered what turning into a gas was going to feel like. And then he was fizzing, from his head to his toes, and it wasn't unpleasant, it was rather nice, and everything went velvet-dark, as though he'd shut his eyes. He was on a carousel in a fairground, still fizzing, but whirling around and around and up and down. No music or voices filtered through, just a background hiss like radio static. Slowly, the feeling subsided, and his vision returned.

He was standing in the middle of a small dome-shaped room. Cushions were scattered everywhere, a Turkish-style rug lay among them (although it couldn't hold a candle to Nimby), and some books were piled on a low brass table. Two doors led out of the room — both closed. Betony suddenly materialized next to him.

She turned to Felix. "Would Rhino *know* how to make those chain saw and machine gun things?"

"Probably not," said Felix. "But he could explain the general idea, and perhaps magic could provide some shortcuts."

"It is said that magic and science are like japegrins and ragamuckies, or milk and vinegar," said the brandee. "They don't mix. I never believed in science until recently, of course."

"And I didn't believe in magic, either," said Felix. He turned to Betony. "Come on. We might as well get started." He walked over to the nearest door and opened it. A smell of old parchment and candle wax drifted out, and he had to wait a moment as his eyes adjusted to the gloom.

"It's the brandee's study," said Betony. "And Rhino isn't in it. Let's try the other one."

"No, hold on a moment," said Felix. "I want to take a look. He's got his own library."

Betony lit one of the candles with a wave of her hand, and the interior was illuminated with soft yellow light.

The room was like an exhibit from one of those museums that shows life the way it used to be. No calculators, no computers, no telephones. Just shelves and shelves of leather-bound books, a desk, a chair, and a vase of dried flowers. Felix glanced at the spines of the books — dictionaries, spelling books, histories, biographies. There was even something entitled *The Compleat Brandee*. Felix took it down and opened it. There was a chapter called "The Venus Question: How to Decide on the Most Beautiful Female of Any Given Species."

"Hey," said Betony, "look at this."

It was a book of mythical beasts — the mythical beasts of *her* world. There were ones he knew — river-fatties (hippopotamuses), humungallies (elephants), no-horns (horses). There were also some he hadn't encountered before, such as spike-backs (hedgehogs) and poo-rollers (dung beetles).

There were clearly some Betony hadn't encountered before, either, because when she turned to the next entry and found a drawing of something called a bonecrusher, she clapped her hand to her mouth and said, "Oh!"

"That's a hyena," said Felix. The front-heavy doglike beast was unmistakable. "It looks sort of like a sinistrom, doesn't it? I didn't realize a hyena — sorry, bonecrusher — was one of your mythical beasts."

"Neither did I," said Betony. "But then, I've never seen a picture of a spikeback before, either. I think this is a rare book; it's probably worth a fortune."

Felix turned his attention to the desk. A thick pad of expensive creamy paper lay there and, beside it, a quill pen and a silver inkwell full of purple ink. Although the feather had seen better days, it was still a rich golden brown, and it was a big one.

"That's a brazzle feather," said Betony. "I'd stake my cap on it. I bet that pen's magic." She picked it up, dipped it in the inkwell, and tried it out on the paper.

To begin with, the pen behaved itself and wrote *Betony* in Betony's untidy scrawl. Betony looked disappointed, despite the signature being a classy violet color. Then her hand jerked slightly, as the quill got going again. She grinned and glanced up at Felix while the pen continued to write of its own accord.

Felix leaned over, so that he could see better.

To search the library catalogue, wrote the pen, in an immaculate copperplate script, *indicate either the book title or the subject you wish to research.*

"Wow," said Betony. "That's better organized than we are in Andria, although once Ironclaw's system is properly installed, things will improve. It's taking longer to set up than Thornbeak expected — some problem or other, I'm not sure what, exactly. Admin doesn't really interest me. Now then, what shall we look for?"

"Snakeweed," said Felix.

Betony wrote down the japegrin's name. The pen responded with the titles of several books of various sizes, and gave their locations on the shelves.

Felix picked out the smallest volume, and he started to laugh. "It's an advertisement for the Castle of Myths and Legends," he said. "Listen . . ." He read out a description of the castle, skipped the parts about the restaurant and the opening times, and went to the section headed MAIN ATTRACTION: ROOM 13.

The tapestries in this room are all of mythical beasts. Note the spinning wheel standing just inside the door. A four-poster bed holds center stage, and upon the bed lies the japegrin Snakeweed, deep in an enchanted sleep that will last one hundred years. Snakeweed sold untested spells and potions on a massive scale, causing many deaths, and he used sinistroms to do his dirty work. He will be on display year-round, excluding dance days.

"Poetic justice," said Betony. Then, "Oh! I've got an idea." She picked up the pen and wrote: *Brandee.*

Once again, the pen responded with book titles, the first of which was, not surprisingly, *The Compleat Brandee.*

Betony pointed to the last entry the pen had written and said, "That's the one."

Felix read, *"The K'Faddle Magic Lamp ~ an Owner's Guide."*

"Don't you see?" said Betony, keeping her voice low. "All the commands will be in there. If we've got the manual, we can find out how to make the brandee do exactly what we ask."

Felix nodded, went to the appropriate shelf, and took down the book.

"Put it in your backpack," whispered Betony. "We don't want the brandee to see that we've taken it."

But Felix couldn't resist glancing at the manual. And then he couldn't resist flicking through it. There were advertisements for other products on the last few pages . . . wands . . . crystal balls . . . divining rods . . . a magical-objects repair service . . . He turned back to the beginning, and then he couldn't resist reading just a *little* bit:

Thank you for purchasing a K'Faddle magic lamp, which should last you several lifetimes. Before you start to use your new lamp, please read all the instructions carefully . . .

"*Felix*," hissed Betony. "Put it *away*. It wants you to read it, because that's the way K'Faddle sells products. Spellbinding prose."

Reluctantly, Felix placed it in his backpack. And it was just as well that he did, because the brandee came in a moment later to get a book.

"Still nosing around?" said the brandee. "I'd have thought it was as obvious as a flea on a bald quaddiump that Rhino isn't in here."

"I've been admiring your cataloguing system," said Betony.

"Oh, yes?"

"It's similar to the computerized systems in *my* world," said Felix.

"That's magic for you," said the brandee. "Dividing things into subjects. What an amazing idea."

"It isn't magic," said Felix. "It's logic."

"The quill's magic, though," said the brandee. "It thought up that subject stuff all by itself. State-of-the-art, that quill is."

Felix peered at it more closely. "It's a little tattered," he said. "As though the owner didn't preen it often enough."

Betony burst out laughing. "Do you think it's one of Ironclaw's feathers?"

"I found it," protested the brandee. "I find lots of things, the places I go."

"Oh, yes?" said Felix. "And where *exactly* did you 'find' it?"

"Oh, come on, Felix," said Betony. "It doesn't matter. We're supposed to be looking for Rhino."

"It does matter," said Felix. "Brazzle feathers are extremely valuable. You stole it, didn't you? It's the pen Ironclaw made for Thornbeak, to reorganize the cataloguing system there. That's why the reorganization is taking so long. Because they don't have it anymore."

Thornbeak strode into the Shadow-beast Reference Section of the Andrian library, a sheaf of papers neatly tucked under one immaculately preened wing. She spotted the person she wanted. He was leaning over one of the desks, peering at something. The sleeves of his white linen gown were pushed up to his elbows, and he had a quill tucked behind one of his pointed ears. There was a noticeable smell of an expensive peribott cologne. Thornbeak walked over. "Grimspite," she said, "have you seen Fuzzy anywhere?"

The white-clad figure looked up from the grimoire he was studying. "No," he said, "I haven't."

"I don't know whether to be angry or worried," said Thornbeak. "She was supposed to be checking these dates for me, but it looks like she's gone off somewhere. Probably

some wretched talon salon — all she thinks about is what color she should paint her claws next."

"I liked the turquoise and purple," said Grimspite.

Thornbeak clearly hadn't known about that, for she looked shocked. Her own claws were the natural gold they'd been when she hatched.

Grimspite took the opportunity to change the subject. "When's Ironclaw arriving?" he asked.

Thornbeak recovered her composure. "Today sometime."

"I need to ask him to explain some numbers to me. You see, I've found the Big Bang spell."

The brazzle looked impressed for just a moment; then she fluffed up her feathers and got straight back to business. "The *real* purpose of Ironclaw's visit is to pay for his daughter's further education. I don't want you distracting him with a mathematical puzzle."

Grimspite hung his head. Thornbeak could be quite scary — and so very *decisive*. He watched her leave, then he went back to the book he'd been studying.

Sinistroms were very unwelcome in Andria, where the library was situated, so Grimspite had to do his research in his two-legged lickit form, and pay particular attention to his personal hygiene. Sinistroms were unwelcome everywhere, really. In their four-legged guise, they were enough to give anyone nightmares. They were the most vicious and ruthless and smelly of all the shadow-beasts — but Grimspite wasn't a normal sinistrom. He had come to realize that being told you smelled as sweet as a sewer wasn't a compliment. Since his pebble had been mislaid, he could no longer be ordered around, and he had rejected a life of maiming, torturing, and killing for a more meditative existence. Initially, this had involved writing a cookbook called *Dining Out on Mythical Beasts*. The book had been very successful, and Grimspite was spending the proceeds on tackling another little project, provisionally entitled *The History of the*

Sinistrom. He hoped to show that not every sinistrom was the irredeemable brute of popular belief.

He stared at the page in front of him, trying to make sense of the text. The Big Bang was the spell that had misfired all those centuries ago, creating 169 sinistroms. He had been delighted to find the thing at all — and then he had realized that it was a numerical spell, and way beyond his comprehension.

One thing was clear, however. The sinistrom stink was hidden in those numbers somewhere, and if Ironclaw could extract them and get rid of the smell, Grimspite might be able to have a regular social life and attend some conferences. He sighed with pleasure. Life as an academic was so much more rewarding than a life of unbridled violence.

Felix turned the ornate brass handle of the other door that led out of the magic lamp's main chamber, wondering what a magical greenhouse would be like. The brandee's study had been harmless enough — although they hadn't found Rhino, nor any evidence that he'd been there. Things were not always what they seemed in Betony's world, however, and dangers lay in the most unexpected places.

After a second or two, the most beautiful perfume wafted through the opening, and a shaft of sunlight skittered across the floor. Felix and Betony smiled at each other, relieved, and stepped into a tangle of flowering plants and little ornamental fruit trees, with trellises and rock gardens and winding paths. There was a small stream with a tiny waterfall, which appeared to go from nowhere to nowhere.

"Water," said Betony, and she took off her cap and scooped some up. She sniffed it. "Smells all right," she said, and she took a sip. "Tastes all right," she said, and drank deeply.

"Well, that solves one problem," she announced, wiping her mouth with the back of her hand and passing the cap to Felix, who did likewise. She looked at the fruit trees. "And that'll solve the other, when we get hungry."

They explored the greenhouse from one end to the other — it seemed to be about the size of Felix's backyard at home — but they didn't find Rhino. There were little statues here and there that smiled at them. Insects with bright metallic bodies were busily pollinating the flowers, and joking with one another as they worked. The jokes were really bad ones about things like blooming idiots and budding geniuses.

"It's awfully late," said Betony, stifling a yawn. "I'm tired. We could go back to the main room and spend the night on the cushions. The greenhouse might be different tomorrow."

"Not a bad idea," said Felix.

"What's that?" said Betony, pointing behind him.

He turned to look. "It's a marble pedestal. Probably had a flowerpot or something on it at one time."

"No, it isn't. It's a silk-covered box."

Felix stared at it. "You're right," he said. "It's not at all as big as I thought it was — must be a trick of the perspective. And how could I have thought it was made of stone?" He got up and went over to look at it. The pattern seemed to shift as he changed his position, swirls of golden yellow one moment and a vivid lime-green the next.

"That's the most delicate pink I've ever seen," said Betony. "Like the inside of a shell."

"It's not pink, it's green," said Felix.

"You're color-blind," said Betony.

"It's purple now."

"Turquoise."

"We can't be seeing the same thing." Felix reached out his hand to check that the padded surface felt as soft as it looked.

"No!" shouted Betony suddenly. "Don't touch it! It's a jinx box."

Felix pulled back his hand. "What's a jinx box?"

"All I know about them is that they were originally a mistake," said Betony. "They were created centuries ago, to store information, but they changed things. They were incredibly malicious, so they were all destroyed. Then — quite recently — K'Faddle found a way of removing the malice. They made their inconsistency and contrariness the selling points, and sold thousands of them. Thornbeak called it a triumph of marketing."

"Oh, hang on a minute," said Felix, opening his backpack. "That owner's guide . . . there were advertisements for other K'Faddle products in the back. Here." He spread the book out on a shelf, and he and Betony read the following:

Special Offer!

The K'FADDLE JINX BOX is a must! Amaze your friends, entertain your offspring, humiliate your teachers. . . . The K'FADDLE JINX BOX comes in three different designs — Invisible, Subtle, and Lurid. It has been manufactured to the very highest standards, and bewitched by a certified sorcerer.

The Invisible design comes with its own Here-I-Am case, so that you can find it. A favorite with japegrins, because it can be used as the basis for innumerable practical jokes!!!

The Subtle design suits the discerning buyer who is looking for a sound investment. We expect this model of the K'FADDLE JINX BOX to become a collector's item.

The Lurid design is for fashion freaks who want to be one flap ahead. It'll get you loved, get you hated, get you barred from Squeak & Squawk clubs.

You can store all kinds of information in a K'FADDLE JINX BOX — but what comes out won't always be quite the same as what went in!!! Read what some of our clients, past and present, have to say:

"After we'd played Hunt the Haunch — it was my birthday—I got everyone to throw an equation into my K'FADDLE JINX BOX. I drew something called Pythagoras' Theorem. Never looked back after that."

—Bronzepinion, mathematician

"I used my K'FADDLE JINX BOX to collect recipes, and every so often, it would change one of them. That was how I got my Rotten Toadstool Soufflé. It made my name as a chef."

—Flourface, chief lickit in the palace kitchen

Order your K'FADDLE JINX BOX today, and be the envy of the roost!

K'FADDLE & OFFSPRING, ZIGGURAT THREE, KAFLABAD

"That one must be the Subtle design," said Betony, glancing at the box sitting on the shelf. "The collector's item. You only see the colors and designs you like best. Unless . . . No. Surely not."

"What?"

"Well . . . if it's been here for ages . . ."

"It might be one of the old ones?"

"No," said Betony. "No, they were all destroyed. I'm sure they were."

Hmm, thought Felix. *Once something bad's been created, it's very hard to make sure it gets destroyed. Unexploded bombs and land mines are always turning up in my world.* But all he said was, "I wonder what's stored in it?"

"I'm not sure I want to know."

"Whatever it is, it's only words," said Felix, thinking, *At least it won't be nuclear waste or toxic chemicals.*

"What do you mean, *only* words?" said Betony. "Words are the most powerful magic of all. They create pictures inside your head — how amazing is that?"

"You know what I mean. It'll just be words that come out

59

of the box, not a sinistrom or a vamprey or a mad japegrin with an ax. We could take it with us."

"You're joking," said Betony. "I wouldn't touch that thing for all the emeralds in Andria."

They ate a few fertle fruits. Then they went back to the main chamber, where the brandee was curled up on his cushion, reading a whodunit about brass rubbing. They sorted out some cushions for themselves, said good night, and went to sleep.

Despite the stone-throwing incident and the ragamucky's curious preference for carrionwings over brazzles, Fuzzy was still really excited about spending a few days in Yergud. She'd heard about the view of the double mountain from the main square, and she knew about Yergud's world-famous bookshop. There was a reference book on squawk music she particularly wanted, which laid out the mathematical structure behind the work of the most experimental bands — the ones her mother said sounded like waggle-ears in pain.

There was also a fly-in restaurant with a top-notch reputation, some spectacular scenery, and some seriously weird wildlife. It was about time she saw some of the world. Her brother, Stonetalon, flew all over the place. She'd show him.

She found it quite difficult to get to sleep that night, although perhaps it was the fact that she'd eaten a little too much of the house carcass and drunk three whole buckets of fertle juice.

*   *   *

"Fertle fruit can lose its appeal, can't it?" said Felix, wiping the scarlet juice from his chin. He and Betony were having breakfast in the main room of the lamp; it bore a remarkable likeness to supper the night before.

Betony nodded. "And you can't eat more than a couple of those custardy vamolins; they're too rich." Then she said, "Oh, hang on a minute. What about that cake your mother made?"

The cake was a little beat-up, but it still tasted wonderful and reminded Felix of home. It was a lot more filling than fruit, and they ate half of it between them.

The brandee looked up from the book he was reading. It was a leatherbound autobiography, written by another brandee, called *Getting on My Wick — Two Hundred Years of Solitude*. "I think I may spend the rest of the day as a gas," he said. "I am consumed with jealousy by your consumption of that cake, for it is clearly a very pleasurable experience."

"We're going to take one more look in the greenhouse," said Felix, "and if it's still the same size, we're giving up and assuming that Rhino got out. Any ideas about how he might have done it?"

"*Zizzipadoo*," said the brandee, and he turned himself into vapor.

"What did he mean?" asked Felix.

"It was a joke," said Betony. "*Zizzipadoo* is the word children use when they're not old enough to do magic but they're pretending to. Come on, let's get on with it."

The greenhouse looked very different this morning. The little stone paths turned to gravel after a few yards, then to dirt, and then they more or less petered out. The vegetation seemed a lot thicker. Clusters of orchidlike flowers dangled from fleshy stalks; yellow speckled with cerise, lilac, and powder blue, pink dappled with white. Bulbous pitchers hung from the slender stems of pitcher plants, lime-green bodies splattered with purple blotches. Strange little trees spread their leaves into fan shapes, and curious spiny fruits clustered at the ends of the branches. It felt hotter than before, more humid.

"It's going to be really difficult to find him in here, isn't it?" said Betony.

"I'm not sure we're going to," said Felix. "I've been thinking. This greenhouse must be a bit like a balloon. Sometimes it's inflated, and other times it's quite small. But there's only one way in and one way out — through the door."

"So we might as well give up?"

"Might as well."

One of the little insects zipped past, giggling. "Why did the firefly bump into the tree?"

"Because it wasn't very bright!" replied another, chortling.

Felix smiled.

"Look at that pitcher over there," said Betony. "It's absolutely enormous."

Felix looked. It was so huge, it had to rest on the ground. "What do you think it eats?" he asked.

Betony looked shocked. "Eats? What do you mean?"

"Pitcher plants are carnivorous. At least, they are in my world. Ours are much smaller than these; they catch flies, which drown and then get digested."

Betony made a face, which quickly turned into an expression of horror as the implications hit home. "What do you think these eat, then?" she asked.

"I don't know," said Felix. "Some pitcher plants have been known to eat frogs. Perhaps this one's big enough to tackle small birds?"

"And not necessarily that small," said Betony, backing away. "I think you're right about Rhino not being here. Let's go."

But Felix was overcome with curiosity. Although physics and chemistry were his favorite subjects in school, biology was a very close third. Insectivorous plants fascinated him; they were just so *weird*. Despite the lid of the pitcher plant being firmly shut, he couldn't resist going over to peek inside.

"I wouldn't," said Betony, but it was too late.

As Felix lifted the green oval lid, a voice said, "Well, hello." It was so sudden and so unexpected that he nearly jumped out of his skin.

"It's not a pitcher plant at all," said Betony. "Look, it's not attached to anything. It's the jinx box — and you've gone and opened it."

"Perhaps you'd prefer me in a different guise," said the plant, becoming a box once more.

"Shut the lid, Felix," said Betony.

"Oh, I wouldn't be in too much of a hurry," said the box. "I've been eavesdropping, you see, and I know whom you're looking for. A human child called Rhino. And I know where he is."

"Really?" said Felix. "Where?"

"Sit down, both of you," said the box silkily, "and watch the show."

Felix looked at Betony.

Betony shook her head.

"It can't hurt," said Felix obstinately, and he sat down. Betony pursed her lips in annoyance, but after a moment or two she sat down as well.

One side of the box darkened, and Felix realized that he was looking at the interior of — well, a bathroom. Shelves full of potion bottles lined one wall, and another was taken up by a big window through which he could see a mountain, like a two-pronged version of Mount Fuji. Someone was looking out the window, with his back to them.

"It's a japegrin," said Betony. "Look, he's got bright-red hair."

"So does Rhino," said Felix.

"Really?" said Betony. "How odd."

It looked as though the figure could hear them, because it turned around to face them immediately. It was definitely Rhino. The box seemed to be acting as a window.

"Oh," said Rhino, zipping up his trousers. "It's you. Is there no privacy anywhere? What do you want?"

"We don't belong in this world, Rhino," said Felix.

"Speak for yourself."

"I've come to take you back."

"No way, José. I'm an important dude here. I'm telling those japegrin-pixie-whatsits how to make gunpowder. They think I'm the bee's knees."

Felix blanched. "You're doing *what*?"

Rhino smiled. "Yeah, how about that? *I'm* the professor now."

"But what you're doing is *wrong*, can't you see that? I've seen magic at work in our world, and it was a nightmare. Science doesn't *belong* in this world. If it got into the wrong hands . . . Actually, I'm surprised you even know how to *make* gunpowder."

"It probably won't come to anything," said Rhino innocently. "I may know the ingredients, but that doesn't mean they'll be able to get hold of them."

"Oh, come on," said Felix. "Charcoal, saltpeter, and sulfur aren't that difficult to find."

"The charcoal's no problem, sure, but sulfur? No school laboratories to steal it from out here."

"Is that what you used to do?"

"Used to take all sorts of stuff and sell it. Didn't get pocket money like *some* people. Mind you, you wouldn't

65

know where to get sulfur, either. Just because your parents are loaded doesn't mean you know everything."

Felix could feel a tightness in his throat. He realized he was clenching his fists. "*Volcanoes*, you idiot," he said, between clenched teeth. "You get sulfur from *volcanoes*. The mountain we arrived on was a volcano, but I wouldn't expect *you* to know that. Gunpowder's only ten percent sulfur, anyway."

"Are you sure?"

"Of course I'm sure!" shouted Felix. How dare Rhino question his scientific knowledge?

"So what percentage is the saltpeter, then?"

Felix told him. Then he said, "Hang on. I thought you knew . . ."

"Thanks," said Rhino.

Thanks? Felix stared at Rhino, aghast, realizing what he'd done.

"Like I said, I'm an important dude here," said Rhino, still smirking. "Hey, is that a tangle-girl with you?"

"Yes."

Rhino laughed. "You want to watch who you mix with, Felix. Tangle-folk are trash."

Felix dug his nails into the palm of his hand. He knew Rhino was deliberately winding him up for his own amusement, and he knew there was nothing he could do about it. He didn't even know where Rhino was. He needed to figure that one out, and fast. "Where are you, exactly?" he asked.

Rhino laughed. "That would be telling. Listen, wimp, I'm not going back to England, do you copy? I'm staying here."

Betony elbowed Felix out of the way and took over the conversation. "Your world is full of bombs and battles," she said evenly. "You must think it's better here, or you wouldn't want to stay. But if you keep doing what you're doing, you'll turn my world into yours."

"Good," said Rhino. "You could use a few hamburger joints. I think you should run on back home, Felix. Your parents will be worried sick — *so* awful for them after all the worrying they did in the past, when you were at death's door. . . ."

This was the last straw. Forgetting that Rhino was just a magical image on the side of a jinx box, Felix lunged at him. Instantly, the picture vanished. He thumped his fist on the box in a rage, jolting the lid shut and pinching his finger.

"I have an idea," said Betony, suddenly looking pleased with herself. "We'll use my first two wishes to get us out of the lamp. Then, when we're back in the Pink Harpoon, we'll use the third wish to get Rhino. The brandee has to cooperate, once he's granted the first wish of the trio."

"It's too risky," said Felix, sucking his injured finger.

"We're not achieving anything by staying here," Betony pointed out.

"OK. But this time, we're taking the jinx box with us. If your idea doesn't work, we'll try to get it to tell us where Rhino is."

"That's stealing."

"It's probably stolen property already. Remember what the brandee said about *picking things up* on his travels?"

Betony's expression wavered slightly.

Felix looked at his finger. A blood blister had started to appear. "It could have important historical information in it as well," he said. He felt that the brandee had caused him quite enough trouble, and the jinx box was a small price for him to pay. Besides, the box was something new, a magical object he'd never encountered before. He was intrigued. "Thornbeak would be fascinated," he added craftily. "*She'd* open it safely."

"True," said Betony.

Felix picked up the jinx box. To his astonishment, it was now small enough to fit into the palm of his hand. He put it in his backpack. His finger was throbbing badly, and he made a face.

"Oh, come here," said Betony, picking a leaf from a nearby plant and crushing it between her fingers. Then she recited the standard healing incantation, and the blood blister shrank to a tiny dot, then disappeared.

They left the greenhouse and went back to the lamp's main room. The brandee was oblivious to their presence — he had bottled himself, and his vapor was swirling gently behind some blue glass as he spent his day as a gas.

"I'm going to get Ironclaw's pen," said Felix, "while I've got the chance. Keep a lookout."

"OK," said Betony, stationing herself at the door of the study.

Felix slipped back inside and picked up the pen. He was about to put it in his backpack when he had an idea — he wrote *Jinx Box* on one of the brandee's creamy sheets of paper. After a moment, his hand started to move — and however hard he concentrated, he couldn't figure out whether *he* was operating the pen or it was some outside agency. It directed him to an encyclopedia of magic, so he took it from the shelf and looked up the definition. After a straightforward description, similar to the one in the K'Faddle advertisement, he read:

Jinx boxes cannot be trusted to store information without corrupting it. In the past, it was assumed they were totally accurate. This was why a jinx box was used to store the Common Language, which was collected several centuries ago from another world by a sorcerer — although, at the time, everyone assumed he had traveled into the future. Nowadays, of course, we know that time travel is impossible.

The crossover from one world to another had some odd effects. Words that, in the other world, were merely pretend magic turned into powerwords with the capacity to do both great good and enormous harm. Fortunately, the jinx box would be able to remember these words only if a suitably scientific event reminded it of their existence — an unlikely occurrence in this world.

The jinx boxes of old could be extremely malicious, and deliberately tampered with anything stored inside them. They also tricked people into saying and doing things they would later regret. These days, however, the malice has been removed, and jinx boxes are used simply for entertainment.

For a moment, Felix wondered if taking the jinx box was such a good idea. It was very possible that it *was* the sole survivor of the malicious boxes of old — forgotten about because it had been stored inside a magic lamp. He did feel uneasy every time he looked at it or touched it by accident — but it also had a kind of magnetism, which he couldn't explain. He closed the encyclopedia and slid it back onto the shelf. Then he put the quill in his backpack, slipping it between the pages of his notebook to keep it from getting damaged, and started to wonder what deprivations might lie ahead. He forgot all about the jinx box and led Betony back to the greenhouse to pocket a few more fertle fruits.

"It hasn't been much of a vacation for you, has it?" he said. "Back in your world again, chasing Rhino all over the place."

Betony didn't say anything.

"I'm sorry," said Felix, feeling really guilty. "I'm always dumping my problems on you. We never get the chance to just chill out and talk about stuff; there's always some crisis going on. Your world's much more exciting than mine, you see."

"Only when *you're* around," said Betony, giving him a playful push.

The tickling match that followed lasted until neither of them had sufficient breath left to continue it.

5

Rhino had stopped being dumbstruck by the extraordinary things that had happened to him. There wasn't much point — they kept on happening, so he might as well go with the flow. He couldn't begin to explain any of it, so why waste time and effort trying?

Once he'd realized that the brandee had turned back into a gas and left the lamp via the spout, he started to feel scared. Life wasn't playing by the rules anymore, and now he was on his own. Being held hostage by a nutcase was bad enough; but at least the weirdo had been company. Then Rhino had remembered the X303/D49 Battle-Monger box, so he went back into the greenhouse.

"Hello there," said the box. "What can I do for you?"

"I need to get out of here," said Rhino.

"So do I," said the box. "Places to go, plans to blow, you know how it is."

"Tell me how to get out, then, and I'll take you with me. And don't bother suggesting that magic stuff again. The brandee nearly throttled me last time. I'm not risking it. He's got a *dagger*."

The box paused. "If you were touching the brandee's cloak when he was summoned, you would turn to a gas and leave as well," it said finally.

"Too late. He's gone."

"But he's got a spare cloak."

"Really?" said Rhino. "Where?"

"Say *abracadabra* and I'll remember," the jinx box replied in a dulcet tone.

But Rhino remembered the feel of the brandee's hands around his throat and the point of his dagger in his back only too well. "Maybe I'll just go and look for it," he said.

"Oh, all right. In the bottom drawer of his desk. You can put me in your pocket now; I'll shrink myself to fit."

Rhino smiled broadly and shut the lid of the box, thereby silencing it, and left it in the greenhouse. Keeping a promise to a lump of cardboard wasn't one of his priorities. Then he went back to the brandee's study and retrieved the cloak. It was as black as night, and surprisingly warm for something that seemed so thin. He put it on.

He was in luck, too. No sooner had he returned to the main room than it turned upside down. The cushions seemed to inflate like airbags, breaking his fall, and the room turned over and over. The moment it came to rest, he felt himself start to fizz and then, before he knew it, he was outside and had returned to his normal self. The lamp lay beside him in the snow, and a little furry squirrel-like thing was chattering at him.

Rhino found himself compelled to bow from the waist and say "Greetings" in the most subservient way imaginable — followed by: "I am your brandee. I assume you want either wealth beyond your wildest dreams, or the most beautiful doe in the world?"

The creature's reply had been inconclusive, but nuts might have been involved. After a lot of chattering, the thing ran off, and Rhino realized he was his own boss once more.

Coming out of the lamp was like surfacing after swimming underwater — the real world came as something of a shock. Rhino had arrived in Vattan ("Fish Emporium of the North"), but at that stage, he had no idea that he'd crossed over into another dimension.

It was bitterly cold, but the cloak was equal to it. He trudged along the road for a while, heading out of town. As to where he was, he had no idea. Scotland was a possibility. The little furry thing could have been a red squirrel; the lamp must have bumped against it and the friction had been enough to summon his magically cloaked self. It was as if the creature had rubbed the lamp with the palm of its little pink paw. He wondered whether it would have been in his power to grant it a sackful of hazelnuts. He tried clapping his hands the way the brandee had done, but, sadly, nothing happened.

Eventually, he managed to hitch a ride on a sleigh pulled by what he assumed were cattle (although the horns on their noses were a little confusing), in the hope of reaching somewhere with reception for his cell phone. He didn't have to ask what the sleigh was carrying. The smell of fish that wafted over his shoulder spoke for itself.

The driver was bundled up in a greasy sheepskin jacket and leggings, and he was wearing the most extraordinary pair of feathered earmuffs. He didn't look quite human — if the earmuffs were anything to go by, his ears would have looked better on a garden gnome. He seemed to think that Rhino was something called a japegrin, and, as a diggeluck (whatever that was), he had a lot of bones to pick with japegrins.

"Your kind think they're the only ones with any idea of how to run things," he grumbled, "but diggelucks know more about mining than anyone else. Used to be a miner myself, before I took some of Snakeweed's cough potion. Can't work underground anymore, so I takes fish to the airstrip instead. . . ."

Rhino sat bolt upright. "Airstrip?"

"You didn't think I was going to *drive* all the way to Tiratattle? Can't take chances with fish, you know; fish has to be fresh. No, I drops them off and they gets air-freighted the rest of the way."

"Er . . . right," said Rhino, his mind working overtime. Perhaps there would be a radio tower in Tiratattle? But how

74

much would the flight cost, and how would he pay for it? He felt in his pockets: a handkerchief, his remaining firecrackers, a knife, the cigarette lighter, a candy bar, a few coins . . . He pulled out the coins.

The diggeluck glanced across. "Never seen any like those," he said. "A collector would pay a fortune for them, I reckon."

"I'll give you a special price," said Rhino, scarcely believing his luck, "seeing as you've done me a favor."

So Rhino got the money for his ticket. After a while the movement of the sleigh had a hypnotic effect, and he dozed off. When he woke up, dawn was breaking and they were at the airstrip.

It wasn't like any airstrip he'd seen in a movie. There was a runway, certainly, the snow packed down hard. But it wasn't very long, and instead of wheel marks, there were huge three-toed footprints, like dinosaur tracks. It looked as though there hadn't been a flight for a while. Rhino went inside the shack, which was the so-called terminal, to buy a ticket and, hopefully, a cup of coffee. He purchased his ticket without any trouble, but he would have to wait for the next flight to arrive so that it could be turned around. It was a tiny airport — there were no planes on the ground at all.

No one seemed to know what coffee was, so he sat there and studied his fellow passengers-to-be. They were an odd group. This clearly was not Scotland. There were a few diggelucks, a one-eyed mutant in a pink frock, a goaty-legged thing with horns — a costume, surely — and one lone human being. He had a mass of curly red hair, not unlike Rhino's own, and squinty green eyes. Just as Rhino was gearing himself up to go over and say hello, the man ran a hand through his hair, revealing a pointed elfin ear. *Oh, well*, thought Rhino. *I may be dreaming, round the twist, or dead, but it could be worse. It could be history class.*

A few minutes later, it did get worse, a lot worse. First of all, he noticed a light in the sky. Then he realized it was winking on and off — some sort of identification signal, probably. By the time the light reached the end of the runway, he'd figured out that its source was a jet of flame, not a lightbulb, and it was coming from the mouth of — well, a dragon. He watched the creature touch down at a gallop and slow to a waddle. EASY-FLAP had been painted on its flank, and it wore a long, many-seated saddle. Rhino watched the passengers disembark. None of them looked normal. A radio tower in Tiratattle was seeming less and less likely by the minute. He walked out of the airport and took the next passenger sleigh out of town. It was going to a place called Yergud.

He eavesdropped on the conversations in the sleigh as it jolted along, and he learned a lot. It became clear that, somehow, he had crossed over into another world. Whether it was a real world, or a world inside his head, remained to be seen. He couldn't do anything about it, so there was no point in agonizing over it — but based on his experiences so far, he would be able to live like a king if he played his cards right.

He was feeling pleased with his curly red hair for the first time ever — and it was long enough to hide his ears.

The landscape was changing, for they were going uphill all the time. They passed gigantic frozen waterfalls, and lakes waxed with ice. There didn't seem to be any trees anymore, just great expanses of shoulder-high bushes with silvery trunks and snow-laden branches. Although Rhino had seen tundra on television, actually *being* in such a bleak environment was a very new experience. The sunrise was far more protracted than it was in England, and the light was strange — a pearly lilac-gray.

Gradually, the grayness seeped away until the sky was streaked with turquoise and pink, and the sun appeared, red and raw. They stopped at a roadside café for breakfast. When they came out, a blizzard was in progress. Five minutes later, it was bright sunshine again. A little later, the sky darkened to a bruise, and then the mountains disappeared behind a veil of white. Rhino pulled up his hood, but once again, the snowstorm didn't last long.

Yergud itself looked like a toy town. There weren't any buildings over two stories high, and they were all painted in pastel colors. He made his way to the market and looked at the produce, considering lunch. Some things were familiar — loaves of bread, crocks of honey, dried mushrooms, cheeses.

The livestock section was completely *un*familiar. There were several pens full of goaty things that quacked and waggled their ears every so often. Beneath the bleating of bright-blue domestic fowls and the bellows of cuddyaks, there was a non-stop background track of haggling voices and clinking coins.

Rhino took out his cell phone and turned it on. He was being very careful about saving power since he didn't have his charger with him. Once again, there was no signal whatsoever.

"I'll take that," said a voice over his shoulder, and before he had time to react, a hand had relieved him of his phone.

Rhino spun around in a fury. It didn't matter that the cell wasn't his in the first place — having the tables turned on him didn't please him one bit. The japegrin responsible for the snatch pressed a few buttons and accidentally called up Rhino's ring tone, which was a bloodcurdling scream he had downloaded from the Internet. The japegrin went very pale and nearly dropped the phone. "What lives inside it?" he asked.

"Give it back and I'll tell you," said Rhino.

The japegrin shook his head. "Squill needs to hear about this."

"Yeah, right," said Rhino, and he lashed out with his foot, catching the japegrin on the shin, and followed up with a swift right to the stomach.

Despite the fact that the japegrin was taller than Rhino, he doubled over, making a satisfying *oomph* sound — but much to Rhino's surprise, he didn't give up the phone. What he did was to pull out a sort of dull black stick and wave it in a figure eight. Rhino felt the coldness arrive like a sudden and violent dose of flu. It was as though his body were changing seasons, from summer to autumn to winter. The frost seeped through his veins, settling around his bones and chilling his flesh from the inside. His eyes fixed in one position so that he no longer had any peripheral vision, and everything grew blurred and foggy. He couldn't swallow anymore, and the moment he stopped breathing was the scariest of all.

When Rhino regained consciousness, he found himself lying on a couch. The japegrin who'd taken his phone was nowhere to be seen, but there were several others sitting at little tables and going through paperwork.

"Hey," said one of them, glancing in Rhino's direction. "The human's awake."

Rhino sat up, trying to remember what had happened just before he passed out. Everything was a bit confused. He could remember someone waving a stick at him, but that was about it.

"So," said a different voice, "we have another human being in our midst. You look far more like a japegrin than the last one."

Something clicked in Rhino's mind. "What do you mean, the last one?"

"Felix Sanders. Felix had brown hair and blue eyes. You, on the other hand, have hair the color of congealing blood, and eyes of the finest mud. Allow me to introduce myself. My name's Squill, and I'm the Thane of Yergud."

"Stephen Rheinhart," said Rhino, trying to take in the fact that Felix had been to this place before and undoubtedly knew a lot more about it. Why hadn't he made his fortune, then? He was good enough at science to be able to explain the internal-combustion engine and probably quite a few other things. Felix wasn't streetwise, though — perhaps that was it. He simply had no business sense.

"Now, then," said Squill. "The Divide spell. You have it?"

Rhino looked blank.

"How did you get here?"

"In a magic lamp," said Rhino faintly.

"So someone else recited the spell. Pity." Squill took

Rhino's cell phone out of his pocket. "You have imprisoned some creature in here. Is it dangerous?"

"It's a machine for talking to people," said Rhino. "The other person has to have one as well. There's nothing actually *in* there."

"So someone was screaming at you through it?"

"No, it was a recording — a copy — of someone pretending to scream."

"Why?"

Rhino couldn't think of any reply that would be worth making.

"It's scientific?"

"Yeah."

"And you are a scientist?"

Pretending to be a scientist might be a good move. "What if I am?" he said, although he realized that he might be required to prove it before too long. Mind you, these pixie folk would be seriously impressed by even the most mundane of inventions. A flashlight, for instance. Which needed a lightbulb. And to make a lightbulb, you'd need to make glass. And to make glass you needed . . . what?

"If you are a scientist, then you are more than welcome," said Squill. "There are various things we're working on. Gold mining, cake design, world domination. Take your pick. Top salary, naturally."

"What exactly are you after?"

"A scientific icing that doesn't go granite-hard. A way

of blowing up rock — drilling spells take forever. We're rebuilding our capital, Tirattattle, way to the south, and we need a lot of stone. We're somewhat behind on production because we had to shut down one of the quarries."

"Why?"

Squill looked evasive. Then he said, "Safety issues," but it didn't ring true somehow.

Rhino put his hand in his pocket. The firecrackers were still there, and so was the cigarette lighter. He suddenly felt that his luck had turned; he could bluff his way through this. "I know a bit about blowing things up," he said. The only time he had ever paid any attention in chemistry was when there were loud bangs involved, and he still had enough fire-crackers to make something fairly destructive. Once those were gone, he'd have to think again.

They dressed him in japegrin purple. Although he felt silly at first, he could pass unnoticed when he wanted to. But he didn't want to — he kept his head bare so that everyone could see his ears. He was famous just for being human, and it felt good when people turned to stare. The only times he'd made an impression in the past were when he'd smashed a window, or spray-painted his name on a wall, or beaten some-one up. He decided to hang on to the brandee's cloak. Although it was black — and consequently unfashionable — it was very lightweight and astonishingly warm.

Squill wanted a scientific demonstration right away, so Rhino packed three of his remaining firecrackers into something that looked a bit like an oversized walnut shell. Squill selected a target — a little ragamucky shack by a rocky outcrop just outside Yergud — and hid behind a tree. Rhino lit the fuse, and then ran like crazy.

The bang was much bigger than Rhino had been expecting,

and he narrowly avoided being hit by flying debris. Dust rose into the air like a mushroom cloud, and a flock of birds lifted out of the trees and wheeled around, dazed and confused. How the heck had three cheap firecrackers managed to produce a result like this? Then one of the birds tumbled out of the sky and landed dead at his feet. Then another, and another. The dust cleared, and he could see that nothing remained of the shack except a few pieces of charred and splintered wood — and two halves of something that looked remarkably like a crystal ball.

Squill turned to Rhino, his emerald eyes bright and intense in his soot-blackened face. "You are a gifted scientist, Professor Rheinhart, that is quite clear. Perhaps you can also show me how to make those talking-together machines. What did you call them? Cell groans?"

The ragamucky suddenly appeared from behind them, carrying a bag of groceries, her face twisted with fury. "That was my home you just razed!" she yelled. "How am I supposed to rent out perching rocks if I don't live on the premises?"

"Slum clearance," said Squill.

The ragamucky's expression darkened. "I demand compensation."

"Only japegrins get compensation," said Squill. "So I suggest you pick up the two halves of your crystal ball — which, clearly, failed to warn you that your house was about to be demolished — and go back to wherever you came from."

*   *   *

That night, Rhino was put up in what appeared to be some kind of hotel, which had once been called the Yergud Valliton, at least according to the sign lying on the grass. The food had all been foreign, of course — no hamburgers, or fries, or hot dogs. His room had been . . . well, different, although the view of the twin volcanoes was magnificent. Hot water came out of the faucet when he clicked his fingers. The carpet was made of moss, like all the other carpets, and the wallpaper was made of birch bark. His bed had asked him if he wanted a lullaby, his mirror had told him he needed a haircut, and his toothbrush had informed him he had a small cavity in an upper right molar. He had some trouble getting to sleep, since the bed had a mind of its own and insisted on rocking him like a baby until it occurred to him to tell it to stop.

The next morning, it had taken him a moment or two to remember where he was. He got up and went to the bathroom. After he'd attended to all the things you attend to first thing in the morning, the mirror suddenly turned itself into a window, and he'd had the most bizarre conversation with Felix, who no longer appeared to be in Wimbledon. Although Felix had asked him where *he* was, he hadn't let on, and after communication was abruptly terminated, he smiled to himself. Felix would never find him — and even if he did, he couldn't force him to go back. Who was at the top of the class now?

Then a white-robed lickit arrived with his breakfast, and after that, a japegrin summoned him downstairs for another audience with Squill.

Rhino had always had a picture in his head of what he'd be like when he grew up. The picture had changed as the years went by — he no longer wanted to be an astronaut or a paratrooper. Most recently, he'd seen himself leaning on the hood of a Ferrari, wearing a sharp suit and shades and talking to someone on the other side of the world on his cell phone. Exactly how he would become that wealthy wasn't quite clear to him.

His new situation changed everything. There weren't any Ferraris here. There weren't any sharp suits or shades, either. What did he really want from life? It sounded like the kind of question a teacher asked when telling you off. He'd never answered, of course — he did *sullen* pretty well — but if he had deigned to reply, he'd have given a cool answer. The one that sprang to mind was the third wish he'd requested from the brandee: "A bit of respect, man."

They reached the foot of the stairs, and then they were outside Squill's office. The japegrin knocked on the door and then opened it with a flourish, bowing low and waving Rhino through. Rhino smiled. His wish had obviously been granted. He had plenty of respect here.

Squill looked up. "Good morning, Professor Rheinhart," he said. "I trust you slept well?"

"Yeah, fine. Did you know Felix Sanders is over here, too?"

Squill looked surprised. "No," he said. "I have encountered him once before, at a dance festival. I was Snakeweed's advertising director in those days." He laughed. "Then I became chief prosecutor to Fleabane, the president of Andria, and when Andria became a tangle-town again, I was sent here. And, as you can see, I've made a success of it. Yes, I remember Felix. What a little troublemaker he was."

"He's trying to get me to go back to my own world," said Rhino. "And neither of us wants that, do we?"

"Well, if we catch him, we could charge him with trespassing," said Squill. "He'd be a popular choice for an execution. We'd get a good audience for him — he's a name, as well as a mythical being."

Execution? It had never entered Rhino's head that the death penalty might be an everyday occurrence here. Had he heard right? Did they give it for impersonating a scientist?

"We could burn him at the stake." Squill smiled. "Now, then. On to other matters. I'm making inquiries about getting hold of the Divide spell so that we can go back to your world and get the recipe for that icing you were telling me about. The one that doesn't break teeth."

"Royal icing," guessed Rhino, but his mind was racing. He could remember every little detail about his encounter with Felix, including *the way to make gunpowder*.

"*Royal* icing," said Squill. "How lovely. I've been thinking lately that *king* sounds much nicer than *thane*."

"If we can get hold of a supply of sulfur," said Rhino, feeling that Squill needed to be distracted from the idea of a trip to London, "I can make you as much gunpowder as you'll ever need."

"Sulfur?"

"Yellow stuff. It comes from volcanoes."

"Volcanoes?"

Rhino gritted his teeth. "Mountain, him spit fire," he said.

"Oh," said Squill. "Spitfire mountains. Yes, we've got plenty of those, although ours are all female. You can leave tomorrow. I'll order you a fire-breather."

"I think we ought to read the owner's guide before we do anything else," whispered Felix, as they sat on the cushions in the main chamber of the brandee's lamp. "Just to make sure your plan will work for summoning Rhino when we're outside."

"I can't believe someone would hand out bombs like candy," Betony whispered back. "He has to be stopped."

"Let's read the guide in the greenhouse. We don't want the brandee to rematerialize and see what we're doing."

Once safely in the greenhouse, Felix opened the manual, and they read the following:

The K'Faddle Magic Lamp — an Owner's Guide

Thank you for purchasing a K'Faddle magic lamp, which should last you several lifetimes. Before you use your new lamp, please read all the instructions carefully. If you have purchased your lamp second-hand, be aware that a previous owner may have customized the brandee.

Parts:

In the box, you should have one brass lamp, one phial of complimentary brass cleaner, two rags, and this instruction booklet. If anything is missing — especially this booklet — please contact our Customer Care department in Kaflabad.

Getting started:

Unpack your lamp and remove the wadding from the spout. Under no circumstance should you attempt to force open the lid. This was welded shut after the brandee was inserted. To summon your brandee for the first time, rub the lamp gently in a circular motion with your fingertips, or some portion of your anatomy free of fur or feathers. A golden gas will stream from the spout until a cloud has emerged and the emission stops. The gas will then change shape, becoming your K'Faddle brandee. He should be dressed in black, loose-flowing robes, and have a dagger in his belt.

Operating the lamp:

Your brandee has certain responses built into his operating system, and *must* materialize in response to direct friction, whether inside or outside the lamp.

Default setting:

Saying, *"I command you, in the name of K'Faddle, the one who cast you . . ."* overrides everything, including half-completed wishes. Memorize this phrase, and do not divulge it to anyone. It is a default setting to enable the makers to summon the brandee for servicing.

Your brandee may grant a trio of wishes at any one summons, using a combination of magic, arcane knowledge, and common sense. Once the wishes are granted, you will not be able to issue another summons until the following moon. There are certain wishes your brandee cannot grant, however. He cannot raise the dead, or turn base metal into gold, or travel in time, or send anyone to another dimension; nor can he influence the weather. Meta-wishes, such as another three wishes or another lamp are not permitted; and no wish may ever be repeated. For a full list of exclusions, write to: K'Faddle & Offspring, Risk Department, Ziggurat Three, Kaflabad.

Servicing and maintenance:

You should polish the lamp only after the completion of a trio of wishes. Your brandee needs neither food nor water and should continue to function for several centuries. A regular one-hundred-wish checkup at an authorized K'Faddle dealer is recommended.

Advanced functions:

MAGIC: Your brandee can perform simple illusion spells, and knows a few useful hexes.

MEDICINE: Although your brandee can do basic surgery in an emergency, performing an illegal operation will cause him to turn blue and crash.

VIOLENCE: Your brandee is capable of killing most beings. Make sure you check local regulations — in some places, murder is against the law. Remember that your brandee can also *be* killed.

Customizing your lamp:

The brandee's flowing robes are designed for subterfuge. However, you may dress your brandee any way you wish.

Your brandee comes with long black hair. You may cut, style, or color it any way you like.

You may purchase any or all of the optional extras or order individually tailored items which will be charged accordingly.

Optional Extras:

Musical ability (lute, crumhorn, and bangithard)
Additional spells
Games and riddles
Sense of humor (anecdotes, banter, irony, and/or satire)
Ping-Pong proficiency

WARNING!

Because your brandee is a magical being, he can be infected by a powerword from another dimension. If he shows any signs of developing free will, return the lamp to our Service Department immediately for fumigation.

If you do not use your brandee for an extended period of time, your registration will lapse and your ownership will be revoked. This is to enable the brandee to take action himself if the lamp is in any danger. You may, of course, reregister at any time.

K'Faddle & Offspring is not responsible for any murder or mayhem perpetrated by the brandee in this or any other world. The owner is responsible for being in control at all times, and therefore legally answerable for the brandee's behavior.

"We're going to have to be careful," said Betony. "No wish may ever be repeated. You get one crack at it, and that's it."

"*Abra* . . . you know, *that* word, the one Rhino said as a joke — it must have been a powerword."

"Must have been." Betony shivered. "Dangerous stuff." She took a deep breath. "All right. Are you ready?"

Felix nodded. They left the greenhouse and went back to the main chamber. The brandee had come out of his bottle and was reading again — a detective story about copper beating. He looked up. "No luck, then?" he said.

Felix shook his head no.

"I'd like my three wishes now," said Betony. "I want Felix to get out of the lamp first."

Felix's last thought as he turned into a cloud of gas was, *I'm the one carrying the owner's guide. I hope Betony remembers everything. . . .*

Felix had expected to find himself back in the Pink Harpoon, but to his horror he was somewhere else entirely. It looked like a general store. He glanced around. A couple of diggelucks were examining some spades stacked against the wall. He pulled his hood over his head to hide his ears and pretended to be very interested in the merchandise. That was when he spotted the picture. It was a pretty good painting of a volcano, shaped sort of like a two-pronged Mount Fuji — and the title said it was a view of the Yergud spitfire mountains, as seen from the Yergud town center. There was no doubt about it — it was the same volcano that Felix had seen behind Rhino in the jinx box. So that's where Rhino was. Yergud. He absently continued looking at some curios sitting on a shelf to his right — and there, among the glass paperweights and the candlesticks, was the brandee's lamp, complete with price tag.

Felix had expected Betony to appear beside him almost immediately, but it was a few minutes before she did, and he was beginning to get worried.

"There's been a snag," she reported, tucking her flaxen hair into her hood. "I have to make the brandee materialize again in order to get the third wish. By rubbing the lamp. Wherever it is." She glanced around.

Felix pointed to it, sitting on the shelf.

"Oh." She peered at the price tag. "What a rip-off! Someone must have found it in the Pink Harpoon and sold it." She pulled out her purse and started to count the silver coins in it. "I haven't got enough," she said. "It's really expensive."

"Well, just pick it up and rub it, then," said Felix.

Betony glanced around. No one was watching. She took the lamp down from the shelf and rubbed it. The brandee appeared immediately — but before Betony could order him to do anything in the name of K'Faddle, he snatched the lamp from her, turned on his heel, and raced out of the store.

The shopkeeper's mouth dropped open. The diggelucks picked up a shovel each, dashed outside, and gave chase.

"They didn't pay for those, either," said the shopkeeper. "Oh, well. At least it was a bit of excitement."

"I think they'll bring them back," said the ragamucky. "Diggelucks aren't thieves." Everyone nodded in agreement.

Felix ran to the door, but the brandee had disappeared. "We can't use our wish now," he said. "Why did the brandee have to kidnap Rhino, of all people? Anyone else would have *wanted* to go back home."

"What you have to ask yourself," said Betony, "is *why* Rhino doesn't want to go home. He must have a pretty horrid life back in your world. If you could make it better for him, he might want to go back."

Felix had no inclination whatsoever to make things better for Rhino, even if it were possible. "He made a lot of other people's lives pretty horrid, too," he pointed out. "And he'll do the same here." He grinned suddenly. "I know where he is, though."

"How?"

Felix pointed to the painting.

A beaming smile arrived on Betony's face. "You are clever," she said. "All we have to do now is get there."

A horrible thought crossed Felix's mind. "How?"

"By magic carp . . ." Betony's voice trailed off. "Nimby," she whispered. "We left Nimby behind in the Pink Harpoon when we entered the lamp."

Nimby had waited patiently for Felix and Betony's return, but as the fire grew lower and the customers went their separate ways, he had begun to get worried. It was all very well pretending to be a brainless floor covering, but he couldn't stay rolled up in the corner forever. Someone would notice. He heard the landlord say good night to his last customer and start to clean up. Nimby could just barely see him with his light receptors. He watched him go over to the table where Felix and Betony had been sitting, look underneath it, pick up the lamp, hold it up to a candle, and examine it. Then he put on his coat and went out.

Nimby unrolled himself and tried to follow. But carpets aren't very good at lifting latches and unlocking doors, and it took him a while to find an open window he could squeeze through, by which time the landlord had disappeared. It was pitch-dark outside, and Nimby knew he wouldn't be able to fly very far. He needed to twisty-strip sunlight for energy, like a plant photosynthesizing, so he decided to find some shelter and lie low until dawn.

It was harder than he'd anticipated. All the outbuildings that looked promising were a little too security-conscious. He had to fly quite a way out of Vattan until he reached the next village, which was farther than he really wanted. It seemed to consist of just a general store, a fishmonger's, two houses, and a small farm. Eventually, he found a door that was slightly ajar and squeezed himself through, catching one of his threads on the architrave. He tried to jerk it free, but it broke off and he let out a little yelp of pain. Fortunately, the room was deserted — it was a storeroom. Nimby just lay there on the floor for a while, exhausted. Finally, his light sensors adjusted to the gloom, and he looked around. Strings of onions were hanging from the ceiling, and sacks of grain were stacked against one wall. There were barrels of salted fish, and casks of fertle juice, and bundles of herbs — and that was when a sudden gust of wind banged the door shut behind him. One cursory inspection of the latch showed him that he wouldn't be able to get out of this one. He was stuck, until somebody needed some onions. He rolled himself up beneath the skylight, so that he would catch the first rays of sunshine, and went to sleep.

It was a long time before anyone came.

The sound of running footsteps alerted him; then the door banged open, and a shaft of light arrowed across the floor. He caught a glimpse of a tall, darkly robed figure, carrying something under his arm. Then the door closed again, and there was the sound of heavy breathing.

After a moment or two, there were more footsteps outside, but these ran straight past. Nimby's light sensors adjusted themselves to the shadows once more, and he found himself looking directly at the brandee. The brandee grinned and held up the red woolen thread that Nimby had left on the door frame like a calling card.

Nimby tried to make a bolt for the ceiling — but the brandee was too quick for him, and he found himself slammed back on the floor with a foot planted firmly in the middle of his central design. He tried wriggling toward the door.

"You're not going anywhere," said the brandee, placing his other foot on the carpet as well. "At least not without me on board."

"I take orders only from my mistress," said Nimby.

"We'll see about that," said the brandee, and he started to recite a change-of-ownership hex.

Nimby knew that these hexes were only temporary — he'd had one put on him before — but it was going to make the heroic rescue of Betony and Felix (if that was what was needed) impossible. "Where do you want me to take you?" he was compelled to ask, but he felt like a cut-rate doormat for failing in his task before he'd even got going. Some hero.

"Yergud," said the brandee.

When they reached Yergud, the brandee rolled up the carpet, admired the view of the twin volcanoes, and went looking for the bookshop. He always visited bookshops, and this one was world famous. He'd once spent fifty years inside his lamp with only *Slobbit's Compendium of Cuddyak Diseases* and a jinx box, and the jinx box had been as mad as a cycad. Since then he had added to his library at every available opportunity. There were a surprising number of cookbooks, although most of them dealt with fish. The brandee's eye was caught by one called *Dining Out on Mythical Beasts*. It was beautifully produced, with some delightful illustrations.

"Bestseller, that one," said the shop assistant.

"Got anything on science?" asked the brandee. It was always worth a try.

She shook her head. "No. You're the third person who's asked me today."

The brandee raised a questioning eyebrow.

"Oh, it's just a fad. Our beloved thane has got himself a scientist, and it's caused an upsurge of interest in all the mythical stuff."

"A scientist? Here?"

"A human being, supposedly."

"Where is this scientist?"

"Squill's headquarters."

"Where's that?"

"Used to be a hotel — the Yergud Valliton. First left at the soothsayer's, and then second right after the hat shop."

"Thanks," said the brandee. He tucked Nimby more firmly under his arm, went outside, and came face-to-face with a brazzle. The carpet wriggled violently, unrolling itself so that half its pile was visible.

"Hey," said the brazzle, a young female sporting the latest craze in black-feather spikes. "You've got Betony's carpet."

The carpet in question started to reply, so the brandee tightened his grip and hissed, "Silence, floor rag."

"What's happened to Betony?" demanded the brazzle. "What have you done with her? Where is she? How come you've got her carpet?"

"I bought it secondhand in a general store," lied the brandee, unrolling Nimby and placing him on the ground.

"Where?" demanded the brazzle.

"On the road to Vattan, Fish Dump of the Spitfire North."

He sat himself down in the center of the carpet, cross-legged, and ordered, "Up!"

The carpet interpreted the command as literally as possible. He jerked upward, tilted suddenly, and tipped the brandee onto the ground. The lamp rolled a little way downhill, and the brandee jumped to his feet and chased off after it.

Nimby moved next to Fuzzy and whispered, "Betony and I got separated. She's got Felix with her. The brandee caught me and used a change-of-ownership hex. It'll wear off after another day or so, but in the meantime I can't go back for them."

Fuzzy nodded. "Where are they?"

"Somewhere near Vattan. They're looking for Rhino."

"*No* chance," said Fuzzy. "I know rhinos are endangered, but Felix won't find any he can reintroduce from over here because they're mythical beasts, and . . ."

"*This* Rhino is a boy, and a very dangerous one. He's telling the japegrins how to make weapons of mass destruction."

"I'd better get going, then," said Fuzzy, thinking, *Smooth. I'm going to have an adventure.*

"*Great balls of wool*, you're not up to something like this, Fuzzy," hissed Nimby, for he could see the brandee returning with his lamp. "If they find Rhino, you'd need to carry three humans at once. I think you should go and get Ironclaw."

"I can deal with it," said Fuzzy indignantly. "I'm not a hatchling anymore."

The brandee kicked Nimby irritably with his foot. "When I

say *up*, I mean like a feather on the breeze, not pumice shooting out of a volcano." He sat down and crossed his legs. "*Up*, curse your knots." The carpet lifted off and bore the brandee away.

Fuzzy was aware that flapping off on a rescue mission on an empty stomach was a bad move, so she treated herself to a peck of lunch at the fly-in restaurant on the cliff face. She got to talking with a chatty old carrionwing called Scoffit, who turned out to be OK and not smelly at all. Scoffit told her the locations of the rescue huts in the mountains, which might be useful in the event of a blizzard. Scoffit also warned her about the molten rock that could spew from crevices, and the super-heated steam that could shoot out of a lake. And for once, Fuzzy was prepared to listen to advice, even if it did come from an old crone on her way to a shrieking convention, with feathers that would have made a moth-eaten duster look up-market. Scoffit was only the second carrionwing she'd met, and she found herself revising her previous opinion. Appearances weren't everything — Scoffit had traveled to the north to guest in a squawk band, and how smooth was that? Mind you, a little scarlet polish on those craggy old claws wouldn't hurt, and a decent feather shampoo . . .

She finished her meal, and said good-bye to Scoffit. Then she launched herself off the cliff with a particularly nifty backflip and reverse plummet, soared upward again, and set a course due north. Fuzzy to the rescue! It had a nice ring to it.

*   *   *

Squill's HQ was a sprawling stone building, with a lot of outbuildings such as stables and storerooms. A huge tree stood within the grounds.

"You can't come in here," said the guard.

"Why not?" asked the brandee, shifting the rolled-up carpet he was carrying to his other arm.

"You're a nomad, aren't you? No nomads. No tangle-folk, no ragamuckies, no brazzles, no brittlehorns, no one-eyes, no lickits . . ."

"I get the picture. However, although I may look like a nomad, I am, in fact, a brandee." The brandee extracted his lamp from somewhere in the folds of his clothing. "I am beholden to no one at the moment."

The guard stared long and hard at the lamp. If he just had the guts to snatch it, he could have wealth beyond his wildest dreams — and the most beautiful japegrin maiden in the world. His fingers started to itch, and he licked his lips.

"Don't even think about it," said the brandee, running his hand over the hilt of his dagger. "I heard you have a scientist here, and I want to meet him."

"Nobody meets him," said the guard. "On the other hand, if you could grant me one little wish I might . . ."

"It's against the rules," said the brandee.

"No one need know. She doesn't *have* to be the most beautiful maiden in the world. Just as long as she isn't thin, or lopsided, and she doesn't bite . . ."

The brandee cast the japegrin a withering glance, turned on his heel, and left.

He waited until they changed the guard, and then he tried again.

"You can't come in here," said the new guard. "No nomads, no ragamuckies, no tangle-folk . . ."

"I'm not a nomad," interrupted the brandee. "I am a prince from a far-off land, and I have come to present this beautiful magic carpet to your thane."

The carpet in question made some muffled remark.

The guard glanced at his clipboard. "Nothing about it in the schedule for today," he said. "Prince . . . er?"

"Prince Goodbody," said the brandee, using the first name that came into his head.

"You could see his secretary."

"All right," said the brandee, and he made his way to the waiting room.

A sorry collection of individuals was waiting to see Squill's secretary. In one corner, a ragamucky was sobbing quietly into a brown handkerchief. The other petitioners were all japegrins, and they gave the ragamucky a wide berth. The brandee found himself a chair, sat down, and laid the carpet on the floor next to him. No one spoke to him, although they gave him a few dirty looks. After a while, a guard entered and beckoned him over.

"Hang on a minute," protested one of the japegrins. "He just came in. I've been waiting since yesterday."

The guard shrugged.

"He's not a japegrin. How come he gets to go in first?"

"It's not right, carpet or no carpet."

"And why is that filthy ragamucky in here?"

"That's not right, either."

The guard took no notice and left the room, gesturing to the brandee to follow.

Squill's secretary was a stunningly beautiful japegrin with shoulder-length auburn curls, and she told him she would have to search him. The brandee found himself wishing — not for the first time — that he had a real body, so that he could fully appreciate it.

"You can't take that in," she said, when she found the dagger.

"Purely ornamental," said the brandee. "It couldn't cut butter."

The secretary seemed undecided, but then she found the lamp. She held it up to the light and admired it. "His excellency likes presents," she said. "I can see that you know it is customary to give them to him three at a time — he'll just love the lamp."

Before the brandee had time to protest this, the secretary ushered him through. The thane looked the brandee up and down and said, "Well?"

"Prince Goodbody," said the secretary.

"*Goodbody?*" said Squill, incredulous.

"I have brought you a gift from my people," said the

brandee, bowing low and unrolling Nimby with a flick of his toe.

"Just the *one* gift?"

"Of course not, Your Excellency," said the secretary hurriedly. "He has a wonderful lamp for you, and a dagger."

"No, I haven't," said the brandee.

Fortunately, Squill didn't hear this remark. He prodded Nimby thoughtfully with his foot. "What does this do?"

"I'm not a *this*," said Nimby indignantly. "My full name is Nimblenap. I'm a top-of-the-line carpet, and I can fly anywhere."

Squill laughed. "It almost sounds intelligent. Yes. I like it. How delightful to have something amusing to wipe my feet on. And the other gifts?"

"There are no other gifts," said the brandee, grinding his heel into Nimby to stifle the carpet's incandescent reaction to Squill's last remark. "To overwhelm you with presents would cheapen our meeting. In my land, you give one present only, but one beyond compare. And receive an equally magnificent one in return."

"I see," said Squill. "You want something."

"Your Excellency is as farsighted as a brazzle," gushed the brandee.

It was the wrong comparison. "What, precisely, *do* you want?" asked the thane coldly.

"To talk to your scientist."

"Come back next week. Professor Rheinhart's gone away for a couple of days."

The brandee's dark eyes suddenly glittered like black glass. "*Rheinhart?* This great scientist's name is Rheinhart?"

"That's right."

The brandee gave a short, harsh laugh. "That human boy is no scientist. I know him."

"And you're no prince," said Squill. He snapped his fingers at one of the guards. "Arrest him. Impersonating a member of royalty is a capital offense."

"It was *I* who brought Rheinhart to this world," said the brandee desperately, "inside my lamp . . ." He stopped, appalled at what he had just revealed.

Squill turned abruptly to his secretary. "Did you search him?"

"Well . . . yes," said the secretary nervously. "I thought . . ."

"And you found a lamp?"

"Yes."

Squill snapped his fingers again. The guard hurried across to the brandee, searched him, retrieved the knife and the lamp, and handed them over.

The thane withdrew the dagger from its sheath, and felt its edge. He nodded, and replaced it. Then he turned his attention to the lamp. "I've always wanted one of these," he said. "So tell me what you know of Rheinhart."

The brandee remained icily silent.

Squill smiled faintly, although the smile never came close to reaching his eyes. "I've made a study of magical antiques," he said. "Little hobby of mine." He turned the lamp upside down and peered at the base. "I *command* you," he said, "in the name of K'Faddle, the one who cast you, to tell me about Rheinhart."

The brandee had no option but to comply. Reluctantly, he told the thane how he had kidnapped Rhino, and that Rhino was a perfectly ordinary human boy — well, somewhat more violent than average — but no budding science buff.

Squill, in turn, told him how Rheinhart's bomb had blown apart the ragamucky's shack. "The explosion even felled the birds from the sky and cracked a crystal ball," said the thane. "It was awesome. Are you sure he is just a nobody?"

Obviously, Squill must be exaggerating. "The boy used ready-made fireworks to produce this scientific phenomenon, Your Excellency," said the brandee, who had read the scorched label on Rhino's firecracker after he'd exploded it in the lamp. "They had been manufactured by someone else in the other world. I have witnessed the detonation of one myself, inside my lamp. The noise was indescribable."

"I'm surprised you're still here," said Squill. "I'd have expected it to kill everyone in such a confined space. The explosion *I* witnessed even split a crystal ball in two, and you know how indestructible they're supposed to be."

The brandee did, and he was puzzled by the differing force

of the two explosions. Perhaps the second batch of fireworks had been more powerful. That wasn't the point, though. "I'm afraid Rheinhart doesn't have enough knowledge to make more of them," he said.

"But he told me the ingredients. I sent him off to get the sulfur."

"On your best fire-breather? I suspect you will see neither the fire-breather nor Professor Rheinhart again."

Squill knew that the form of address he had used had made it impossible for the brandee to lie. "Rheinhart has made a fool of me," he declared. "That's a capital offense, too; I've just decreed it. I'd be better off finding a way to get to his world, wouldn't I? Yes, I could get more fireworks — *and* the Royal Icing." He leaned back in his chair and put his hands behind his head. "All right. I want you — no, I *command* you, in the name of K'Faddle — to follow the boy to the Spitfire Mountains and kill him. And use the carpet to bring back his body. I want to put it on display." He scribbled on a sheet of paper. "Here's an official death warrant, just in case there are any questions."

"I can't kill him with that," said the brandee sourly. He held out his hand. "I'll need my knife."

Squill gave him back his knife.

Without another word, the brandee rolled Nimby into a cylinder, picked him up, and left the room. It was turning into a really bad day.

7

Ironclaw landed in a messy heap on the lawn outside the library in Andria, next to the statue of Flintfeather. He glared up at it for a moment or two, as though the statue of the brazzle had been directly responsible for his own small brazzilian lapse of concentration. Flintfeather had always been rather overrated, in his opinion. A number cruncher, like Bronzepinion. He stood up, quickly preened, which made little or no difference to his appearance, and walked up the steps to the main entrance. Thornbeak dashed out at precisely that moment, and they almost collided.

"About time," snapped Thornbeak. "Our daughter's missing. I want you to go look for her."

"But I just got here."

Thornbeak glared at him.

"She's not a hatchling anymore," said Ironclaw, in what he thought was a reasonable voice. "She's probably gone to some squawk club or something."

"She's not into squawk music, Ironclaw; give her some credit. No. She wants to travel."

"What's wrong with that?"

"I think she's gone to Yergud."

"There's a good bookshop there."

"Oh, *beaks and bills*, Ironclaw, anything could happen to her. Yergud is hostile toward brazzles. I hear things. I live in the real world."

Ironclaw doubted that the library was much of an example of the real world, but just as he was about to point this out, he noticed a dangerous glint in Thornbeak's eye. He thought better of it and said, "So you want me to go flapping off there and bring her back?"

"Yes. But leave me the gold to pay for her chronicling course first."

Ironclaw started to empty his pouch. Every time he paused, thinking he had shelled out enough, Thornbeak would peck him. He continued removing the gold pieces, one at a time, until she finally nodded.

"Off you go, then," she said. Her fierce expression softened for a moment. "And when you get back, Grimspite's got a nice little number puzzle for you. He wants to isolate the stink factor in the Big Bang spell."

Ironclaw's eyes lit up.

"But I want Fuzzy back here first."

*   *   *

111

Felix and Betony stood at the window of the general store, somewhere between Vattan and Yergud, wondering how much damage Rhino had already done, and watching the snow falling. They'd been waiting there for a considerable length of time, and they'd had to buy some fish turnovers for lunch. Felix thought his was horrible, but Betony made him eat it. When she'd watched him swallow the last glutinous mouthful, she said, "We may as well buy you a real cloak while we're here."

There were several to choose from. One of them was much more expensive than the others, and when Felix tried it on, he suddenly felt handsome and brave and as strong as a cud-dyak. "I want this one," he said.

"Take it off," hissed Betony. "Didn't you look at the label? It's magic. For people with depression. And it costs a fortune."

"It's really warm," said Felix obstinately.

"Of course it is. And if you use it when you don't need it, it could have all kinds of unwelcome effects."

"Such as?" said Felix.

"It could make you really reckless, and endanger your life. Take it *off*."

Reluctantly, Felix removed it and selected an oiled woolen garment like Betony's, which she paid for. He couldn't wear both it and his parka, so he opened his backpack to stow away the jacket — and managed to spill everything else out onto the floor. Something clunked and rolled into a corner. It looked like a cylindrical pencil case made of gunmetal. Felix picked it up and opened it.

There was nothing inside, but a voice said, "Well, hi there."

"Hello," said Felix automatically.

Betony gave him a funny look. "Whom are you talking to?"

"The jinx box." He suddenly remembered that he'd thought about getting rid of it. He glanced around. He could just put it on the shelf, with the souvenirs, and leave it there. . . . He placed it next to a particularly horrible cross-eyed wooden fish.

"Don't leave me here," pleaded the jinx box. "They'll sell me to some illiterate who'll use me to store fishhooks. I'd much rather travel around with a mythical being. I could be really useful to you; I'm like one of your encyclopedias."

"Don't listen to it," said Betony.

But Felix couldn't help listening. The oily little voice managed to combine extreme smarminess with a seductive charm. Felix found himself thinking, *How does it* do *it? A politician would pay a fortune to learn a skill like that.*

"You wouldn't have found out where Rhino was without me, now, would you?" continued the box, oozing charisma. "And now you've got to decide which way to go, and you can't agree. How can I help?" The blue-gray gunmetal had taken on an attractive pinkish sheen, like rose quartz.

"Well . . ." said Felix. He had established earlier that there were public sleighs in both directions — to Yergud

("Stone Center of the North") and to Vattan ("Fantastic Freshwater Fish Award three years running"), but after an on-and-off argument with Betony that had lasted for hours, they still hadn't reached an agreement.

"You don't need that horrible box to advise you," said Betony. The pinkish sheen reminded her of fish roe, not rose quartz. "Once we've picked Nimby up from the Pink Harpoon, we can travel anywhere. You should ask yourself why a jinx box wants you to travel by sleigh rather than magic carpet."

"Because it's in your best interests," said the box quickly. "We all *know* Rhino's in Yergud. You'd be wasting time by back-tracking. And what's more, the Yergud sleigh has just arrived."

Felix could just barely see it through the shifting veil of snowflakes. He started to walk toward the door.

"Please," said Betony, dodging in front of Felix in a last-ditch attempt to stop him from boarding the sleigh. "Nimby could be in trouble."

"I'm just trying to do what's best for *everyone*," said Felix miserably, snapping the box shut and absentmindedly putting it in his pocket.

Betony hesitated. Then her expression softened, and she stepped aside. "I know you are," she said.

They left the store, climbed into the sleigh, and tucked the thick woven blankets around themselves. "When we get back to my world, I promise you as many cities and movies and subways as you can take," said Felix. He glanced at the other passengers. There were six of them: five japegrins and a diggeluck. One of the japegrins had a harpoon. Felix looked at it with interest. The actual weapon was a small spear, which was launched by a crossbow. The spearhead itself was a pale cream, either bone or ivory, through which a couple of holes had been drilled. Through this ran a thin rope, the other end of which was attached to the bow. The rope was very long, and was carried coiled up.

"I hope we have a nice uneventful trip this time," said the diggeluck conversationally. "Not much hope of that, though."

The other passengers ignored him, tucking in their own blankets.

"Being as there's a full moon," the diggeluck continued, undeterred.

A couple of japegrins shifted uncomfortably in their seats.

Felix couldn't help himself. "What happens then?" he asked.

"There's a lot of howling."

No one said anything.

"Let me tell you about something that happened to the daughter of a friend of mine," said the diggeluck. "She was sort of an oddball — used to wear a red cloak. Went off to deliver a cake to her grandmother . . ." and he told them a story. He followed this with another, and then another. To begin with, the japegrins reacted with a hostile silence, but gradually they mellowed and even allowed themselves an occasional laugh. There was nothing else to do — no view to speak of, because of the snow.

"He's quite funny really, isn't he?" said one japegrin to another. "Whoever would have thought it?"

The cuddyaks trotted along, impervious to the blizzard, and snorting now and then. The sleigh's runners made a faint whooshing sound, drowned out for a while by the rushing torrent of a river, which ran alongside the road before veering off in another direction. Everyone was huddled beneath the covers — blankets, then skins and furs. These were nice and warm, but smelled rather rank. The cuddyaks smelled, too. It

was the sort of oily smell you get on your fingers when you run them through your hair — particularly if you haven't washed it for a while — only stronger, and mixed with the scent of leather harnesses. After a while Felix got used to it, and it ceased to bother him. The diggeluck finally ran out of stories, and then the snow stopped as suddenly as it had started, and the sky cleared.

The sunset seemed to last forever, streaking the sky with delicate pinks and blues. Eventually, the sun sank below the horizon, and it got noticeably colder. The moonlight was almost as bright as daylight, and the landscape turned to the sort of silver that's almost white and the sort of black that's almost blue. The mountains stretched into the distance, smooth snowy slopes slashed through with dark crags, and

the little dwarf trees made strange lumpy shapes, their boughs laden with snow.

Felix must have dozed off, because he felt himself wake with a jerk. The most eerie sound imaginable was all around him, rising and falling. Then it stopped, presumably as suddenly as it had begun. He sat up. "What was that?" he asked.

"Snagglefangs," said the driver shortly. "Full moon."

A japegrin at the rear of the sleigh lifted his harpoon and rested it on the guardrail. The other passengers looked at one another, but none of them seemed inclined to comment.

Felix looked at Betony. "What's a snagglefang?"

"I don't know," said Betony. "We don't have them down south."

Felix scanned the surrounding countryside. Once or twice, he thought he caught a glimpse of something white moving against the white snow, but it was hard to be sure. It was only when one of the shapes turned a pinpoint pair of luminous green eyes on him that a chill ran down his spine. These creatures were hunting, and they were hunting *him*. It felt as though there'd been a mistake. The people on the sleigh were intelligent, thinking beings. They weren't simply *food*.

"Hold on tight," said the driver. "We're going to see if we can lose them." He yelled at the cuddyaks, and shook the reins. Felix could see the whites of the animals' eyes as they rolled them in protest, but they broke into a lumbering gallop and the sleigh speeded up.

"I don't like this," whispered Betony as they jolted along. "Cuddyaks can't outrun *anything*. Those snagglefang things are getting closer."

Felix glanced out of the rear of the sleigh. Six pairs of disembodied green eyes were following along some ways behind. His mouth went dry with fear; the disembodied smile of the Cheshire cat from *Alice in Wonderland* had scared him half to death when he'd been small. Then he realized that the eyes only *looked* disembodied because the animals had snow-white coats, which were lost against the icy backdrop. They looked like the illustrations he'd seen of Pleistocene dire wolves, and they seemed to be about the same size. Big.

The eyes were getting closer. He could make out the shapes of their bodies now, ghostlike in their pallor, and he could see their paws landing on top of the tracks made by the sleigh, hear the faint *thubbidy-thub* as they sent up little puffs of snow.

The driver started to swear quietly to himself as the japegrin tried to take aim with his harpoon, but the sleigh was bouncing around too much.

The eyes were a *lot* closer now — although it was hard to estimate their real distance since there were no landmarks, just snow. The snagglefangs looked completely at home in this frozen wasteland, and ran so effortlessly they seemed almost to float.

"Go right, go right!" shouted the japegrin suddenly, and the sleigh nearly tipped over as it did a sharp turn, spraying snow in a graceful arc.

Felix felt his knuckles go into spasm as they gripped the guardrail too tightly. The sleigh was heading straight toward a crevasse, and the cuddyaks were galloping flat-out. As they drew closer, he saw that there was a bridge. It was very narrow. It looked as though someone had spun it from sugar, to decorate a wedding cake. Delicate strands of white twinkled in the moonlight, arching over a chasm so deep that Felix couldn't see the bottom until they were actually on the bridge itself. The river below foamed and frothed and battered its way past boulders that were so far away they looked like pebbles. All he could hear was a faint rumble, like white noise. Snow was blowing off the cambered surface like clouds of spray, and there was a grating and a grinding noise from the sleigh as the runners hit stone. Felix bumped his nose on the seat in front, and then felt a tiny trickle of blood reach his lip. He wiped it away with the back of his hand.

When they were halfway across, the first snagglefang loped into sight. It was the creature's long black shadow that Felix noticed first, then the beast itself. For the first time, he got a really good look at it — and so did everyone else. He could see the ears, pricked, fluffy, set at a slight angle on a heavy skull. Its coat was thick and furry, like a husky's, and its fangs were long and thin and pointed, with a slight curve to them. There was a wail of fear from someone, and a stifled sob from someone else.

"Just get us to the other side!" yelled the japegrin with the harpoon. "I'll do the rest!"

The sleigh skidded to the left, and one of its runners strayed perilously close to the edge. Felix heard the diggeluck catch his breath as the driver hauled on the right-hand rein to compensate. The sleigh managed to steer a central course from then on, and they reached the other side without mishap. All six snagglefangs were on the bridge now, their wraithlike bodies coiling and stretching as they ran. They were closing the gap.

"Stop!" called the japegrin with the harpoon, and the cuddyaks slid to a halt, breathing hard.

Felix felt his nose begin to throb where he'd hit it on the seat in front. Was he going to have a full-scale nosebleed? Finding a handkerchief occupied him so thoroughly that the next time he looked up, the japegrin had jumped down onto the snow. But instead of aiming his harpoon, he had drawn his wand. He pointed it at the bridge, and shouted something with lots of Zs in it.

The bridge seemed to crumble to nothing. The snagglefangs fell with it into the chasm below — looking, at that distance, like cuddly toys thrown from a window by a bad-tempered child.

The rest of the passengers burst into spontaneous applause, and the japegrin smiled and bowed.

"Lovely bit of sorcery," said the diggeluck.

"There's just one problem," said the driver.

The other passengers looked at him expectantly.

"Yergud's on the other side of the chasm. We went way off course trying to escape the snagglefangs, and the only route back involves making an even bigger detour to the north."

There was a moment of silence.

"Can't be helped," said someone.

"Are we going to travel all night, then?"

"You're not going to find an inn out here in the wilderness, are you?"

"Oh!" said Betony, pointing upward. *"Blazing feathers!* What's *that?"*

There was an eerie strip of light in the sky, like a wisp of dry ice illuminated by a green spotlight. As they watched, it faded . . . only to reappear somewhere else.

"It's the Sky-mold," said a japegrin. "You get it a lot up here at this time of year."

The light started to behave like a gauze veil, doubling over on itself and streaming away into nothingness, reappearing, fading, intensifying, flickering, fading again.

"It's the northern lights," said Felix, awestruck.

"Are they dangerous?" asked Betony.

"No."

"So what are they?"

"There's something called the solar wind, and charged particles from it collide with gas particles in the atmosphere and make the lights . . ." He stopped, aware that he was losing her. "I need to give you a real science lesson. Several lessons, really."

The lights flickered and danced, and a shooting star went straight through the middle of them.

"For me," said Betony, "it's enough that they're beautiful. I don't particularly want to know how they work."

Felix grinned. "Typical girl."

"I am *not,"* said Betony. She bent down, made a snowball, and threw it at him. Felix retaliated, and for a while they exchanged missiles. As usual, Betony scored more hits than Felix — but when they called a halt, they realized that everyone else had climbed back on board and tucked in their covers. As they walked back to the sleigh, they noticed that the cuddyaks had become very nervous, and after shying a few times, they lowered their horns and stood shoulder to shoulder.

"What's that?" asked someone, pointing upward.

A four-legged shape was flying across the face of the moon. It turned its head in their direction and then veered toward them.

"It's a brazzle!" exclaimed the diggeluck. "*Picks and shovels*, they're really fierce, brazzles are."

The brazzle went into a long glide and landed on the snow in front of the sleigh. Felix had been hoping that it would turn out to be Ironclaw, but this one was a female, and it wasn't Thornbeak. The japegrin leveled his harpoon.

"No!" shouted Betony.

But it was too late. The japegrin had fired already, and the weapon streaked through the air, the rope snaking along behind like a party streamer. The brazzle looked astonished for a moment; then the harpoon hit her a glancing blow and she sank down into the snow.

"It's Fuzzy," said Betony, in a strange, expressionless sort of voice.

"It can't be Fuzzy," said Felix, horrified. "Fuzzy's just a chick."

"Not anymore."

Felix felt sick.

"I meant she isn't just a little chick anymore."

They both ran over to her.

Rhino had never flown in an airplane, let alone on the back of a dragon. His family hadn't gone on vacations, because they never knew which one of them was going to be in prison at any given time. Rhino had five elder brothers, and all but one of them had a criminal record.

There had been no one to witness his cowardice at the airstrip, when he'd taken the sleigh to Yergud instead of the fire-breather to Tiratattle. This time, though, there was no way out. He had to travel to the Spitfire Mountains by dragon, or look like a total wimp. At least he wasn't on his own. Two japegrins, Catchfly and Pepperwort, were accompanying him, and they would do the donkey work of loading the animal's panniers with sulfur. All Rhino had to do was identify the stuff. He knew it was yellow, and that was about it. Maybe there was something else scientific he could turn his hand to? Drilling for oil, maybe? Lots of things came from oil: gasoline, polystyrene, asphalt, paraffin, adhesives . . . He remembered the list only because he'd had to write it out for a detention once.

The takeoff had been horrible. Rhino had barely fastened his seat belt before the fire-breather heaved itself to its feet and galloped off down the runway like a demented goanna. It spread its huge leathery wings, lifted off the ground, climbed for a minute or two, and then banked steeply. The horizon turned nearly vertical, and Rhino felt sick. The japegrins were chatting away to one another as though traveling sideways was perfectly normal. He shut his eyes and willed the time to pass as quickly as possible.

After a while things settled down, and Rhino opened his eyes. They weren't as high up as he'd expected, and they were traveling toward some mountains. The landscape directly below seemed rather featureless because of the snow, although there were lots of rivers and some spectacular waterfalls. Every so often they passed what he assumed to be a factory, because of the steam, and he wondered what they manufactured. He turned his attention to his immediate surroundings and noticed a basket strapped to the seat in front of him with soda and snacks and an in-flight magazine. He read about the rebuilding program in Tiratattle, the stone quarrying in Yergud, and the library in Andria. He also read about the geothermal water that came from underground, bubbling and steaming and heating the glass domes that grew the vegetables in this cold northern land. A little later, he spotted a streak of red in the distance. There was either some smoke or some steam climbing upward from it in a snow-white column. "What's that?" he asked.

"Spitfire fissure," said Pepperwort. "The ground splits open and spews out flame."

"And what's that?" asked Rhino, pointing to a broader

streak of pale turquoise-blue, shaped like a gigantic hot dog bun that tapered away to nothing.

"Glacier," said Catchfly.

The fire-breather started to lose height, going into a long glide. The sun was low in the sky now, but the sunset was taking just as long as the sunrise. Eventually, they landed beside a group of three little wooden huts.

Pepperwort went over to the biggest one, opened the door, and beckoned to the fire-breather. He pointed at something inside, and the fire-breather shot a jet of flame through the open door. "Put the kettle on, now you've got the fire going!" called Catchfly, unpacking a leather satchel and laying some parcels on the snow.

Rhino went into the hut. A log fire was roaring away in the fireplace, as though it had been going for hours. There were some rough wooden cots, a table and some stools, and piles and piles of thick woolen blankets.

Pepperwort filled the kettle with snow and hung it over the fire on a metal hook. Then he pulled the cork out of a gourd, and it popped the way a bottle of wine does when it's uncorked.

Rhino had a sudden flashback to life at home. His mother eating fries, with a cigarette in one hand and a glass of gin in the other — not an easy feat. His brothers, swigging beer straight from the can and watching football on TV. The cat, peeing behind the sofa. He missed the cat.

He looked out the window. The mountains towered above

them, the sheer rock faces black against the florid evening sky, the slopes of snow between them a deep cobalt-blue. It beat the London suburbs hands down. He looked around the hut. The fire danced and crackled, and central heating suddenly seemed dull and pedestrian. What really hit him, though, was the silence that underpinned it all. He could hear Catchfly and the fire-breather outside, barbecuing something, but other than that . . . nothing. No traffic, no sirens, no airplanes, no television. To his astonishment, he actually liked it. He, Rhino, the streetwise city kid. He lived in the poorer part of Wimbledon, the part that wasn't on the hill. He'd grown up in a concrete landscape that smelled of discarded takeout food and exhaust fumes, and he suddenly realized that he hated it.

"Barbecued cuddyak steaks and piffleweed salad," said Catchfly, appearing in the doorway with three plates balanced on his arm, like a waiter from a fancy restaurant. "Just as good as any lickit could produce. Not that I've ever discussed recipes with one. They tend to avoid japegrins. Frightened of us, for some unfathomable reason." He laughed.

Everyone was frightened of me, too, thought Rhino. *The whole school was scared of me. And it felt great. Except when you needed someone to talk to, because they'd only say what they thought you wanted to hear. Best never to* need *to talk to anyone.*

Eventually the night closed in around them, but when the moon came out, it was as full and fat as a Gouda cheese. Catchfly had found some sort of stringed instrument, and

he was trying to tune it. Pepperwort was humming
something — then, suddenly, he was no longer singing by
himself. The most eerie sound imaginable was all around
them, rising and falling. Then it stopped, as abruptly as it
had begun.

"What was that?" asked Rhino.

"Snagglefangs," said Catchfly. "But *we're* all right; we've
got a fire-breather on guard."

8

"Fuzzy?" Betony kneeled down in the snow beside the brazzle's motionless body and stroked her head. She noticed that a few of the golden feathers there had turned black and spiky. "Oh, Fuzzy," she sobbed. "I'm so sorry I took all the interesting jobs in the library and left you the indexing. And I'm sorry I laughed at that squawk song. And I'm sorry I told Thornbeak you weren't serious about history."

Fuzzy opened a bright yellow eye. "So it was *you*?"

Betony's mouth dropped open.

"It doesn't matter," said Fuzzy. "And it explains why she didn't get her feathers in a twist when *I* told her."

"She's alive," said Felix, rather unnecessarily.

"Of course I'm alive," said Fuzzy, standing up and shaking the snow from her plumage. "But it's much safer playing dead when there's a mad japegrin with a harpoon close by. Is he likely to fire at me again?" She wriggled the wing where the missile had caught her a glancing blow.

130

Felix glanced behind him. The japegrin had reeled in his harpoon and was standing there, talking to the driver.

"She's a friend!" Betony called out. "She's not going to hurt you!"

"Don't bank on it," said Fuzzy, under her breath. "That's the second time I've been attacked for no reason."

"I thought you were dead," sniffed Betony, wiping her eyes with her sleeve. "I thought that was why your feathers had started to turn black."

"Had them done at a screech salon," said Fuzzy. "They look pretty smooth, don't they? Anyone who's anyone has black spikes this season. And check out the talons."

"Nice," said Betony, wondering whether pink and orange really did go together.

Felix overheard the driver say, "You were protecting the sleigh, pal. I'll stick up for you if she decides to press charges."

"What are you *doing* here?" asked Betony.

"Rescuing you," said the brazzle. "And some boy called Rhino. I think Nimby must have gotten the name wrong, though, because . . ."

"Nimby?" squealed Betony, her face going pink with excitement. "You've seen Nimby? Where is he?"

"How do you think I found out about you two — and your friend?"

"He's not my friend," muttered Felix.

"Nimby's been hexed by a brandee," Fuzzy continued. "It should wear off soon. Then he'll come and find you."

131

"Are you two getting back in the sleigh or what?" demanded the driver.

"They don't need *you* anymore, squinty-eyes," said Fuzzy. "They've got *me* to take them to Yergud now."

The japegrins looked at one another. Riding on a brazzle was unheard of. The driver shrugged and shook the reins, and the sleigh creaked and squeaked its way into the distance.

Felix and Betony climbed onto Fuzzy's back, where the sleek bronze feathers changed to tawny fur. Fuzzy twisted her head around to look at them — her neck was far more flexible than theirs. "There's supposed to be a group of rescue huts around here somewhere," she said. "A carrionwing told me about them. Drew me a map, even."

"What was a carrionwing doing in Yergud?"

"Going to a shrieking convention," said Fuzzy. "She was guesting with a squawk band as well. How smooth is that?"

Felix just listened as the conversation moved on to music. He was still having trouble accepting that this fashion-conscious brazzle was the scrawny little chick he had tucked under his arm the previous summer.

"I can't fly any farther," said Nimby to the brandee. "It's getting dark. I'm going down. I have sensors that detect comfort facilities and there's some rescue huts up ahead. We can shelter in one of them. Rhino's execution will have to wait."

It was clear that the biggest hut was occupied, because a fire-breather was curled up asleep beside it, snoring. Inside, someone was wailing a tuneless song about carousing on ice-bound ships, and someone else was accompanying him on a bangithard. There was a sleigh parked outside the middle hut, but it was covered with snow, so it couldn't have been used for a while.

The brandee opened the door of the smallest hut and dragged the carpet inside. He lit the fire with a wave of his hand, but it was a while before it burned up enough to provide much warmth. Nimby settled himself by the hearth, and the brandee made himself comfortable on one of the cots.

"It's not very nice being at someone's beck and call, is it?" said Nimby conversationally. "Now that Squill's got your lamp, he's got you sewn up like a stuffed pillow."

The brandee poked the fire and said nothing.

Nimby could feel the hex beginning to wear off, and he wanted a piece of the action. No carpet had ever won the Magical Objects Bravery Award. It had long been a dream of his to beat the crystal ball that had won first place for the past three years for rolling into extreme danger to predict catastrophes. "Funny thing, free will," he said. "I know a sinistrom who developed it when he became separated from his pebble. His name's Grimspite."

The brandee looked around. "The one who wrote the cookbook?"

"Yes, him. He said that the trouble with free will is that once you get it, you don't always know what to do with it."

The brandee snorted.

"Me," said Nimby, "I don't want it. Give me a nice under-standing mistress who goes to interesting places, and I'm as silky as a carpet can be."

The brandee scowled. "You don't want free will because you've never had it. I keep getting it for a while and then los-ing it again. If I were a human being, I wouldn't be beholden to anyone ever again. And the only way to achieve *that* is with a scientist . . ."

"Or possibly the right powerword," said Nimby. "If they really exist."

"They exist, all right," said the brandee. "They're stored inside my lamp, in a jinx box. It's forgotten what they are, though. A jinx box always forgets a powerword once it's got someone to use it."

There was a moment of complete silence. Then Nimby said, "Are we talking about the jinx box that was used to col-lect the Common Language, by any chance?"

"You know the story, then."

"Of course. There was once a sorcerer who convinced our world he'd discovered time travel," said Nimby. He was very well-educated, for a carpet. "The guilds sent him off to find a language that was either extinct or hadn't yet been discov-ered, so that *everyone* had to learn the new language from scratch. Except he wasn't time traveling, because it's impos-sible. In fact, he'd discovered the Divide spell."

"Not exactly," said the brandee. "It was the *jinx box* that created the Divide spell, by accident. The sorcerer had stored

134

his useless time-travel number-string in there, and the box fiddled with the figures."

"Well, anyway, the sorcerer went to Felix's world, using the spell," said Nimby, "and he brought back English."

The brandee nodded. "When he came back, he kept the jinx box in my lamp. Nice quiet place to work while he compiled his dictionary and got it ready for Quillfinger the scribe to copy out. He didn't realize that the box kept changing things. Hippopotamus to river-fatty, djinn to brandee, that kind of thing."

"Is it still there? Inside your lamp?"

"In the greenhouse. It looks very nice next to the evening flumpett — it's pretending to be a marble pedestal at the moment. It doesn't take a lot to amuse it."

"What would happen if it remembered the powerwords?"

The brandee didn't answer for a moment or two. Then he said, "It's a nasty piece of work, that box. Malicious. Fortunately, the powerwords are only effective if they're spoken by a mythical being. Rhino said one of them by accident — *abracadabra*. That gave me partial free will, which is a good thing for me; but unfortunately, you get both good *and* bad effects."

"What might make the box remember them?" queried Nimby.

"The book I read wasn't too clear about that," said the brandee, looking slightly worried. "I'm hoping it's nothing to do with explosives. Rhino set off a firecracker inside my lamp." He poked the fire again. "The sooner I execute Rhino, the better, I think."

The air outside was suddenly filled with an eerie sound that rose and fell in a cadence of howls, composed of many voices — although, even with Nimby's sophisticated sound sensors, it was impossible to say how many.

The brandee got up, went over to the window, and peered out. Then he hurried over to the door and barred it shut. After that he drew his dagger and tested the edge, then threw more logs on the fire.

"What are they?" asked Nimby, as the chorus intensified.

"I don't know," said the brandee. "But it is quite possible they are hungry enough to gnaw on a carpet."

"They won't come any closer with a fire-breather out there," said Nimby.

"As long as it stays there. Male fire-breathers are all cowards, despite their size."

Suddenly, there was silence.

The brandee looked through the window once more. "Whatever they are, they're camouflaged even better than a riddle-paw on a rock," he said. He sat down on the cot and studied his dagger. "I happen to know that the fire-breather outside is Squill's," he said eventually. "So Rhino must be in the hut next to us, with two japegrins. If I had free will, I could let the boy go. As it is . . ."

"Why don't you wait a while?" said Nimby. "You never know, after all."

"I could always kill him in the morning," agreed the brandee, sheathing his dagger again.

"Spoken like a human being," said the carpet.

"There!" cried Felix, pointing at three dark smudges in the distance.

"Fuzzy saw them ages ago," said Betony, who was sitting in front of Felix. "They're the rescue huts."

"What's that lump, by the biggest one?"

"A sleigh, I think," said Fuzzy. "But it's so covered with snow, it's hard to tell."

"No, next to it."

"Oh, yes — it's a fire-breather. And I can see firelight through the window. There must be people inside."

"The smallest hut's occupied as well," said Betony.

"We'll use the empty one, and fly on to Yergud in the morning."

The brazzle spiraled down as silently as the snowflakes that accompanied her, and landed behind the middle shack. "Gotta hunt," she said. "I'm famished. You two go inside and warm yourselves up. I won't be long."

Felix opened the door, and he and Betony stepped inside.

"Quite cozy, really," said Betony, shaking out some of the brightly colored blankets and fluffing up a few cushions.

"What's Fuzzy going to find to eat out there?" wondered Felix.

"No idea," said Betony. "But I hope she brings us back a

137

haunch of something. There's a roasting spit in the corner. Otherwise, there's dried fruit, dried mushrooms, or dried fish."

Felix kneeled down by the fire and recited the only spell he could do, waving his hand across the dry tinder. To his delight, a flame licked out, and before long the wood had caught fire, too.

"Here." Betony had recovered from her fright over Fuzzy and was back in bossy mode. She handed him a kettle. "Fill it with snow, and we'll have a hot drink. There's some powdered stuff in this jar; it smells quite nice."

Felix went outside into the moonlight and walked a little way away from the huts, so that he could scoop up some clean snow. The blizzard had stopped. He noticed that the fire-breather had woken up, and he stood there and watched it for a moment. It didn't look terribly happy. It couldn't be the cold, because it had built-in central heating, and it couldn't be hunger, because the japegrins had brought a carcass for it, which it had nearly finished.

Felix watched it treading down the snow with its feet and circling on the spot — the way cats do when they've chosen a bed but it isn't quite to their satisfaction. Every so often it looked around, scanning the surrounding countryside with bloodred eyes. Somewhere in the distance, a swivelneck called *hoo-hoo-hoo*, and the fire-breather nearly jumped out of its skin. *I suppose they must shed their skins like reptiles or insects*, thought Felix. *Maybe it's about to do that and that's why it's behaving oddly — could be interesting.* He'd watched a mantis molting once. It hung upside down from a twig and pulled one leg after the other out of the old skin like someone peeling off thigh-high boots.

But the fire-breather wasn't about to shed its skin. Instead, it stood rooted to the spot, and stared very hard into the distance. Then it looked wildly around, selected a downhill route, and ran like blazes until it had sufficient speed to take off. Felix watched it spread its wings and lift into the air.

The door of the biggest hut flew open and a japegrin dashed outside, swearing, just as the fire-breather disappeared behind a mountain. Then the japegrin saw Felix, and he stopped dead in his tracks. "Who in the name of a bent wand are *you*?" he demanded.

"I could ask you the same thing," stalled Felix.

"Catchfly. Here on Thane Squill's business."

Squill had become a *thane*? The last Felix had heard, he'd been chief prosecutor for the late President Fleabane — and he'd lost his case against Snakeweed, who'd been just a smidgen cleverer than he.

The japegrin looked at the patch of melted snow where the fire-breather had been. He turned to Felix, his face livid. "*What did you say to it?*" he yelled. "You *idiot*. That wasn't just our transport, it was our insurance against attack."

Felix stiffened. "Attack? Attack by what?" And then he didn't need an answer anymore. The unearthly wail that had started up told him everything he wanted to know. "Snagglefangs," he said, and both he and the japegrin dived simultaneously for the nearest door. They squeezed through it wedged together, neither wishing to give way, and slammed it shut behind them. The japegrin locked it, barred it, and bolted it.

"Well, well," said Rhino, leaning back in his chair and placing his hands behind his head. "Fancy meeting you here."

Felix just stared, lost for words. *Rhino, here?* He'd been in Yergud the day before. The coincidence was beyond belief. Or was it? Fuzzy had known where to find the huts, and the japegrins presumably had known where they were, too. And the reason for their visit didn't take a lot of brainpower — sulfur. He'd even told Rhino where to find the stuff himself. He stood there, meltwater running down his neck, feeling stupid. Then he thought, *We've found him. We've found Rhino. We've just got to get him to come back with us now.*

There was a second japegrin sitting on one of the cots, a bangithard between his knees, and he looked decidedly familiar. *I remember you*, thought Felix. *Pepperwort. Snakeweed's sidekick, but very junior.*

"I could tell them to throw you out into the snow," said Rhino. "But I don't think we want to open the door really, do we?"

The song of the snagglefangs was all around them now, and so close that the singers had to be right outside. *It's a good thing Betony's safely inside the other hut*, thought Felix. *If truth be told, it felt rather more substantial than this one.*

140

He suddenly realized that Betony had no idea where he was, so he decided to take a look out the window and see if he could signal to her. The pane of glass was thick and old-fashioned, with a greenish tinge to it. He could see the other huts, warped by the glass so that they seemed to lean at crazy angles. And then a face appeared — and it appeared so suddenly that Felix let out a gasp of shock.

The snagglefang's snout was pressed right up against the glass, and its slanting green eyes were looking straight into his. Although the animal remained there only for a moment, its image stayed etched on his retina as clearly as if he'd taken a photograph. The head itself was huge, as big as a bear's, and covered with shaggy white fur. The muzzle didn't taper  the way a true wolf's would have; it was heavy and blunt, and armed with ferocious teeth. He caught a glimpse of thick black gums and a scarred black nose. And then the creature was gone, and he remembered to start breathing again.

Catchfly looked at Pepperwort. "Wand fully charged?"

Pepperwort shook his head.

Catchfly tossed a notebook over to him. "There's a recharging spell in there I keep for emergencies. Use it."

Pepperwort used it.

Felix turned back to the window, glad that the glass was

141

so substantial. The snagglefangs had stopped howling. They'd discovered the remains of the fire-breather's dinner and were tucking into it with relish, snarling and batting one another out of the way with paws the size of shovels. Table manners clearly weren't their thing. Felix could see two of them having a tug-of-war with a length of intestine. It broke in the middle, and they both did backward somersaults. He laughed — but the laugh sounded slightly hysterical, as though it belonged to someone else. He tried to be constructive and counted them: six, fewer than he'd expected. It was only when he saw the door of the middle shack open a fraction that he realized Betony was going to go outside and look for him. She couldn't see the snagglefangs from where she was, but surely she could hear them? He banged on the window, but it had no effect.

"What?" said Rhino.

"Betony," said Felix, heading for the door.

Catchfly reacted like lightning, and reached the door before Felix. He stood there, his back against it, shaking his head.

Felix tried to push him out of the way, but he drew his wand.

"Here," said Rhino. "You can share my window if you like."

"No, thanks," said Felix, and he went back to his previous vantage point. Betony had come right out of the hut now and was bravely following Felix's tracks through the snow, carrying a blazing torch as protection. In a moment, she would turn the corner and come face-to-face with the pack.

Felix kept banging fruitlessly on the window, harder and harder until his knuckles bled. If only Fuzzy would come back. He heard himself asking the japegrins if snagglefangs were shadow-beasts, as though this were some scene from a film and nothing to do with him.

"No," said Catchfly.

"Yes," said Pepperwort.

"What's a shadow-beast?" asked Rhino.

Felix saw Betony turn the corner, spot the snagglefangs, and drop the torch into the snow. It went out almost instantly. The northern lights chose precisely that moment to renew their display; the sky was suddenly awash with emerald, and the bloody remains of the carcass turned black beneath the green light. Felix watched helplessly as the first snagglefang raised its bloodstained snout and turned its head to look at the small blond figure standing there. Felix dug his nails into the palm of his hand; he was powerless to prevent this appalling tragedy.

And then, astonishingly, the door of the littlest hut opened just a fraction and a *carpet* squeezed itself through the gap.

Felix wanted to cheer at the top of his voice, but he kept quiet just in case he might spoil Nimby's plan. One of the predators took a pace forward, then another, and then the first one was padding forward and the lights seemed to dance in time with its steps. The carpet flew across the snow like an arrow and swept Betony's feet from beneath her as the snagglefang broke into a run. Lifting his edges to keep his pas-senger in place, Nimby swooped upward. The snagglefang sprang, but the carpet was too quick for it.

The scene blurred; Felix realized that his eyelashes were wet, and he brushed them dry with the back of his hand.

"Nifty bit of flying, that," said Pepperwort admiringly. "Top-of-the-line carpet, has to be."

"The werewolves are going," said Rhino. "Look."

"They're not werewolves," said Felix.

"I thought they only came out at night? Werewolves only come out at night."

"I told you what they are — snagglefangs," said Pepperwort. "They turn to stone at sunrise, and come alive again at sunset."

The creatures seemed very jumpy all of a sudden. They jibbed and shied and snapped at one another, and two of them slunk off with their tails between their legs. *How odd*, thought Felix. One of them looked up into the green-and-black night sky, and after that the other three followed suit. And then they were streaking away across the snow. All they left behind was a welter of paw prints, a patch of blood where the carcass had been, and two lengths of intestine. As he watched, a dark shape swooped down on the pack from above.

Fuzzy.

The snagglefangs scattered in different directions — all except for one, which seemed to have decided that attack was the best form of defense. It was no match for a brazzle, though. Fuzzy seized it in her talons and rose into the air once more. When she was high enough, she simply dropped it, and the snagglefang must have broken its neck as it landed, for it didn't move again. It didn't turn into something else, either, so that proved snagglefangs weren't werewolves.

This time Catchfly didn't stop Felix from opening the door and dashing outside. Nimby had circled around, and now he floated gently down. Betony jumped off, and Felix ran over to her and flung his arms around her.

Betony didn't hug him back. "Were you in the other hut all the time?" she said coldly.

"Yes."

"And you didn't try and stop me from going outside?"

"I *did*," protested Felix. "Look." He showed her his skinned knuckles. "There are two japegrins in there, though, and they wouldn't let me out."

"Two japegrins and me," said Rhino, appearing in the doorway wearing the brandee's black hooded cloak and looking like the grim reaper. Then he saw Fuzzy overhead, and froze. It was the first time he'd seen a brazzle. Fuzzy's sheer size alone was intimidating — and then there were the razor-sharp claws and the curved aquiline beak to consider.

"What a result," said Nimby. "Betony, do you think you could nominate me for the Magical Objects Bravery Award?"

Fuzzy swooped down and landed next to them. "I couldn't find anything," she said. "But I can eat the snagglefang. I don't suppose that you . . . ?"

"No, thanks, Fuzzy," said Betony.

"I'm not sure *I'd* fancy eating a shadow-beast, either," said Pepperwort. "They smell terrible when they're alive. Goodness knows what they smell like once they're dead."

"Snagglefangs aren't shadow-beasts," said Felix. "Surely you know all shadow-beasts vanish when they die?"

"Will someone tell me what a shadow-beast *is*?" said Rhino, keeping his distance from the half-eagle–half-lion creature he had now realized was a griffin. Fuzzy was much too soft a name for something that looked capable of ripping his head off.

"Shadow-beasts are magical creatures created from spells that went wrong," said Betony. "They're all horrible."

"I've heard of sinistroms," said Rhino. "Is a sinistrom a shadow-beast?"

Betony nodded.

Fuzzy suddenly noticed Rhino, angled her head, and peered at him with an acid-yellow eye. "So you're the human that's been causing all the trouble, are you?" she said. "Is it the japegrin hair that makes you so unpleasant?"

Rhino seemed to lose his voice all of a sudden.

Betony snickered. Fuzzy could be every bit as intimidating as Thornbeak.

146

Fuzzy looked at her. "What?"

"Nothing," said Betony.

But Felix was smiling as well now. Fuzzy had sounded just like her mother — severe and headmistressy, and not to be messed with.

Fuzzy turned to Felix. "What?"

"It's easy to see whose daughter *you* are," said Felix.

Fuzzy glared at him.

"Oh, look," said Betony tactfully. "The fire-breather's coming back."

They watched it land and skid to a halt in front of them, looking sheepish.

As if on cue, the door of the smallest hut banged open, dumping some snow from the roof onto the ground in a miniature avalanche. "Well, this is excellent," said the brandee, emerging from within and unsheathing his dagger. He surveyed Rhino for a moment — then he said, "You're wearing my second-best cloak. Oh, well. Condemned being's last perk, if you like."

"Who are *you*?" asked Catchfly.

"Stephen Rheinhart's executioner."

There was complete silence while a few mouths dropped open.

Rhino is the only reason we're here, thought Felix. *We've just found him; we* can't *lose him now. I may hate his guts, but I don't want him* dead.

"Squill has taken possession of my lamp," explained the brandee. "He has ordered me to eliminate you."

Quick as a flash, Betony began to recite, "I command you in the name of . . ."

"Sorry," said the brandee. "I've already been commanded in the name of K'Faddle by Squill, so that won't work. Brandee law is awfully complicated. People do doctorates on it."

Rhino looked at Catchfly. Catchfly looked at Pepperwort. Pepperwort looked at the brandee. "But *why* does the thane want him dead?" he asked. "He sent us up here to collect sulfur to make that gunpowder stuff."

"The boy's a fraud. His science won't work because he isn't a scientist." The brandee felt among his flowing robes and pulled out a sheet of paper. "This is a death warrant."

Catchfly seized it and read it. He looked at Pepperwort. "It's genuine," he said.

Rhino had gone as white as a sheet. "You can't *kill* me for impersonating a scientist," he said.

"Of course I can," said the brandee.

Rhino looked at Catchfly. "You're not going to let him, are you? I thought we were friends."

Catchfly didn't answer.

Rhino turned to the other japegrin. "Pepperwort? You were teaching me that song. 'Mallemaroking' . . . remember? And you were going to show me how to play the bangithard."

Pepperwort wouldn't look at him.

"You see, Rhino, I need a body," said the brandee, as though he were discussing an item of clothing. "Squill wants to put it on display. Only after that will I be free to continue my search to become a human being."

Everyone looked at everyone else. The brandee tested the edge of his knife, then wiped it on his clothing.

Suddenly, and without any sort of warning, Rhino surprised them all by leaping aboard the fire-breather and yelling "Move!" in its ear. And, equally surprisingly, the fire-breather did precisely as instructed and took off.

"Stop him!" shouted Catchfly, making a grab for Nimby. The carpet fluttered feebly and fell back onto the snow. There was a moment of complete chaos as everyone fell over everyone else.

In the midst of all this, the brandee suddenly and inexplicably turned to gas and streamed off into the distance, apparently becoming one with the Sky-mold.

"Quick," said Fuzzy to Felix and Betony, crouching for a moment to enable them to climb aboard. Then she took off and hovered over Catchfly, snatching Nimby from him with a flick of her beak and transferring him to her talons.

"No energy," said Nimby weakly. "It's all this night flying."

"I know," said Fuzzy, rising higher into the air. "Hold tight, humans. We're going to catch that fire-breather!"

The japegrins watched Fuzzy rise above the snowy landscape, the carpet held securely in her talons like a furled flag.

"What now?" said Pepperwort.

Catchfly drew his wand.

"Why didn't you use that earlier?" asked Pepperwort.

"Because it's going to be far more effective once they're all up in the air," said Catchfly. "There's a warrant out for Rhino. If we bring him back, there'll be a promotion in it, you mark my words."

"Dead or alive?"

"Oh, dead," said Catchfly. "He's never going to survive this. It's a long-distance plummeting spell I learned from a carrionwing."

9

Ironclaw circled above Yergud, looking for the perching rocks. He couldn't see anything that fit the bill, although he did spot a carrionwing sitting on a rocky outcrop on the outskirts of the town. He homed in with his magnifying vision. There was a battered old sign, which read: ONE SILVER PIECE PER NIGHT, PAID IN ADVANCE. The rocks themselves had obviously seen better days, and there was a sort of blackened crater in the middle of them.

Ironclaw spiraled down and landed on the rock next to the sole occupant. It was numbered, the way rocks always were when they were rented out. Ironclaw glanced around. No one was collecting any money.

The carrionwing looked Ironclaw up and down and said, "Don't you have any manners? There are plenty of vacant perches farther away."

"I'm not here to roost," said Ironclaw irritably. "I'm looking for my daughter."

151

"Oh," said the carrionwing. "As it happens, I did meet a young female in the fly-in restaurant on the cliff face. Spiky black feathers and pink-and-orange talons?"

"I don't think so," said Ironclaw.

"She's the only one I've seen around here. Fuzzy, her name was. Into squawk music in a big way."

"Where is she?"

"I thought you said she wasn't your daughter?"

"I made a mistake. Where is she?"

"She's been to a talon salon without telling you, hasn't she?" cackled the carrionwing. "Adventurous in the food department as well. Tried the rotted fish, and it's not everyone'll do that."

"Yes, but *where is she?*"

"Talking of dinner," continued the carrionwing, "that restaurant I mentioned serves a very good fermented fertle juice. The name's Scoffit, by the way. And you are?"

"Ironclaw," said Ironclaw, clenching his toes in annoyance. It looked as though the information he wanted was going to cost him at least a couple of drinks, if not a whole meal. "Lead the way, then," he said bitterly.

"Jolly decent of you," said the carrionwing, and they took off.

It took three whole buckets of fertle juice and two portions of cadaver à la carte before Scoffit seemed inclined to talk. By this stage, both parties were rather less coherent than they'd been when they arrived.

152

"So where is she?" asked Ironclaw eventually, punctuating his sentence with a hiccup.

"Gone to the spitfire mountains, to find a tangle-child and a couple of mythical beings. A human and a rhinocerosh."

"Oh," said Ironclaw, wondering what a rhinocerosh was, though he'd be plucked before he'd ask.

"You'd better pay the bill if you're to get off before night-fall," said the carrionwing.

"Yes, all right," said Ironclaw irritably. He had a slight case of indigestion, and an uphill flight was definitely not appealing.

The meal turned out to be quite expensive. He passed over two gold coins from his leg pouch. Then he jumped off the precipice in what he hoped was an *I-do-this-all-the-time* sort of way, and opened his wings.

Scoffit watched him bank sharply, nearly hit the cliff face, turn to the north, and fly off into the distance.

Catchfly held his wand out in front of him, pointed it at the distant speck that was Squill's fire-breather, and waved it rather theatrically in a figure eight. Then he declaimed the spell as though he were taking his Level Thirteen Magical Elocution Exam. After a moment or two, his expression darkened.

"What?" said Pepperwort.

"Nearly out of range." He tried again — but he was in a hurry, and his aim was not what it could have been.

The wand fired its spell at Fuzzy instead, who was a lot

closer. She had been having a hard time gaining height because she was carrying both Felix and Betony on her back, as well as a rolled-up carpet in her talons. The Sky-mold seemed to gather itself together into a streak of green lightning, which hurtled down and enveloped her in a blaze of shimmering emerald. For a moment, Fuzzy's dark shape was silhouetted, and then it disappeared behind a billowing cloud of green smoke.

"Nice," said Pepperwort admiringly. He glanced sideways at his superior. To his surprise, Catchfly had dropped his wand as though it had bitten him and was just standing there with his mouth open. He looked sort of silly. "What?" said Pepperwort.

"That wasn't supposed to happen."

"I thought you said it was a plummeting spell?"

"It is. And that's all she was supposed to do — plummet. I don't know where all that green fire came from."

Pepperwort shrugged. "It doesn't matter, does it?"

"Of course it does," said Catchfly. "I was after Rheinhart, not them. What good are their deaths going to do us?"

When the green fire enveloped them, Felix thought they were all done for. Out of the corner of his eye, he saw Rhino's fire-breather turn to a small speck and disappear. Then Fuzzy let out a strangled squawk, Betony screamed, and Nimby made a noise like wet laundry flapping in a hurricane. The emerald flames were all around them, weaving about in a

154

crazy tarantella, but they didn't burn at all. The flames felt more like a cool breeze licking against damp skin, hinting at winter. The heat came from elsewhere — somewhere much closer to Felix's heart. He felt something start to scorch a hole in his pocket. Hot, hot, hot — he turned the fabric inside out in an attempt to escape it. There was a sudden beam of light. He must have knocked the switch of his flashlight into the ON position. It rolled out, hit him on the knee, and then tumbled away like a parachutist leaving an airplane. He caught one last glimpse of it as it fell, glowing like a live coal.

Fuzzy was spiraling slowly down, autumn leaf–style, and as long as her rate of descent remained the same, none of them risked much more than a twisted ankle. Nevertheless, Betony was clinging on for dear life. Nimby was unable to do likewise, and after a moment, as Fuzzy's talons relaxed their grip, he drifted away from them like a skydiver in free fall, and Felix lost sight of him.

The snow-covered ground rose to meet them — not in a great rush, but certainly fast enough. Before Felix had a chance to collect himself, they had all landed *plop* in a deep drift, and he was struggling to breathe. He wiped the snow from his face and fought his way out. Betony joined him a moment later. Fuzzy shook herself and looked disoriented.

"Are you OK?" Betony asked her, her voice filled with concern.

Fuzzy shook her head. "I've chipped a couple of talons."

"No harm done, then," said Betony.

Fuzzy glared at her. Then she stretched out a wing and peered at it.

"Where's Nimby?" asked Betony, looking around.

Felix looked around, too, but he couldn't see him.

Fuzzy stretched out her other wing and gave both of them an experimental flap. Nothing much happened — she should have lifted a couple of feet off the ground, but she didn't. "I feel dead craggy," she said. "I think we should try and get some sleep."

Felix peered into the distance, but he couldn't remember exactly where the fire-breather had gone. They'd lost Rhino *again*. He wanted to scream — but to be honest, he was simply too exhausted.

"I'm going to look for Nimby," said Betony, and she wandered off.

Felix remembered the time he and Betony had been crossing the mountains with Ironclaw and they'd dug a shelter in the snow. He started to dig, and Fuzzy joined him. After a while, Betony came back empty-handed, but they were all too tired to do anything further. The three of them curled up in the shelter they'd dug, and fell asleep immediately.

When Felix woke up the next morning, the sky was blushing a delicate coral-pink at the horizon. Dawn was so different here — a long, lazy, unhurried procedure. For a moment he lay there, watching it through the opening in the ice cave —

then he remembered that Rhino had gotten away from them again, and his heart sank. He wasn't very comfortable, either; something was digging into his hip. He felt in his pocket, and pulled out the jinx box. This morning it seemed to be covered with skin, and the touch of it welcomed him like a handshake. For a moment, he was tempted to open it — then he realized that Betony was already up. He could see her scouring the immediate vicinity for her magic carpet. After a while, he saw her coming back, looking despondent, so he put the box in his backpack. Somehow, he knew she wouldn't want anything to do with it.

Fuzzy climbed out of the shelter and shook herself. Then she spread her wings and flapped them a few times. Once again, nothing happened. "I've been hexed," she said finally. "I didn't think it was possible. Brazzle feathers are supposed to act like a shield."

"Even when *not* attached to their owners," said Felix, who had Thornbeak's feather to thank for his current good health. "I've used them to ward off vampreys, too."

"It doesn't make sense," said Fuzzy.

"That hex turned my flashlight red-hot," said Felix. "No idea where the thing is now. I dropped it. It won't work anymore, anyway, not when it's been half-melted."

"I think that might be important," said Fuzzy. "Although, at the moment, I'm molted if I can think why. I don't feel too good."

"Does that mean you can't fly?" asked Betony.

157

Fuzzy nodded.

"The hex will wear off, won't it?" asked Felix, worried.

"Of course it will," said Betony. "Nimby had one put on him, remember? They don't last long." She glanced around, as though the mention of his name might help to summon him.

"So we'll just have to walk for a while?"

"Brazzles aren't built for walking long distances," said Betony, scanning her surroundings again. "I was hoping that Fuzzy would be able to see Nimby from high up, with her magnifying vision. We'd better go back to the rescue huts."

"The japegrins are there," said Fuzzy. "With those heavy-duty wands."

"What we need is a sleigh," said Felix.

"And who's going to pull it?" snapped Betony. "Just the two of us, with a brazzle on board?"

Felix grinned. "Have you ever tried pulling a sleigh?"

Betony glared at him. Then she shook her head.

"It's much easier than pulling a cart."

"I may be much bigger than you," added Fuzzy, "but my bones are hollow. I weigh less."

"I think I remember a sleigh parked next to one of the huts, but it was covered with snow," said Felix.

"I bet we could sneak up and nab it," said Betony, perking up. "The japegrins will be inside, keeping warm." She glanced back at the snow-covered landscape, now tinged with lilac and pink. "I wish I could see Nimby."

They left Fuzzy behind, since she was too ungainly on the ground to make any real progress through the snow. It took longer to get back to the huts than Felix expected — it had taken only a minute or two to fly the distance the previous night. Walking was harder than it looked. Sometimes the snow was quite firm, and other times they sank down to their knees in it. There was no way you could tell; the surface was crisp and white no matter what it covered. Occasionally, there were patches of bare rock, dappled with bright orange lichen where the wind had swept the snow away, and sometimes there were tussocks of yellowish grass poking through, which also helped.

It was a depressing journey. For just a moment that previous night, things had been OK. They'd found Rhino, and they'd had transportation — and then everything had gone wrong. Rhino would probably try to sell his gunpowder recipe to someone else now.

Felix could see a wisp of blue-gray smoke curling out of the chimney of the biggest hut, and as they dodged into its shadow, they could hear voices, although they couldn't make out the words. The sleigh was still there.

"We'll have to be really careful about this," whispered Betony. "We need to push it in *that* direction, so that they can't see us through the window."

Felix nodded.

"And before we do it, I think we should go into the other hut and get some supplies."

Felix nodded again. Betony was so much more practical than he was — neither of them had had any breakfast, and dried fruit and biscuits would be a lot better than nothing. They sneaked into the hut and grabbed a couple of blankets and a kettle as well. They needed something in which to melt snow to get drinking water. Felix seized a bundle of kindling, too, and Betony nodded her approval.

The next thing they had to do was to clear the snow off the sleigh, which was piled so high with the stuff that it looked like a giant marshmallow. They discovered a brown leather cover, which protected the wooden seat beneath which the cuddyak harnesses and the harpoon were stored. It wasn't going to be the height of comfort, but it was clean and dry. Felix buckled one section of the harness to the shafts — they needed something they could use to haul the sleigh along, and that was as good as anything.

When everything was ready, they nodded to each other, and each placed a strap over one shoulder. Then they pulled. Nothing happened. They tried pushing. That was no good, either. Then they tried one pulling and one pushing, with the same result.

"Stop," hissed Felix. "The runners are frozen in their tracks."

Betony looked at him, unsure what to do.

"We have to break them out. I read about it, in a book by Jack London. First this side, then that. It's worth a try."

They put their backs against the side of the sleigh, braced themselves, and leaned against it, hard. Then they went around to the other side and did the same thing again. There was a cracking sound, and the sleigh seemed to shift slightly. They moved to the back of it and tried pushing it again. This time, it inched forward. They smiled at each other, their faces red and shining from the effort, their eyes twinkling with victory. The sleigh moved very slowly at first, but as the runners freed up, it moved more easily until they could go around to the front and pull it steadily.

The next few minutes were nerve-racking, for at every moment they expected to hear the japegrins call out to them to stop. But as the huts grew smaller and smaller and nobody challenged them, they dared to hope that they'd gotten away with it. By the time they reached Fuzzy, they were feeling very pleased with themselves.

"Smooth," said Fuzzy, looking equally pleased.

"Where to?" asked Felix.

"Yergud, I guess," said Betony. "Unless you've got any better ideas."

"So which way is it?"

Fuzzy pointed a wing.

Felix looked surprised.

"Brazzles have a really good sense of direction," said Betony. Her face clouded for a moment. "Like magic carpets."

"Let's have breakfast *before* we get going," said Felix, wanting to distract her. "I'm starving."

"I'll preen, then," said Fuzzy. "I don't need to eat as often as you humans do."

161

Felix opened his backpack, feeling around inside for the breakfast supplies. His fingers closed over something squashy and furry, and he quickly withdrew them.

"What?" said Betony.

"I think something's made a nest in there."

"Don't be ridiculous," said Betony, and she upended the backpack in the bottom of the sleigh. Dried fruit and crackers tumbled out, as well as some disgusting-looking dried fish and a green velour overnight case, shaped like a hippopotamus.

"Wow!" said Betony. "A river-fatty! You kept that pretty secret." She grinned. "Don't be embarrassed — I've got a cuddly brazzle in Andria that I take to bed with me." And before Felix could protest that he'd brought nothing of the kind with him, Betony had picked it up and unzipped it. She wasn't used to zips, and she caught her finger in it.

"Hi there," said the jinx box.

"Oh," said Betony, disappointed. "It's you." She put her finger in her mouth. The zip had drawn blood.

"I know some really good words," said the box. "They get amazing results."

"Well, I suggest you keep them to yourself," snapped Betony, sucking her finger.

"Even if they reverse the effects of plummeting hexes?"

Felix pricked up his ears. "Go on."

"They need to be spoken by a mythical creature — but *wow*, that's not a problem here, is it? I'll list them for you. There's hocus . . ."

"Felix, don't listen to it. You can't trust jinx boxes," Betony interrupted.

The jinx box sighed theatrically. "I'm only trying to help," it continued. "Traveling by fire-breather is an awful lot faster than lugging a sleigh. Your friend will be far ahead of you by now."

Felix gritted his teeth. "Rhino is not my *friend*," he muttered, "but the box does have a point, Betony. We'll never catch up with him like this."

Betony shook her head. "It's nothing but a troublemaker, Felix. Put it away." And before Felix could say anymore she grabbed the jinx box and stuffed it back into the backpack. "We'll ask Fuzzy about it when she's finished her preen," she said firmly. "After breakfast."

But by the time Fuzzy had rejoined them and they had finished their meal, it was as though the incident hadn't happened at all.

Pulling the sleigh was hot work, because when they came to soft patches of snow it was much harder to keep it moving. Felix stripped down to his T-shirt, and Betony put her cloak on the seat next to Fuzzy, who treated them to a few rather rude songs her father had taught her. Eventually, they came to something resembling a road — a track made by hoofed animals of some sort. Things then got a lot easier, so easy that they were able to take it in turns, with one of them pulling and the other one riding.

Felix felt a bit guilty to begin with, when Betony was

being the cart horse. It didn't seem very gentlemanly. Felix's parents were extremely particular about manners — men opening doors for women, and everyone waiting until everyone else was served at the table before starting to eat. It wasn't until Betony made a noise like a cuddyak, pranced a few paces, and called out, "Hey, this is fun," that he felt OK about it and started to take an interest in his surroundings.

And the surroundings *were* spectacular, no doubt about it. After an hour or so, they came to a puddly sort of area, with patches of bare wet rock crusted with yellow and interspersed with tiny lakes. For a moment, Felix didn't understand — why wasn't the rock treacherous with ice? How come there was water everywhere? They stopped for a rest and some more dried fruit and crackers.

Suddenly there was a loud whooshing noise, and a column of water shot up into the air in front of him. Betony leaped backward, slipped on the rock, and fell over. Felix knew better than to offer her a hand up — she had to be seriously injured to accept help. The column continued to spurt into the air for a moment or two, giving off clouds of steam, and then it subsided, and everything was quiet once more. Betony stood up, trying to look dignified about it.

"That was a geyser," said Felix. "The water around here comes from underground, and it's hot. That's why it hasn't turned to ice."

"Natural hot water?" scoffed Betony. "You've got to be

kidding." She dipped her finger in the nearest lake and pulled it out again sharply. "Ouch!" she said. "You're right. But how?"

"We have a subject called geology," said Felix. "The scientific study of the structure of the world. The core of the earth is a lot hotter, and there are faults in the crust called vents and fissures and fumeroles. Water for this geyser probably comes from an underground river, flowing over the hot molten rock deep down below, which superheats it."

"So is it forced through the crack?"

"Yes. The steam comes first, followed by the column of hot water. Conditions underground tend to remain the same, so the eruption will happen at regular intervals. If a geyser suddenly changed its pattern, it could be predicting an earthquake."

"Oh," said Betony, looking at it suspiciously. Felix suspected she didn't know what an earthquake was but wasn't going to ask. She pointed at the ground. "What's that yellow stuff?"

"Sulfur," said Felix, noticing it for the first time. "It's what Rhino came up here to collect, to make gunpowder."

"I wonder where he is now?"

"He'd be a fool to go back to Yergud," said Felix. "There's a price on his head. I don't think we'll find him there. What would *you* do if you were Rhino?" He picked up his section of the harness and looped it over his shoulder.

"I don't know," said Betony, doing the same.

They got the sleigh moving, and trudged along for a while in silence. Fuzzy seemed to have dozed off. Her eyes were shut, her eyelids as mauve and wrinkly as her skin had been when she'd first hatched.

"More to the point," said Felix, a little later, "what are *we* going to do?"

"Try a crystal ball parlor?"

"They're not very reliable, are they?"

"Not really. They get it right sometimes, though."

"So does sheer chance."

"I know what *I'd* do," said Fuzzy, opening an eye.

"What?"

"I'd think about what the fire-breather might decide to do. Has Rhino piloted one before?"

"No," said Felix. "But it's not difficult. All you have to do is tell them where to go. Politely, of course. They may not be able to speak, but they understand everything. Especially abuse. They hate abuse."

"Rhino won't realize that. If he insults it, the fire-breather could simply decide to do its own thing."

"Go back home, you mean, to its stable in Yergud?"

"Perhaps, or it might rejoin some wild ones. Rumor has it that they live in fire craters," said Fuzzy.

Betony gulped. "That's just a story. There aren't any wild ones left. And what would they live on, out here?"

"Whatever made this track," said Fuzzy. "I'm hoping we come across a herd of them before too long, because that snagglefang wasn't terribly filling. You could roast a haunch."

A roast dinner sounded wonderful.

"We'd need a fire to do that," said Felix miserably. "The little bit of kindling we've got will boil a kettle of water, and that's about it."

"No problem," said Fuzzy, pointing a wing. "Look."

They had breasted the top of a small incline and were looking down into the valley below. Felix was instantly reminded of stubble burning in a field — the flames stretched out in a line of warm, bright color against the dull blues and grays of the snow-covered rocks. White smoke rose in a lazy wedge above it, hanging in the still air like a gauze curtain.

"It's one of those fissures I told you about," said Felix. "A crack in the earth's crust."

"It's like a wound," said Betony. "That red stuff . . ."

"Molten rock."

"It's like blood . . ."

"See those dark specks, over to the right?" said Fuzzy. "I've just magnified them. They're nobble-heads."

"Nobble-heads?"

"Just one of them would feed all of us," said Fuzzy wistfully.

"We're forgetting something," said Betony. "Fuzzy can't fly. And if she can't fly, she can't hunt."

167

"We can't pull this sleigh indefinitely on dried fruit and crackers," said Felix.

"Oh, right, let's buy some eggs and cheese, then," said Betony sarcastically. "The market is which way?"

"Are you suggesting *we* kill one of those nobble-head things? I've never hunted *any*thing; I wouldn't know how." His stomach chose that moment to tie itself into a knot, and then to rumble rather loudly.

"Fine," said Betony shortly, letting go of the harness and picking up the harpoon. "Fine. I'll do it, then."

"Have you used a harpoon before?"

"No. But it can't be too difficult, surely." She cranked back the crossbow, but she couldn't make it go all the way. She scowled and said something under her breath.

Felix held out his hand. "Let me try," he said. And to his astonishment, he was able to cock it. Not only was he taller than Betony now, he was stronger than she was as well. He caught a glimpse of the expression on her face — outright admiration. Then she noticed him watching and stuck out her tongue.

They left Fuzzy in the sleigh, and set out across the icy volcanic landscape toward the herd of nobble-heads. As they got closer, Felix could make out more detail. They looked a little like a cross between elk and reindeer — they had the coloring of reindeer, a sort of dirty gray and white, but the antlers of the bucks were more reminiscent of the great Irish elk of prehistory. They were huge spreading hand-shaped horns, like exotic plants sprouting from the creature's fore-heads. Even at this distance, Felix could tell that they were big animals. They made him feel very puny indeed. He glanced at Betony.

She caught his eye, misinterpreted his look, and gave him a thumbs-up. She clearly thought their roast dinner was just a matter of time.

10

As he lay in the snow after he'd fallen from Fuzzy's talons, Nimby realized he was soaking wet. This was very bad news; not only would he be paralyzed until he dried out, but he would lose his voice. He would be no better than a bedspread, or a tablecloth, or that torchlike thing of Felix's, lying dead on the ground nearby. Worse, actually. People would wipe their feet on him — assuming anyone ever found him out here in this cold, bleak place. He lay in the snow, shivering, hoping Betony would come looking for him. But as the day wore on, he realized that he wasn't going to dry out — his damp fibers simply froze, and he became as stiff as a board.

He grew more and more despondent. Fuzzy had had sufficient altitude for the fall to be fatal for both her and her passengers — creatures with backbones were very flimsy compared to carpets, and they broke far more easily. He thought about the hex the brandee had placed on him. There had been something very strange about it. The brandee had used the "inky, pinky, now you're mine" hex to bind him, which felt like being hung from a clothesline in thick fog. And, like fog, these hexes never lasted all that long. The Skymold hex had been something *far* more powerful. He looked at the flashlight. One end of it seemed to have melted. A scorched torch. He liked the sound of that. Maybe he should have stayed with Turpsik and learned some poetry. That "Mallemaroking" song of hers, now . . .

Your mind's wandering, Nimby, he said to himself. *Careful. That's what happens when things die of hypothermia. Think about the torch thingy. It must have gotten terribly hot to have ended up like that. But how — and why? It was a scientific instrument . . .*

The solution hit him like a kick from a cuddyak the moment he recalled the conversation between Rhino and Squill. There had been a colossal otherworld explosion in a ragamucky's shack, and there had been a *crystal ball* in there. It had cracked in two — the magic in the ball had reacted to the science of the firework. The plummeting spell and the torch had done exactly the same thing. The combination of science and magic wasn't as straightforward as thirteen plus thirteen. It was more powerful — like thirteen *times* thirteen — or even thirteen *to the power of* thirteen.

Nimby wanted to wriggle with excitement, but he couldn't even move a tassel. Just imagine, a *carpet* coming up with an idea as sophisticated as this. Ironclaw would be

171

seriously impressed, the other magic carpets he met would be in awe of him, and Betony would be *so* proud.

And then he heard voices. He wanted to twist himself around to see who it was, but it was impossible. And then someone said, "Inky, pinky, now you're mine; winky, dinky, stay in line."

It really wasn't fair. Why did it always have to happen to *him*? He felt himself lifted into the air, and he got his first look at his new master. It was Catchfly. Once he had a higher vantage point, he could see that he'd landed very close to the rescue huts, and the japegrin had spotted him when he went outside to get some more logs from the wood-shed. The hut loomed large in front of him, and the door banged open.

"Thaw him out by the fire," said Catchfly to Pepperwort, throwing Nimby across the room. "And then make us both a hot drink."

Pepperwort glanced around. "There's no kettle," he said.

"Well, go and look in one of the other huts."

Pepperwort went outside and felt instantly uneasy. He wasn't worried about snagglefangs — they didn't hunt by day. Rumor had it that they turned to stone; no one he knew had ever seen one in daylight. There was something different out here, though, but he couldn't quite put his finger on it. Something was missing. Perhaps he was still expecting to see the fire-breather. He went into the middle hut and rooted around for a kettle. There wasn't one. *Odd*, thought

Pepperwort. And the blankets are missing, too. He went back outside, intending to visit the smallest hut — and then he realized what was different. The sleigh was gone. He could see the tracks of the runners, disappearing into the distance. He could see footprints as well. Two sets, leading to where the sleigh had once been. Then two sets leading away again, although the runners had almost obliterated them. It didn't make sense. He went back to the biggest hut and told Catchfly what he'd seen.

"It's perfectly obvious, simpleton," said Catchfly. "The plummeting spell didn't finish them off after all. But the brazzle can't fly anymore, and they need the sleigh to carry her. I don't see that it's any of our concern, to be perfectly honest. It's Rheinhart we're after."

"Where do you think he is?"

"The fire-breather will head back to Yergud."

"So we're going back to Yergud? Empty-handed?"

"Once that carpet's defrosted," said Catchfly. He kicked the offending object with his foot.

Nimby coughed. He was getting his voice back as pieces of him unfroze and then dried out, and the Magical Objects Bravery Award seemed farther away than ever. It was mid-afternoon by the time he was fit to travel, but the japegrins didn't want to waste any more time. "I can't fly after sunset, you know," he said, his voice still a little hoarse. "I twisty-strip sunlight for energy, like a plant."

The sky had darkened and was now the color of tarnished silver.

"It's going to snow," said Pepperwort. "I wish we didn't have to go back. Squill will be furious."

"I'll think of something," said Catchfly. "We'll be heroes by the time I've finished my tale."

Ironclaw was getting hungry. The double portions of cadaver à la carte at the fly-in restaurant had been prepared nicely, with a piquant bittersweet sauce — but the portions had been a little on the stingy side. Haute cuisine was all very well, but it didn't fill you up. What he needed was a nice meaty carcass. He lost some altitude and scoured the snow-fields below with his magnifying vision — both for his daughter *and* for something to eat. There were two of those spitfire mountains ahead, and the one on the left was a big one. He could see the smoke curling out of the top of it. A live one, then. No one with any sense would live close to something like that, so finding a roadside eatery and buying a haunch of something was out of the question.

He flew even lower, and when he spotted the herd of nobble-heads, he couldn't quite believe his luck. He'd had nobble-head only once, when he'd taken Thornbeak out for a meal in their courting days, half a century or so before. It had been the most expensive thing on the menu (decorated with a set of antlers), and his suggestion that she pick something else had not been well received. She'd sent back the fertle juice *twice*, and asked to be moved to a perch with a better view. Ironclaw had begun to wonder whether she really *was* the hen for him — then she'd lashed her tail and wiggled her hindquarters, and he'd taken a deep breath and paid the bill without quibbling, even though he'd spotted a small mistake in the service charge.

He went into a long glide, selected his prey, and dispatched it with the minimum of fuss. It tasted even better than he remembered. It tasted so good, in fact, that he ate far more than was strictly necessary. After that, an afternoon nap seemed like a constructive idea — when he woke up, he'd be in top condition to go off looking for Fuzzy. Thornbeak was being overprotective; Fuzzy would be all right. She had the strongest peck on her of any pullet he'd ever come across. He would have loved to take the credit for that himself, but it was something she was more likely to have inherited from her mother. He yawned and looked around for a likely roost. There wasn't one. All the trees were stunted little things that wouldn't have supported a carrionwing, let alone a brazzle, and there wasn't really any shelter anywhere. Unless . . .

There would be a crater in the spitfire mountain. A nice sheltered area, with its own central heating. Just the ticket. He left some of the carcass uneaten — it really was too big for just one, and when he found Fuzzy, he could offer her a snack. Then he took off and winged his way up to the crater.

Ironclaw had spent most of his life on Tromm Fell, a rocky outcrop above a temperate forest. There weren't any extremes of climate there — it didn't snow, and the summers were pleasantly warm. Snow wasn't a novelty, nor was desert — he'd traveled quite widely for a brazzle, actually. But this fire-and-ice landscape was an unknown quantity.

The geyser came as a total surprise. He was flying low because the temperature was dropping as the altitude increased, and he was right over the top of the geyser when it blew. He found himself shot upward into even colder air by a jet of hot water to his backside. It was a good thing he hadn't been even lower, because the water had cooled down a little by the time it hit him. At least there hadn't been any witnesses; the whole episode was most undignified. Then he came to some bubbling mud, which made belching noises and spat at him, and a flaming fissure that spewed out a curtain of smoke.

The summit of the mountain was wreathed in clouds. He flew on, and the next time the clouds cleared, he was nearly there. A moment later, he was over the lip of the crater and landing on a ledge. The ledge was on the warm side, so he hopped around until he found somewhere more comfortable.

He was just dozing off when he heard wing beats. He opened his eyes, wondering if it was Fuzzy. He hadn't thought to look — she could have had exactly the same idea and been roosting somewhere close by.

It wasn't Fuzzy. It was a fire-breather — a fire-breather without a saddle, or a harness, or the name of a travel company painted on its side. And it was heading straight for him.

Ironclaw leaped into the air, doing the first vertical take-off he'd done for decades, and hovered on an updraft. The fire-breather overshot and skidded to a halt on the ledge. It turned its head toward him, its bloodred eyes pinpointing his position, and breathed out a jet of flame. Ironclaw flapped his wings furiously and rose higher. The fire-breather was hunting *him*. The sheer nerve of it! He was so incensed that he didn't take the sensible option and turn tail. He just hovered there, out of reach of the beast's breath, but close enough to take a good look at it with his magnifying vision. What he was looking for was some evidence of the corporation that employed it, because he fully intended to report its behavior to the appropriate authorities. It was outrageous behavior, absolutely outrageous. Perhaps the creature was mentally ill, because it certainly wasn't old and doddery and two kidneys short of a pot pie. Nor had it downsized and decided to retire here; it was far too young. It was in tip-top condition, and it looked very mean indeed, although it didn't seem inclined to chase him into the air — which showed some sense, at least. Fire-breathers were no match for brazzles in the air; they couldn't maneuver as well, and they were usually rather leery of them. Scared, even. Your average fire-breather was something of a coward.

177

Unless it was a female.

Ironclaw felt sort of silly. Why hadn't he noticed that this one was a much lighter green than the ones he'd encountered in the past? He'd never seen a female before — travel companies hardly ever used them, for they were far too aggressive. Females — on the rare occasions they were used at all — transported goods, not passengers.

She sat on the ledge and watched him, her tail flicking back and forth and striking sparks when it hit the rocky side of the crater.

That was when Ironclaw noticed the crack in the rock wall, a little farther along. The fire-breather saw him looking, and her tail went rigid.

She's made herself a lair, thought Ironclaw. *Well, I never. I'd have expected her to be lost without a nice comfortable stable. I wonder what's in there — a pile of old bones? Or does she have some sort of instinct to make her home in a cave, the way female brazzles just seem to* know *how to construct a nest? And has she remembered that fire-breathers used to collect gold, when they were wild animals?*

Suddenly, the fire-breather looked the other way and started to behave very strangely. She went stiff-legged, and her head bobbed up and down. The ridge of scales along her spine stood up, and her throat blushed a deep, startling red. Then she rattled her wings threateningly, advanced a couple of paces, hissed, and bobbed her head up and down again. Ironclaw allowed himself to lose a little altitude so that he could see what had attracted the fire-breather's attention and caused this reaction.

It was another fire-breather.

Ironclaw didn't hesitate. His leg pouches were practically empty — Thornbeak had relieved him of most of the gold he'd brought home with him. The fire-breather wouldn't have made an inventory of everything she had collected — if indeed she *had* collected anything. Good grief, she couldn't even speak, let alone add — and if she couldn't add, she could hardly be called an intelligent being, could she? She wouldn't miss a few nuggets. The nuggets would have been stolen from elsewhere in the first place, anyway. He felt a little uncomfortable with this reasoning — he could hear Thornbeak saying, *Two wrongs don't make a right, Ironclaw.* Perhaps he could return the gold to its rightful owner, if any of it had been engraved with an identity mark — minus his commission, naturally. He landed on the ledge a couple of paces from the fissure, and slipped inside while her attention was elsewhere.

A flock of birds lifted off the ground as Felix and Betony approached them, and scattered like windblown litter.

"What are they?" Felix asked.

"Don't know," said Betony. "I'm not one of those sad beings who go around with notebooks, jotting down things like the 'lesser spotted tease.'"

"The what?"

"Lesser spotted tease. It hardly ever stays still long enough for anyone to identify it. Those white things are just birds, OK?" They were taking turns carrying the harpoon, and it was proving to be heavier than she'd expected. Getting close to the nobble-heads was nearly impossible as well. A while back, one of the creatures had spotted them. The rest of the herd lifted their heads and turned to look. Then — rather than galloping away in fright — they just moved off a little, out of range. Every time Felix and Betony got close enough to think that maybe, just maybe, it was worth cocking the crossbow, the same thing happened.

"Those birds," said Felix. "I think they've been eating something. Let's go take a look."

And sure enough, there were the remains of a nobble-head on the ground. Betony made a face.

"This is a real piece of luck," said Felix. He noticed Betony's expression. "I'll carry it. You carry the harpoon."

Betony handed it over and looked the other way as Felix hefted the remains of the carcass onto his shoulders. It was unpleasant business, messy and a bit smelly, but it had to be done. The terrain was too bumpy for the sleigh, and Fuzzy had to eat. They started to walk back.

"There's something very odd about this," said Felix.

"What?"

"Something killed this, presumably. My first guess would be snagglefangs — those rocky outcrops over there look just like them."

Betony turned to look, and a smile crossed her face. "They do, don't they? That could be one sitting on its haunches, and that lump there could be two of them lying down. . . . The only thing that spoils the effect is that they're covered with snow. There weren't any paw prints leading to the kill, though."

"Maybe it died of old age."

"Maybe."

They made their way back to the sleigh. Fuzzy said she'd butcher the remains of the carcass for them when they reached a fissure they could use as a makeshift stove. The snow began to melt as the ground got hotter, and the sleigh runners grated on the rock a couple of times. Eventually, they found a suitable spot. There was a kind of natural chimney, and they could see glowing red magma deep down below. Fuzzy climbed out of the sleigh and sliced off a couple of steaks for them. She then retired to a polite distance and started to consume the rest of it.

Felix was thinking very practically now. He speared their dinner right through with the harpoon, and rested the two ends of it on the ledges on either side of the chimney. The meat began to cook right away, and before long there was the most delicious smell.

Betony grinned and said, "You're learning." She produced some herbal tea she'd stuffed in her pocket, and they hung the kettle from one end of the harpoon and made themselves a hot drink. Then they unfolded the blankets they'd packed and wrapped them around their knees. Felix decided to use his backpack as a pillow, but it seemed to be very lumpy all of a sudden. He reached inside. His hand closed around something hard and round and knobby, so he pulled it out.

"Where did you get that?" asked Betony.

"What is it?" asked Felix. The object was actually rather ugly — sort of a sickly green, with orange lumps all over it like a rash of boils, and a bulbous little lid. He unscrewed it and sniffed.

"It's a gourd of fertle juice!" exclaimed Betony. "It's the really expensive stuff, too. Let's have a swig."

She leaned over to take it, but Felix lifted it high above his head and said, "Me first."

"*I* asked first," said Betony, trying to snatch it.

"Tough," said Felix, pushing her out of the way.

"Ouch!" said Betony, and she lunged for it again.

Felix tried to fend her off, but he was too late. Her hand caught the top of the gourd, turned it on its side, and flipped off the lid. There was no splash of bright red liquid — in fact, nothing whatsoever spilled out of it.

"Well, hi there," said a familiar voice. "Sorry, ran right out of fertle juice. Disappointed? Never mind. I've got something else that might interest you."

Felix and Betony froze.

"It's the jinx box," said Betony. "I might have guessed. Throw it *away*."

"Don't listen to her, human child," wheedled the box. "I do have something you want . . . something you *need*. . . . All you have to do is say a couple of words for me . . ."

"Don't be an idiot, Felix," snapped Betony. "Get *rid* of it. Can't you see, it wants something from you?"

Felix hesitated. OK, jinx boxes didn't sound altogether trustworthy, particularly the old kind, but there was something special about this one. It knew all about their search for Rhino, and it *had* helped them in the past. It had actually *shown* them Rhino, in Yergud, the two peaks of the volcanoes behind him like a legend on a map. They'd never have found him the first time without the box.

"Stop worrying, Betony," he said, not quite meeting her eye. "Let's listen to what it's got to say."

Betony's eyes flashed with annoyance. "It's out for number one, Felix; it has no one else's interests at heart except its own. In fact, it doesn't even have a heart. It's a *box*. I wish you'd talk to Fuzzy about it."

"And what would she know?" said Felix impatiently. "She's still just a chick."

"She studied K'Faddle products in her last history module."

"So?" He knew he was being unreasonable, but suddenly he didn't care all that much. "It's no one else's business but ours."

"It's trying to turn us against each other," said Betony sharply, "and so far, it's succeeding pretty well."

They glared at each other.

"What are you talking about?" asked Fuzzy, coming over. She'd finished her own dinner a little too quickly. Nobblehead was unbelievably delicious, and she suspected she'd pay for it later with a touch of indigestion.

Felix put the lid back on the gourd, looked hard at Betony, and returned it to his backpack. "Just complaining out loud that my backpack was too lumpy to act as a pillow," he said. "Ow! I think it's bruised my shoulder."

"No, you weren't," said Betony.

Felix looked at her, confused. He knew they'd had a quarrel, but he couldn't remember what it was about. "What was I saying, then?"

"Can't remember," said Betony. "Are those steaks done yet?"

A little later on, as they sat with their backs to the warm rock, sipping their drinks and eating their meal, things didn't seem quite so bad anymore. Of course, Rhino was still out there somewhere, either in or out of control of a fire-breather, with a gunpowder recipe for sale to the highest bidder. Fuzzy's hex still hadn't worn off, and Nimby was still missing. But life always seems a little better when you're warm and you have a full stomach.

As the brandee turned from a gas to a solid once again, he discovered that he had materialized in an office of some kind — and that the creature that had summoned him was no less than a sinistrom. He felt sick, which was really unpleasant because he could never actually *be* sick and get it over with. Being summoned by a sinistrom was no laughing matter. How on earth had it happened? He couldn't see his lamp anywhere. He glanced around. The walls of the room were lined with books, and there was a big wooden desk in the middle of the floor, covered with papers — along with a plate of cookies and a little plaque that read THORNBEAK, with a picture of a brazzle beneath it. Nothing made sense.

The sinistrom just stared for a moment, his jaws agape, which gave the brandee a particularly good view of his canines. Then he shook himself, padded across to the door, and checked that it was locked. After that, he sat back on his haunches and shook his head in bewilderment.

"Greetings," said the brandee, between gritted teeth. "I suppose you want either wealth beyond your wildest dreams or the most beautiful female of your species in the world."

"I'm a sinistrom," said the shadow-beast. "Sinistroms don't have a gender. We've always been referred to as males because we're so violent. Other than me."

"Well, that's a relief," said the brandee, trying to sound convinced. He glanced around the room. "Look," he said, "I don't know how you've managed this, because you don't have my lamp, do you?"

"No," said the sinistrom. There was an awkward pause. Then he said, "My name's Grimspite, by the way."

"*Grimspite?* Not the Grimspite who wrote *Dining Out on Mythical Beasts*?"

The sinistrom looked ridiculously pleased all of a sudden. "Yes."

The brandee managed a weak smile. "Terrific production values," he said. "The illustrations are first-rate. I know quite a lot about you, you see. You became separated from your pebble, and now you have free will. That's what *I* want."

"You may already have it," said Grimspite. "You see, I've been researching the Big Bang spell, and I found this reference to a word that was stored in a jinx box. I think it may have been a powerword. . . ."

The brandee stiffened.

"I wasn't sure it *was* a powerword," the sinistrom continued. "So I spoke it out loud, just to see what would happen . . . and there was this flash of green lightning, and *you* appeared. Listen, I'm going to order you to do something, and I want you to disobey me."

"You'd have to use the right words," said the brandee slowly.

"What are they?"

The brandee hesitated. It was one sandstorm of a dilemma. If he told this sinistrom how to command him and the powerword stuff had been a lie, he would be the servant of a shadow-beast. But would it be any worse than being the slave of a thane? Not really. Might as well go for it. "In the name of K'Faddle, the one who cast you . . ." he recited.

"In the name of K'Faddle, the one who cast you," repeated Grimspite, "I command you to stand on your head."

"I'm useless at acrobatics," said the brandee. "Can't you ask me to do something else?"

The sinistrom was smiling now, his jaws stretched wide.

"What?" said the brandee.

"You're not standing on your head," said Grimspite. "Have a cookie."

"I can't . . ." The brandee stopped mid-sentence.

Grimspite pushed the plate of cookies toward him with his paw.

The brandee took one. Then he bit into it, and the sugary sweetness that flooded his mouth was quite indescribably wonderful. "Exquisite!" gasped the brandee. "Delectable! Magnificent!"

"Welcome to the real world," said Grimspite. "Have another cookie. The honey ones are particularly nice."

"That powerword has turned me into a human being, then?" said the brandee, his mouth full of cookie. "With no going back?" Then he choked, and found out about coughing.

"Have a slurp of rainbow juice," said Grimspite. "It helps."

The brandee had a slurp of rainbow juice, and found out about hiccups.

"Not a human being," said Grimspite, glancing at the brandee's ears. "A nomad. A desert-dwelling being, of an old and noble race."

"Oh." He hiccupped again.

Grimspite gave him a thump on the back, which came as a surprise, but the hiccups stopped.

"In that case," said the brandee, once he'd recovered, "I can go back to Kaflabad, the Jewel of the Desert. Yes. That will suit me very well."

Grimspite went over to one of the bookshelves and took down a thick volume entitled *Craggy Magic*. "There's a section in here about powerwords," he said, reading the entry. Then he said, "Oh, dear."

"What?"

"A powerword can do great good and enormous harm, in equal measure."

"So something awful's happened somewhere," said the brandee. "And speaking of awful . . ." He took a deep breath and told Grimspite all about the jinx box in his greenhouse.

"We have to retrieve your lamp," said Grimspite, when he'd finished. "That jinx box must be destroyed."

"I think it's the last one in existence of the old kind."

"I know a little about them," said Grimspite. "They react very strangely to scientific events. The explosion inside your lamp was a scientific event. That may have restored its memory of otherworld things — in which case, it will be raring to get those powerwords spoken by someone. And it'll be a real charm merchant. Those old jinx boxes could sweet-talk even the best-intentioned people. They were all dedicated mischief-makers, but some were downright wicked and wanted only to create chaos. I'm afraid it sounds as though this box is one of them, and with every powerword spoken, it will become more self-confident and more destructive. We have to stop it. There's only one good side to it — once it releases a word, it forgets it."

"So the one you've just used is gone forever?"

"Yes. Let's take one thing at a time, though. You're a brandee no longer, so you need a proper name."

"Goodbody," said the brandee.

Grimspite looked surprised, but he nodded.

"There's something else," said Goodbody. He thought for a moment. "Will that word have released all the other brandees from bondage? Or anyone else, for that matter?"

189

"I don't know," said Grimspite.

Goodbody looked thoughtful, had another swig of rainbow juice, and astonished himself with a burp.

Many, many miles away, in a four-poster bed in a castle in the forest, a japegrin opened his eyes.

II

"I don't know anything about magic lamps," grumbled Scoffit the carrionwing. "I'm in waste disposal." She had been asked — at wandpoint — to present herself at Squill's headquarters.

Squill threw the lamp across the floor. It landed with a loud clunk against the opposite wall, and rocked back and forth a couple of times before coming to rest.

"It should have been foolproof, that K'Faddle summons," he said. "I want you to fly the lamp to Kaflabad for me and take it to the Service Department. Ziggurat Three."

"I'm in Garbage," repeated the carrionwing. "I'm not a courier."

"You're whatever I say you are," snarled Squill. "If you want to keep your feathers, that is."

Squill's secretary came in, her auburn hair tumbling over her shoulders like a spray of autumn leaves. "Catchfly and Pepperwort are outside," she said.

191

Squill brightened. "Do they have the human boy with them? We don't have any executions lined up for next week."

The secretary shook her head.

Squill's mouth set in a thin, hard line. "Send them in."

Pepperwort walked in rather hesitantly, but Catchfly was far more composed. He dumped the rolled-up carpet he was carrying in the corner of the room, and told the story of Rhino's escape with great flair, placing the blame squarely on Felix's shoulders. According to him, Felix had called down the Sky-mold with a scientific torch, allowing Rhino to steal Squill's fire-breather, and the others to get away on the carpet. He explained how he'd shot the carpet out of the sky at almost maximum wand range, tracked it down, wrestled it free from a snagglefang, and come straight back to Yergud on it to tell the thane what had happened.

The carpet in question didn't comment — in fact, it sounded as though it were snoring.

Squill looked extremely thoughtful. "You think this torch contraption acted in conjunction with the hex and did something unexpected?"

Catchfly nodded.

"This science and magic combination sounds too unpredictable to be really useful. A well-functioning magic lamp would be much more to the purpose. So where is the brandee?"

"He escaped as well, Your Excellency, streaming off into the sky and becoming one with the Sky-mold."

"So he could be anywhere, if he's still alive." Squill turned back to the carrionwing. "On your way, stink-feathers," he said. "I want you to get that lamp to Kaflabad as soon as possible."

Scoffit stuffed the lamp in her leg pouch and went. Kaflabad was a tall order. Andria was a lot closer; there would be a real courier service operating out of Andria. She could charge it to Squill's account and make herself scarce. She took off, heading east.

Ironclaw looked around the cave in amazement. The fire-breather had obviously been in residence for a long time. There were jeweled bangles, necklaces, ankle rings, piles of coins, ingots of silver, nuggets of gold. A leg ring, with enameled toadstools in pink and orange. Fuzzy would like that; it would match her talons. He could give it to her when he found her. He felt so pleased with this idea that he completely forgot to actually *put* it in his leg pouch. There were even entire *crocks* of gold — some lined up like loaves of bread in a baker's window, others lying on their sides, cracked and damaged, their terracotta lids askew. Ironclaw gulped. There was a king's ransom in here. His noble intention of restoring all the things to their rightful owners was totally unrealistic. *Ten* brazzles would not have been enough to carry all this treasure away.

There was still a lot of hissing and wing rattling going on outside, so Ironclaw decided to stay where he was for a while.

He examined a few of the objects for ownership marks, but the only name he found — K'FADDLE & OFFSPRING, inscribed on the base of a crystal ball — was the maker's name. He peered into it. Nothing. He'd never had much faith in the things, but he'd never tried to use one before, either. He wiped it with his wing, and looked again. This time he could see swirls of gray moving around like speeded-up clouds, and a streak of green in the midst of them, but that was all. He gave up. K'Faddle & Offspring had a dreadful reputation; the company was always being sued by someone or other. He continued rummaging — but the next thing he found made his tail flick back and forth with alarm.

In a small depression in the rock lay two oval white eggs, which were splattered with scarlet streaks. These glowed with an inner light that moved like tiny rivers of red syrup. He wondered how long it would be before the eggs hatched into replicas of their antisocial mother.

He suddenly became aware that everything had become very quiet outside. He went back to the entrance and tried to angle his head so that he could peer through the opening without his beak advertising his presence. The fire-breather had her back toward him, and her tail was curled into a question mark. The new arrival was pressed against her, flank to flank. Their heads were close together, and their long blue tongues were flickering like flames. For a moment, Ironclaw thought he was in danger of interrupting a rather private moment — then he wondered whether it was a form of communication. The creatures could roar, but their vocal cords weren't any good for speech. The new one was a deep sea-green, which meant it was a male. He couldn't be the father of the eggs, though — could he? He wasn't wild; he was wearing a saddle. And what was more, he had Squill's kicking-boot emblem daubed on his flank with scale paint.

Then Ironclaw saw the young japegrin standing behind them, quaking with fear. It did look like a japegrin at first glance, with its flaming red hair — until you noticed the rounded ears. Ironclaw was very good at putting two and two together, and he didn't like the answer he came up with one little bit.

The female was a wild fire-breather. She was probably very attractive, in the way fiery females frequently are. The male was a tame one — and a magnificent specimen, too. He would be, if he was Squill's personal vehicle. But somehow he had met up with the wild female when he was on his own, and it had been love at first sight. The hissing and wing rattling hadn't been signs of hostility at all. Squill's fire-breather was the father of the eggs in the cave, and he'd brought his secret mate a little present. Supper for two — a human child. Ironclaw had never seen this youngster before, so presumably it was Rhino, the boy his daughter had been looking for.

He wondered if the female had forgotten about him. Then both the fire-breathers turned their heads toward the cave entrance, and he knew they'd been discussing him. He slipped out of the cave and into the open as quickly as possible — being trapped in an enclosed space would be very bad news indeed.

The boy hugged himself with his arms, glanced to his left and right, and then stayed where he was. The wall of the crater, though not sheer, was very steep, and a fire-breather could have picked him off it at its leisure.

Squill's fire-breather didn't seem to know what to do. It was unlikely that he'd ever had a confrontation with a brazzle before. Brazzles would have been on the Friendly Creatures List, and it was doubtful that years of training could be overturned without a second thought. He shifted from leg to leg, fidgeting his wings and looking agitated.

The female was an entirely different matter. She had already attacked Ironclaw and would undoubtedly do so again — she had seen him coming out of her lair, and for all he knew, she assumed he'd eaten her eggs. He disliked eggs intensely, but the fire-breather wouldn't know that. Somehow, he needed to do another one of those tricky vertical takeoffs, and scoop up the boy with his talons.

Ironclaw waited until the female charged, galloping along the ledge toward him in that ungainly way that fire-breathers had. He knew she wouldn't be able to belch her flamethrower breath at him with sufficient accuracy while she was running. Nevertheless, it was a close call, and as Ironclaw lifted into the air, he was aware that she'd managed to singe a couple of his feathers. She skidded to a halt and spun around as he flew over her head — but it was too late. Ironclaw had seized the boy by his clothing and was up and away. He glanced back as he reached the rim of the crater, and saw her lash out at the male with her hind legs. Such indiscriminate displays of temper didn't bode well for their long-term relationship.

The human child wriggled and squealed. This was very stupid behavior; if Ironclaw dropped him from that height, he would certainly die. After a little while, the boy seemed to realize this, for he stopped struggling.

Ironclaw was none too sure what to do with him. He wanted to continue searching for his daughter, but he couldn't just dump the boy in the snowy wastes below. He decided to land and discuss the matter with him. He started to look for somewhere suitable among the fissures and geysers, and then he spotted a sort of natural chimney. He turned his magnifying vision on it — and that was when he saw Fuzzy, sitting beside a sleigh with Felix and Betony. He let out a screech of delight and spiraled down.

"It's my dad!" squawked Fuzzy, leaping to her feet and spreading her wings. This time, she managed a little hop and hover, and although she landed again fairly quickly, it was a good sign. The hex was beginning to wear off.

Felix could hardly believe his eyes. Life had suddenly started to look up.

Ironclaw set Rhino gently onto the ground, and gave his daughter a quick greeting-preen. "Got a present for you,

Fuzzy," he said. He looked in his leg pouch for the pink-and-orange leg ring. "Oh, droppings!" he said. "Left it behind."

"You look a little worse for wear," said Felix to Rhino. His clothes were torn and dirty, and his face was scratched.

"So do you," said Rhino. He was recovering fast from his ordeal. His brothers had used him as target practice for all sorts of horrible things. Bouncing back from adversity was a life skill in *his* family. "Listen," he continued, "I've had enough of all this. That flaming dragon was going to make a present of me to its mate, like a box of chocolates. I want to go back to Wimbledon. Wave a magic wand or something and get us there."

"It doesn't work like that," said Felix. "We have to find a Divide, which means going back to the place we arrived at. But that shouldn't be too hard now that we've got *two* brazzles." He glanced at Ironclaw, who was talking animatedly to Fuzzy. "Have you been properly introduced?"

"Get real," said Rhino.

Felix sighed. "I'd advise you to be civil to Ironclaw," he said. "He doesn't suffer fools gladly, and you've been a pretty big one. And tell me how else you're going to get home?"

"Yeah, yeah, all right," said Rhino. "Do the honors, then."

Felix did the honors.

"Yes, yes," said Ironclaw impatiently, which made the whole procedure a waste of time. "But we'll have to wait a little longer for Fuzzy's hex to wear off."

"Isn't there a spell that will speed it up?" asked Rhino.

"Of course," said Ironclaw. "But I don't fill my head with trivia like that."

They all sat down, and Rhino polished off the last of the roast nobble-head. It was snowing again, but it was warm where they were, and as long as the snow didn't get too heavy, it didn't really matter.

"My cloak stinks," said Felix, taking it off and wrinkling his nose in distaste. There was dried blood on the shoulder, from when he'd carried back the dinner.

"Don't worry," said Betony. "I think I can remember a spell to clean it." She sprinkled some snow on it and recited a little rhyme about washing. Felix's woolen cloak turned into a bunch of flowers. Betony hurriedly recited the countercharm. Then she tried again. This time she got the words right, and the stain faded away.

"The nice thing about magic," said Felix, "is that magic is always reversible."

"Science *isn't* reversible?" Ironclaw looked shocked.

"Some of it is," replied Felix. "At school, we divide science into physics, chemistry, and biology. Physical reactions *are* reversible — water to ice, ice to water."

Ironclaw looked skeptical. "We call that *stuff studies*."

"Chemical reactions are trickier. Some of them are reversible. Manmade glues have solvents, for instance. But other things don't degrade, like plastic bags. You can't get rid of them."

"What's biology?"

"The study of *living* things."

"Magic *can* do some irreversible things," said Ironclaw. "You can kill someone with a wand, but you can't bring them back to life. You can burn a building to the ground, but you can't restore it to its former state. But most charms *do* have countercharms, and most hexes have antidotes. It's disgracefully irresponsible to release a spell or a potion that doesn't have an *undo* facility, the way Snakeweed did."

"The rules sound similar to the things in the magic lamp handbook," said Felix, opening his backpack and fishing around for it.

His fingers closed over something feathery. *Ironclaw's cataloguing quill*, he thought. *I must give it back to him so he can return it to the library.* But as he tried to pull it out, he realized it was caught in something. Something square but soft and silky at the same time. The jinx box! He'd forgotten about it yet again. Suddenly, he remembered he'd forgotten the magic lamp, too, the last time he'd crossed from Betony's world back to his own. Was that some peculiar property K'Faddle products had? An ability to get themselves carted around all over the place, because people forgot they had them? He tried to separate the jinx box from the feather, but somehow the box ended up outside the backpack, while the quill remained inside.

"Oh, no," said Betony. "I'd forgotten about that."

"Wow," said Rhino, wiping his greasy fingers on his tunic. "A laptop. Imagine bringing that with you."

"What on earth are you talking about?" said Fuzzy. "It's a really smooth bangithard, with built-in echo. I've been dying to try one."

"Your eyesight's not back to normal yet, Fuzzy," said Ironclaw. "It's a math book from the other world; it has to be. *Fermat's Last Theorem*. How exciting."

"It's a jinx box," said Felix.

"Oh," said Ironclaw, sounding disappointed.

"What a pity," said Fuzzy.

"What's a jinx box?" asked Rhino.

"A storage facility," said Felix quickly, glancing at Betony. "It was in the brandee's lamp. It looks like whatever you want it to look like. Except when it's playing a practical joke. It's got a sense of humor, apparently."

"You're putting me on," said Rhino. "It's a laptop." He leaned across, slid the catch to one side, and opened it. He did it so quickly that Felix didn't have time to stop him.

Betony's hand went to her mouth in an involuntary expression of dismay, and Fuzzy said, *"Fangs and talons.* That was a pretty craggy thing to do, Rhino."

"Hi, everyone," said the jinx box cheerfully. "Nice to meet you all. Don't shut my lid just yet — I have information each one of you wants, one way and another."

"I know that voice," said Rhino. "It's the X303/D49 Battle-Monger."

"And I know *you*, Stephen Rheinhart," said the box. "You promised to take me with you if I told you how to get out of

201

the lamp, and then you went back on your word. But hey —
I don't carry grudges. I still have something you want."

"I don't think a jinx box could possibly have anything *I*
need," said Ironclaw pompously.

"Oh, I've got lots of lovely little puzzles," said the box.
"Try this one. There's a boat lying at anchor in a harbor, with
a rope ladder hanging over the side. Each rung is one and a
half toe lengths apart, and there are eight rungs. The tide is
rising at a rate of half a toe length a cuddy."

"What's a cuddy?" asked Rhino.

"A unit of time," said Betony. "As long as it takes a cuddyak to drop a cuddypat."

"How many cuddies will it be before the ladder is
submerged?"

"Twenty-four," said Ironclaw instantly.

"No," said Fuzzy, "the ladder won't *ever* be submerged,
because boats float."

"Hmph," said Ironclaw. "Trick questions for chicks. Not
interested."

"How about Fermat's Last Theorem, then? Picked that up
quite recently. Fascinating little problem, stumped human
beings for centuries. Or chaos theory. That's my speciality, of
course."

The brazzle raised a feathery eyebrow. "Go on."

"The science of nonlinear systems."

Felix knew something about this. "A butterfly flapping in a
rain forest, causing a typhoon thousands of miles away," he said.

"Very good," said the box, sounding surprised. "It's when some tiny event has what seems to be an unpredictable effect — although, if you had *all* the information, you could, in fact, predict it."

"Go on," said Ironclaw, now hopping up and down with excitement.

"Not just yet," said the jinx box. "The other brazzle — Granitefuzz?"

"Fuzzy," said Fuzzy. "I only use Granitefuzz on official documents."

"Love the head feathers, Fuzzy," said the box. "Seriously smooth. I do, of course, have the words to some fantastic squawk songs — in Ancient Brazzle, what's more. Shriek-shriek, whistle-cackle . . . Interested?"

Fuzzy ruffled her feathers. "You're a jinx box. What's the catch?"

"The only catch is on the outside of my box, darling."

Betony looked worried. Fuzzy and Ironclaw weren't reacting the way she'd thought they would. "I think we should shut it now," she said stubbornly.

"Not just yet . . ." said Fuzzy and Ironclaw together.

"There's nothing *I* want from it," snapped Betony.

"Not even the correct antidote to the spell that froze your parents?" said the jinx box in its oily voice.

The color drained from Betony's face. Then she recovered herself and said, "So what is it that *you* want, box?"

"That would be telling," said the jinx box. "Stephen

Rheinhart. You want *respect*, don't you? But, my little pachyderm, I'm afraid you'll have to earn it. "

"What do I have to do?"

"Just say a couple of words for me. I'm dying to hear them said in a real flesh-and-blood human voice . . ."

"I'm not so sure that's a good idea," said Felix uneasily. The box seemed more menacing than it had previously — it was uncanny the way it could find the very thing to tempt each one of them. Even Fuzzy and Ironclaw seemed to have been taken in by it.

"What a spoilsport you are, Felix," said the box. "A couple of years ago, it would have been easy to offer you your heart's desire — the spell to cure you. There's something else you want now, though. Above all else."

"Oh, yes?" said Felix, his chin lifting defiantly.

"Yes. And I'll tell you how to get it if you say *hocus pocus* for me."

"No way," said Felix. "That's a powerword."

"*Open sesame*, then."

"That's another one." He reached out to close the box, but succeeded only in knocking it away from him. It slid a little way down the slope. He got to his feet and started to scramble down the incline after it.

"Fermat's Last Theorem," mused Ironclaw. "There's more to that box than meets the eye."

"It knows some tail-tapping squawk songs," agreed Fuzzy. "In Ancient Brazzle, as well. How awesome is that?"

204

"I don't understand any of you," said Betony. "I'm almost certain it's one of the old jinx boxes. The nasty ones."

"They've all been destroyed," said Fuzzy.

"I think this is the last one left, and it's out to wreak havoc."

Fuzzy looked skeptical. "If it is, Betony — and I don't think for one moment you're right — we're going to have to be very careful how we dispose of it, because it will try to protect itself. I studied K'Faddle products last semester . . . but, er, that seems to be about all I remember of the syllabus . . ."

As he scrambled down the slope, Felix was surprised at how far the box had fallen. As he picked it up, it changed its appearance once again. This time it really did look like an open laptop — a laptop playing a movie. Felix caught a glimpse of himself, straddling the Andrian Divide. Betony was watching him, tears streaming down her face. He took a deep breath and slammed the lid shut. The box became a watered-silk eyeglass case, small enough to put in his pocket. He did precisely that, and climbed back up to join the others. "There's only one person who knows how to deal with this particular jinx box," he said. "The brandee."

"He could be dead," said Betony. "He turned into a gas and merged with the Sky-mold."

Ironclaw looked interested. "Sort of like a green streak in the cloud?"

"Yes. Sort of all swirly."

"Hmph," said Ironclaw. "There's a crystal ball up there, in a cave in the crater. Not that I set all that much store by them, of course, but just occasionally . . . You see, I thought I was just seeing patterns in it. But maybe I wasn't. Maybe it was showing me what happened to the brandee — and if it was, it might just show me what happened to him after that."

Rhino shuddered. "You're not suggesting we go back up there, surely?"

"If that jinx box is what I think it is, we'll need all the help we can get," said Betony adamantly.

"I'm up for it," said Fuzzy.

"You can't fly," said Ironclaw.

"Wanna bet?" Fuzzy scrambled to the top of the chimney and launched herself into the air. This time, there was no immediate return to earth. She started to gain height, slowly and steadily, circling in wide sweeps.

"All of you had better stay here," said Ironclaw. "We won't be long."

"Hang on, Ironclaw . . ." said Felix, wanting to give him back the quill. But Ironclaw was now thinking solely about Fermat's Last Theorem, and nothing was going to divert him. Felix watched the two brazzles fly off through the snow. What might happen if they didn't come back, he couldn't bear thinking about. Before he had a chance to do much of the not thinking, Betony turned on Rhino.

"This is all your fault!" she shouted. "You really are the

206

nastiest creature I've ever met, and I've faced sinistroms and vampreys and even a riddle-paw! I was supposed to be having a vacation in *your* world, trying out elevators and escalators and double-decker buses. I was supposed to be eating apples and apricots and hot dogs, and meeting humungallies and river-fatties."

"You what?" said Rhino, laughing.

"Elephants and hippos," said Felix. "And don't you dare laugh at her. She's ten times the person you are."

"*And* I've lost my carpet," said Betony, her eyes flashing. "And now Ironclaw and Fuzzy are doing something really dangerous, and . . . and . . ." She bit her lip.

"Well, there's one good thing, surely," said Rhino. "What was that part about unfreezing your parents?"

This was a more sympathetic remark from Rhino than Felix had been expecting.

"You don't understand, do you?" snapped Betony. "Of course I want them back. But they're going to hate what I've chosen to do with my life. They wanted me to be an herbalist, but instead I'm studying to be a historian. My brother's failed all his exams and is playing in a squawk band. My sister's OK — but she always was the goody-goody. Mind you, she's got a boyfriend now, and he plays in the same band as my brother. It's all really complicated."

"Actually, I do understand," said Rhino. "Bill was always my mom's favorite, because he was so good at forgery. I couldn't draw a fifty dollar bill to save my life."

"Oh, I'm sure you could do even *better* than that," said Felix. "Like drawing cash out of an ATM — with someone else's credit card, naturally."

The brandee now known as Goodbody (or Brad Goodbody, when he needed the minimum two names necessary for a nomad) waited at the fire-breather terminal with Grimspite, who was in his two-legged lickit form. They were going to Yergud, to — hopefully — get the lamp from Squill, which was where the brandee-that-was had last seen it. Grimspite knew that in his four-legged form he'd have a real chance of persuading the thane to hand it over. It was amazing what a set of really long fangs could achieve.

There were a lot of japegrins boarding the Yergud fire-breather, and neither Grimspite nor Goodbody felt comfortable with japegrins. Andria was back to being a tangle-town these days, so you could be any species at all (apart from a sinistrom) and still be treated civilly. Once in Yergud, however, it would be a different matter. They asked to be seated at the rear, to enable Grimspite's smell to waft backward. Naturally, he had drenched himself in the peribott cologne he favored, but it would wear off before the flight reached its destination. They were nearly the last to climb aboard. They both wrapped themselves up in their thick woolen cloaks; since Yergud was at a much higher altitude than Andria, it would be a lot colder. Grimspite's cloak was, of course, lickit-white. Goodbody's was black. The final passenger almost didn't make it — he had come in on another flight, which had been delayed. He had also invested in a heavyweight cloak, which was purple, so he must have been another japegrin — but he had wound a scarf around his face so that only his eyes were visible. When he was finally seated, the pilot was able to order the fire-breather onto the runway.

Initially, the trip was uneventful, and Grimspite and Goodbody passed the time by flicking through the in-flight magazines, drinking spiced milk, and eating the little complimentary packets of nuts. Goodbody couldn't wait to try fermented fertle juice, but the caterers had run out. This was probably just as well, because he hadn't gotten used to all his bodily functions yet, and some of the ones below the belt were taking him by surprise. He hadn't realized that bits of nut could get stuck between his teeth, either.

"Vattan sounds interesting," said Grimspite, passing him a toothpick. "If you like fish, that is, and I do."

They were climbing steeply now, and the ground below was white. Grimspite hadn't traveled to the north before, and he thought the frozen waterfalls were really beautiful. It was so nice being able to appreciate beauty; this had only happened since he'd acquired free will. They flew into something called the Icicle Pass, the only official flight path through the mountains, which enabled them to avoid having to go right over the top. There was a fair amount of traffic, and they passed three other fire-breathers and a triple-head. The pass was very narrow, and the fire-breather's wingtips occasionally grazed the branches of the little trees that clung to the rock face, shivering snow down onto the path below.

Grimspite had been ignoring the snatches of conversation that he was catching from the japegrins seated in front of him, until one of them mentioned the name *Snakeweed*. He tried to prick up his ears, forgetting he was in lickit mode, and merely succeeded in waggling them.

"Disappeared, apparently," said the speaker. "This raga-mucky went in to clean his room, and — gone."

"Who'd steal an enchanted body?" asked the second jape-grin. "You couldn't exhibit him, because everyone would know he'd been stolen."

"Maybe he isn't unconscious any longer," said the first japegrin.

"Oh, don't talk nonsense. A spinning-wheel hex lasts for a hundred years. How did you hear about it?"

"A carrionwing told me."

"Oh, you can't trust anything *they* say. No better than ragamuckies."

"Or diggelucks."

"My mother used to have a half-and-half chimney sweep," mused the first japegrin. "Half ragamucky, half japegrin."

"Disgraceful," said someone.

"I know. Anyway, *she* said . . ."

Before he could elaborate, the fire-breather went into a dive, and some of the other passengers screamed. Grimspite felt as though he'd left his stomach behind; the icy wind rushed past his face and blew off his hood.

"This is fun!" shouted Goodbody, who had no idea that feeling as though you'd left parts of your body elsewhere was unusual.

Grimspite caught a sudden glimpse of a carrionwing, flapping desperately to get out of the way of the fire-breather — then the two creatures collided and tumbled to earth.

"Everyone OK?" shouted the pilot, as the fire-breather's passengers stood up and brushed the snow from their clothes.

Grimspite found himself tangled together with the japegrin in the purple scarf. For a moment their eyes met, and Grimspite wondered if his cologne had already worn off. A good hard sniff persuaded him it hadn't, but he nevertheless disentangled himself as quickly as he could. Someone's wand was lying in the snow, and the japegrin picked it up. For a moment he stood there, looking at Grimspite; then he turned abruptly on his heel, handed the wand back to its owner, and had a coughing fit. He seemed to be in delicate health, and was using his scarf to cover most of his face and warm the icy air before he breathed it in. Grimspite buttoned up his white woolen cloak, and wished he were in his four-legged form so that he could really appreciate the snow. He could just imagine rolling around in it and snapping at the snowflakes that were drifting down. There weren't a lot of them, but they awakened the hunter within him the way a swarm of juicy flies would have.

The fire-breather itself was lying on the path at the foot of the pass, winded. The carrionwing touched down a moment later — she'd had the presence of mind to use her wings as a parachute, so she had made the final descent with a bit more dignity. Then she spoiled the effect by stubbing her toe and swearing loudly, fluently, and imaginatively.

Something metal hit the rock face with a loud clunk, rolled a little way, and rocked back and forth a couple of times before coming to rest.

"I don't *believe* it," cried Brad Goodbody. "It's my lamp, I know it is. I'd recognize it anywhere," and he dashed over to the foot of the escarpment and picked it up.

The pilot was trying to get the carrionwing to consider a compensation claim.

"Don't talk guano," said the carrionwing. "No one's been injured."

"That was dangerous flying, that was, and in a mountain pass as well. You were the one traveling north to south — you should have dropped down and yielded the right-of-way. I want your name."

"Scoffit," said the carrionwing irritably, glancing down at one of her forelegs. There was a leg pouch strapped to her ankle, but the lid was open and it was empty. She glanced around.

The nomad in the black cloak was trying to hide something

in his clothing, but he wasn't fast enough. The magic lamp glinted a dull and depressing gold in the weak wintry light.

"I saw you!" screeched the carrionwing. She hopped over and peered into his face. "Well, *rot my offal*," she said. "You have the look of someone just released from bondage. I know it well — I free creatures from predator hedges all the time. If they're dead already, I eat them, of course."

"I used to be a brandee," said Goodbody, clutching the lamp to him. "I'm a nomad now."

"And that was your lamp, I gather."

The fire-breather was back on its feet, and everyone else was getting ready to re-embark. "We're leaving!" shouted the pilot. "Are you two getting back on board, or what?"

"We don't need to," said Grimspite. "We got what we came for."

"Hold on," said Scoffit. "My life's at stake here. I'm supposed to be taking that lamp to Kaflabad, to get it fumigated. The Thane of Yergud is using me as a courier. If I don't deliver that lamp to K'Faddle and Offspring, Squill will have me plucked for sure."

"We'll figure something out," said Grimspite. "I'm not quite what I appear to be."

The fire-breather broke into a run and took off.

Scoffit sniffed. Then she sniffed again. After that she started to back away. "You're darned right you're not what you appear to be," she said, her face turning a chalky white. "You're not a lickit at all. You're a sinistrom."

"My name is Grimspite," said Grimspite, "and these days, I'm a writer." He transformed himself back to his four-legged form, and tried to look sweet. It was something he hadn't quite managed yet, but he was working on it.

There was a very long pause, when no one said anything.

"So what now?" asked Scoffit finally, when it was clear he wasn't going to disembowel her. "Am I supposed to hope that Squill forgets all about the lamp?"

"Join forces with us," said Grimspite. "We're on a very important mission. We have to destroy the jinx box inside that lamp before it runs riot with some powerwords."

"Oh, come on! Powerwords don't really exist."

"It was a powerword that turned that brandee over there into a nomad," said Grimspite, and he told the carrionwing the whole story.

"There's something I don't understand," said Scoffit. "Even if powerwords aren't just a myth — and I suppose the evidence *is* right here in front of me — I thought the only beings who could use them were the ones who invented powerwords in the first place. *Human* beings. But you used one. And it worked."

"He spent a year in the other world, didn't he?" said Goodbody. "Maybe some humanity rubbed off on him. He doesn't like disemboweling things anymore. I don't think the speaker *has* to be a human being, though — just a mythical beast."

"I think I became one," said Grimspite. "A mythical

being called a bonecrusher. They call them hyenas in the other world, where they really exist. I suspect that if I'd been in lickit form when I spoke the powerword, it wouldn't have worked. But because I was in my four-legged guise — and I had free will, just like a *real* hyena — I was as effective as any human being."

"Why don't you just destroy the lamp?" said Scoffit. "Then the jinx box will be destroyed as well."

Goodbody stiffened. "You can't do that!" he said. "There's a whole library in there, some rare plants, and a magic cata-loguing pen." A strange expression crossed his face. "I've got a really unpleasant feeling in my stomach."

"You're hungry," said Scoffit.

"But there's nothing to eat," said Goodbody, grimacing as another hunger pang hit him.

"That's how life is, sometimes," said Scoffit. "Pretty often, actually."

"What's that rumbling noise?" asked Goodbody, clearly shaken by the unexpected things his flesh-and-blood body was doing. "Is it my stomach?"

"I don't think so," said Grimspite. "I can sort of feel it through my paws. As though the landscape itself is angry about something."

Much to Felix and Betony's surprise, the two brazzles returned from the crater in no time at all, screeching with mirth.

"My dad is *ultra* smooth," giggled Fuzzy, who was sporting

216

a pink-and-orange leg ring. "Squill's fire-breather had gone, and the female was off hunting. So Dad leaves me on guard and goes into the cave. Then I see the female coming back, and I do my alarm squawk and hide, like we arranged." She couldn't continue, she was laughing so much.

"There was a large silver tray among the treasure," said Ironclaw, "so I polished it with my feathers and stood it against the end wall. As the female entered, she saw her own reflection and she thought there was another fire-breather in her lair. She let out a huge jet of flame, rushed the mirror, and banged her nose. I was able to slip out with the crystal ball, and we made our escape."

No one else seemed to think it was quite as funny as the two brazzles did, but the crystal ball was there in front of them, and ready for use.

Ironclaw peered into it with one eye, his head to one side. Then he peered into it with the other. He looked disappointed and shook his head.

"Let me try," said Fuzzy, but she had no better luck — although this could have been because her black spiky feathers kept getting in the way.

Felix was rummaging in his backpack again. He pulled out the magic lamp handbook and turned to the back. There was an advertisement for the K'Faddle crystal ball in there, as he'd suspected, with a few rudimentary instructions. "You can't use it in bright daylight," he said, running his finger along the text. "That's why it worked in the cave, Ironclaw."

"I'll make an umbrella with my wings, then," said Ironclaw, "and you can do the honors."

Felix placed the crystal ball on a little rocky ledge and kneeled in front of it. Ironclaw spread his enormous azure wings, and everything darkened. *Useless*, thought Felix. *I can hardly see the ball, let alone anything in it.* Then he remembered that he had to cup his hands around it.

Right away, the glass began to glow with a pearly light. Felix took his hands away, as if he'd burned himself, and the light faded. He took a deep breath and tried again. The glass began to glow once more, although it didn't heat up. At first, all he saw were swirling gray shapes, like fast-forwarding clouds.

"Well?" said Betony.

"I think I'm getting something." The shapes went grainy, and Felix realized he was looking at snowflakes. Then, like a picture coming into focus through the viewfinder of a camera, the snowflakes dissolved and the scene behind them became visible. He stiffened. That four-legged shape was unmistakable . . . the heavy head, the pricked-up ears, the sloping back, the silly little tail . . . "I'm getting a sinistrom," he said. His voice had sunk to a whisper.

There was a chorus of indrawn breaths.

"What else can you see?" asked Betony.

Felix fought to suppress the fear that had suddenly taken over his body, making his heart race and his skin prickle and his palms perspire. The fact that he had faced sinistroms and lived to tell the tale — had even been friends with one — was no defense against this knee-jerk reaction. Sinistroms were absolutely terrifying, with their knifelike fangs and their calculating eyes. He moved his hands and realized that they were behaving like a cursor on a computer, allowing him to survey different parts of the curved crystal screen. He concentrated on another area of the globe, and this time he saw a two-legged figure — one he recognized. "Yes!" he shouted, punching the air. "I've got the brandee!"

"Who's about to be killed and eaten by a sinistrom," said Betony dryly. "Yes, Felix. Just what we needed."

The brandee didn't seem especially perturbed by his proximity to the sinistrom. Felix moved his hands a little farther, and to his surprise he discovered a carrionwing.

"Does it look like she's been dragged backward through one of those predator hedges she patrols?" Ironclaw mused. "Sounds like Scoffit. Can you figure out where they all are? My wings are getting tired. It's most unnatural, holding them at this angle."

"Take another look at the sinistrom," said Fuzzy. "There's something odd about this. Sinistroms and carrionwings don't just sit there, discussing the price of carcasses."

"All sinistroms look the same to me," said Felix.

"They don't to me," said Betony. "Let me look."

Somewhat reluctantly, Felix moved over.

"It's Grimspite!" declared Betony.

"So is this scene in the past, the present, or the future?" asked Felix.

And that was the moment when one of the twin spitfire mountains decided to erupt.

There was the most tremendous bang, and they all turned to look. A shower of rocks and lava shot into the air, and a little streak of red treacle started to make its way down the side of the mountain. A tiny winged figure took to the air and headed east.

"The wild fire-breather's decided to move on," said Ironclaw. "No doubt she's taken her eggs with her. I think we ought to get going, too."

But Felix had first seen the eruption in the crystal ball, just before Ironclaw let in the light, and he was able to pinpoint their friends' position. "They're not very far away at all," he said, and he pointed. "Over there. But they're right in the path of the lava. Is a carrionwing capable of carrying them all to safety?"

"I don't think Scoffit could carry more than one at a time," said Fuzzy.

"All right," said Ironclaw. "We'd better get moving, then. Come along, Rhino, up you go. You can sit behind Felix."

Betony and Fuzzy were already in the air and winging their way across the snowfields toward the mountain.

Squill was leafing through an advertising brochure for K'Faddle & Offspring, and wondering whether to order one of the magic lamps from their latest line. There was a waiting list, apparently, despite the fact that the lamps were ludicrously expensive; they only manufactured one every thirteen years. "How long *is* the waiting list?" he asked the rep, who was sitting cross-legged on the floor.

"Two lifetimes, Your Excellency."

Squill threw the brochure across the floor in a temper. "Well, that's no use, is it?" he said.

"People usually buy them for their descendants," said the rep nervously.

"I've got a daughter," said Squill. "But there's no sign of *her* deciding to settle down. Anyway, I want one for me, not the children she hasn't had yet. If she ever does. She's a career woman. Breeds fire-breathers."

Squill's secretary came in. "There's a japegrin to see you," she said.

"Name?"

"He won't give it. But he says he knows where your lamp is, and it isn't in Kaflabad."

Squill scowled. "I'll have that carrionwing plucked, poisoned, roasted on a spit, beaten to death, and teased by schoolchildren," he said. "Show the stranger in."

The stranger was wearing a purple cloak, and he had a scarf wound around his neck and covering his mouth. He also had a hat pulled down over his head, so in the end, only his eyes and his nose were showing. His eyes were bloodshot and his nose was red, and he was wheezing a little. "I wish to speak to you alone," he said. His voice was husky.

"You might be here to assassinate me," said Squill suspiciously. "My secretary isn't very good at searching people." He cast her a venomous look, and she blushed.

The japegrin flung open his cloak, revealing a skinny body wearing a tight purple tunic that couldn't have concealed a wand, let alone a knife. His ribs were just visible beneath the fabric.

"You really don't look very well," said Squill. "All right." He waved a hand at the K'Faddle rep and the secretary, who left.

The stranger unwound his scarf and removed his hat. "Your lamp has been intercepted by a sinistrom," he said.

Squill just stared. Then he said, "I don't believe you."

"I think you should," said the stranger. "And I also think you ought to go and get it, because . . ."

"I've seen you somewhere before," interrupted Squill.

"Indeed you have. Pepperwort didn't recognize me, either. I've lost weight, you see. Enchantments play havoc with one's metabolism." He coughed again.

"Metabolism?"

"Just an otherworld expression I picked up."

"Otherworld?" The color suddenly drained from Squill's face, and he put out a hand and rested it on the desk to support himself. "Snakeweed," he said faintly.

"Thirteen out of thirteen. Tiratattle looks like pretty much a dead loss at the moment, with all the rebuilding.

This is where the money is, am I right or am I right? Stone quarrying. I've always fancied watching people breaking up rocks for a living."

"You can't just saunter in here and take over, you know," said Squill, recovering a little of his composure. "You don't even have a wand."

"True," said Snakeweed. "But I do have this." He turned his hat upside down and extracted a small black pebble from somewhere inside it.

Squill went even whiter. "He's *your* sinistrom? That's his pebble?"

Snakeweed rolled the pebble between his finger and thumb, held it up to the light, and admired it.

Squill lunged for his wand.

"I wouldn't," said Snakeweed. "If you try to harm me, he will instantly materialize and rip you to shreds."

"Let me get this straight," said Squill. "You want me to go and face your sinistrom, to retrieve a malfunctioning lamp I was sending back to the makers — or else you'll rub the pebble and summon him here? Heads I lose, tails I lose?"

"That's right," said Snakeweed. "I think you know the area, for I believe your daughter lives close by. If you're quick, you might get there before the sinistrom pays her a visit. Tell him I said he's not to eat her — and he's not to disembowel you, either. There's a password you can use so he'll know you've got authorization."

Squill ground his teeth. "What is it?"

"Cluck-bird," said Snakeweed. He glanced around. "This was once a hotel, wasn't it?" he said. "I'd like a room with a view, a hot bath, some clean clothes, and room service."

Squill couldn't think of a way out. He nodded. As he made his way to the stables, he collared one of his japegrins and instructed him to find a way to relieve Snakeweed of his pebble once he fell asleep. Then he commandeered Pepperwort, opened the stable door, and beckoned to his fire-breather.

Everything was irritating today. The creature seemed to have a silly smile on its face — and some idiot had burned a heart on the wall, with two interlocking flames in the middle.

Nimby woke up on the floor of Squill's office. It had been a tiring day, and the flight from the rescue huts to Yergud had really taken it out of him. He tended to get all tense when he was carrying japegrins, and flying like that was exhausting. The office was empty — it looked as though everyone had forgotten about him. He levitated slightly, so that he could see his surroundings more clearly, and realized that the hex had just about worn off. What he really needed to do was find Betony. He knew she and Felix had made off with the sleigh, so they were probably all right. And he was desperate to explain his theory to someone as well. Magic and science were a devastating combination, and he was the only one who had appreciated quite *how* devastating. It was a huge responsibility for a carpet. The door of the office was closed, though, and he would have to wait for someone to open it.

After a while he heard footsteps, and then, to his delight, the door opened. He watched a pair of purple boots walk across the floor, and stop on the other side of the desk. A japegrin, then. Only japegrins wore purple. The owner of the boots coughed a couple of times — a male cough, not a female one — and after a moment there was the rustle of papers. A drawer opened and closed again, then another. After that there were some scratching and scrabbling sounds. Then the scrabbling stopped, and a drawer slammed shut. Nimby wriggled forward a little, so that he could see.

The owner of the boots was waving a wand around theatrically, as if remembering how to use one. Then he stuck the wand through his belt and flicked through some documents. His face was turned away. He selected a few papers and put them in a leather satchel. Then he took something out of his pocket, placed it on the palm of his hand, rubbed it between his fingers, and laughed.

Nimby gave an involuntary gasp of horror. He would know Snakeweed's chuckle anywhere.

The sound of the gasp took Snakeweed by surprise — he had obviously thought he was alone — and he dropped what he was holding. A shiny black pebble rolled across the floor and wobbled on the spot a couple of times before coming to

a halt. In two strides, Snakeweed was behind the desk. He didn't realize that Nimby was anything but an ordinary carpet, and after a perfunctory search, he shook his head and slapped his ear, as though he'd just been on a long flight that had affected his hearing. He retrieved the pebble, polished it on his tunic, and dropped it into his pocket. It was clearly just an ordinary pebble, although it looked very much like a sinistrom stone. "Excellent," he said aloud. "Time to over-throw the thane, I think. Shouldn't be too difficult. He never was the brightest spark in the spell." He turned on his heel and left the office. Fortunately, he didn't close the door behind him.

Nimby emerged from his hiding place. He suddenly felt very frightened — Snakeweed had that effect on people. Nimby left the building as surreptitiously as he could, then he flew at full speed for a while before the panic subsided and he was able to get his bearings. He needed to head back to the mountains and look for his mistress. He was carrying two pieces of devastating news. Magic plus science equaled big trouble — and Snakeweed had returned. He tucked in his selvage and flew as though he were taking part in the Textile Trophy.

He hadn't gone far before he heard what sounded like thunder. A column of gray-and-white smoke rose slowly into the air, as though it were beginning some stately dance.

13

The nearer the brazzles and their passengers got to the volcano, the more alarming everything became. A thick plume of gray-and-white smoke was rising into the air, and the safety of Scoffit, Goodbody, and Grimspite hung in the balance.

"We've got to keep our eyes open for any *low* rolling clouds," warned Felix, gripping with his knees so that he could turn his head and speak to Rhino. "Pyroclastic flows are killers."

"Pyroclastic flows?" shouted Rhino. "Speak English!"

"Didn't you pay *any* attention in geography?"

"Get real," said Rhino. "I hardly ever went to geography."

Ironclaw banked to take advantage of an updraft, and Rhino tightened his hold around Felix's waist.

Felix felt smug. He was far more experienced at keeping his balance on the back of a brazzle. He decided it was time to be irritatingly superior. "When a volcano erupts," he threw over his shoulder, "the hot air moves upward, and the heavier particles of rock and ash sink. You get this superheated cloud that races down the mountainside, killing everything in its path. Sometimes it reaches speeds of a hundred miles an hour."

"They're probably all dead by now, then," said Rhino, gripping Felix ever more tightly so that he could lean to one side and look down. "Let's turn back."

"There hasn't *been* a pyroclastic flow," said Felix, gritting his teeth. "It doesn't happen *every* time a volcano erupts. There's simply a small stream of lava at the moment. Look up there, you can see it. That red ribbon in the sky."

"I hate this place," said Rhino, with feeling. "Give me a fistfight in the projects any day."

"With pleasure," said Felix.

"You wouldn't stand a chance," said Rhino. "Oh, look. There's that crazy carpet."

"Nimby!" squealed Betony, as the carpet raced toward them.

"She's more fond of that carpet than she is of you, Felix," said Rhino. "Pretty weird, if you ask me."

"I *didn't* ask you," said Felix shortly.

" . . . got some nearly portant views!" yelled the carpet, the moment he was in range. "Silence and madness . . ."

"You can't have a serious discussion in this wind!" shouted Ironclaw. "Can't it wait?"

"No!"

"All right! We'll land for a moment!"

The two brazzles spiraled down, and Nimby landed beside them.

"I've got some really important news," said Nimby. "Science and magic together are big trouble. *Really* big trouble. And I've just seen Snakeweed."

"*Snakeweed?*" said Betony, aghast. "You couldn't have!"

"I did," said the carpet.

Scoffit had tried to carry both Goodbody and Grimspite (in lickit form) to safety, but their combined weight had been too much, and she hadn't even been able to take off.

"I can probably outrun the lava on *four* legs," said Grimspite, reverting to his other guise. "It's moving quickly up here because the mountain's steep. Lower down, where the gradient's more gentle, it'll flow much more slowly."

"Falling ash is the greatest danger," said Scoffit, shaking some flakes of gray from her plumage. "I'll drop Goodbody off somewhere and come back for you."

"*Quicksands and quaddiumps!*" yelled the nomad, as a tiny fragment of red-hot cinder landed on his arm.

"I've got the protection of a fur coat," said Grimspite, making light of the situation and sounding a lot more optimistic than he felt.

Scoffit managed to lurch into the air, gripping Goodbody with her talons, but she didn't climb very high. She went into a long glide that required little energy and would take both her and her passenger safely to the foot of the mountain.

Grimspite didn't hang around — he ran. The terrain wasn't easy. There had been eruptions here before, and beneath the snow, which was melting fast, the ground was ridged and sharp-edged and treacherous. At first, things went well. He outdistanced his fiery pursuer more easily than he'd expected, and he had to stop and roll in a patch of slush only once, when something hot landed on him. He was feeling pleased with himself — he was good at making decisions these days, taking charge of situations, and being unselfish. It just took practice. You really could change yourself and your behavior if you wanted to.

Then he cut his paw. He yelped — it really hurt. He sat down for a moment and licked it. The blood tasted salty and rather nice; his tongue was cool and wet, and it eased the pain. But as soon as he stopped licking, the pain returned. He couldn't run anymore; he could do only a three-legged hobble. This was not good news. He continued downhill — but his progress was a lot slower now, and when he stepped on anything hot or sharp, it was agony. He glanced behind him. The stream of red treacly rock was closer now. It wasn't racing along; it was traveling at a gentle lope, but it was catching up with him. There was something almost hypnotic about it. Pieces of the lava stuck to the rocks as they passed; the red went out of them, and they scabbed into stone. Like water, the molten rock was finding the swiftest route down the mountain, and the lower it got, the less steep the incline. Eventually, he would be able simply to sidestep it — but not yet.

He carried on, trying not to think about the danger he was in. One paw here, one paw there; one paw here, one paw there. The lava was getting nearer; he could feel its heat. He didn't dare look up — he didn't want to see how close it really was. One paw here, one paw there. Every now and then, out of the corner of his eye, he saw one of the dwarf trees burst into flame. It was as though someone was lighting flares for him, to show him the progress of the molten river. One paw here, one paw there. He was concentrating so hard on the ground beneath his feet that he didn't see the shape zoom out of the ash-colored sky until it was almost on top of him.

"Grimspite!" shouted a silky little voice. "Jump on! Quick! I dare not land. I'll just hover!"

Nimby. Grimspite felt a lump come to his throat. *What a carpet!* He scrambled on board — with some difficulty — and lay down. The pain in his paw eased as soon as he didn't have to put any weight on it.

"All the others are waiting for us," said the rug, doing a flashy but unnecessary three-point turn in midair, then heading back the way he'd come.

"Others?" said Grimspite. He sniffed himself. The peribott cologne really had worn off this time, no doubt about it. He wouldn't be very presentable to strangers.

"Ironclaw, Fuzzy, and Felix," chirped Nimby. "Betony,

Rhino, Scoffit, and Goodbody . . . They let *me* come and rescue you, because if I get ash on me, all I have to do is turn upside down and . . ."

"Don't demonstrate," said Grimspite hurriedly. "I believe you."

"And what's more," said the carpet, "I've made a really important discovery about science and magic. Ironclaw said it was a groundbreaking theory. *Ironclaw* said that. And Snakeweed's come back."

"*What?*"

"I saw him," said Nimby.

When the carpet landed triumphantly at the foot of the mountain, with Grimspite safely on board, Betony greeted him: "Nimby, we're *all* going to nominate you for the Magical Objects Bravery Award. You're a hero."

"Do you know about Snakeweed?" asked Grimspite.

The others nodded — apart from Rhino. The color drained from his face as he took in the powerful jaws and the saber-like teeth of their new companion, and he took a couple of steps backward.

"Oh," said Betony, thoroughly enjoying the moment, "I forgot. You've never met a sinistrom before, have you? Grimspite, this is Rhino. Rhino, this is Grimspite."

"Can we go home now?" said Rhino faintly.

"First things first," said Grimspite. "Our friend the brandee here is now a nomad, with a name of his own —

Brad Goodbody — so he can't turn to gas anymore and go inside the lamp. And someone has to get inside that lamp to get hold of the jinx box."

"The fact that my greenhouse, where the box languishes, is inaccessible to me now is as sad to me as a sunny day," agreed Goodbody.

"Jinx box?" said Felix, suddenly remembering about the eyeglass case in his bag. "But we brought it with us. I've got it in my backpack."

"Well, that solves *my* problem, then," said Goodbody. "If you've got the jinx box already, you don't need my lamp. If I take the lamp back to K'Faddle and Offspring at Kaflabad, they'll open it up and salvage my books."

"Why is the box so important?" asked Felix. He'd read something about it somewhere . . . Whatever it was, it seemed to have slipped his mind.

Grimspite explained about the powerwords, and how the box would try to get people to speak them, and that if it succeeded, the consequences could be dire. It was, for instance, highly likely that Snakeweed's return was a result of the *abra* word being spoken.

"So how do we destroy it?" asked Felix.

"I'm not sure," said Grimspite. "The box is cunning, and it will try to save itself. . . . Could be dangerous."

"Count me out," said Rhino. "I just want to go home."

"If it hadn't been for you, human, there wouldn't have *been* a problem," said Grimspite. "Your fireworks inside the lamp enabled the box to remember the powerwords."

"How was I supposed to know that?" said Rhino sulkily.

"I've had enough of the north," said Scoffit suddenly. "*I'll* take Goodbody to Kaflabad."

"Will you be safe there, Scoffit?" asked Grimspite.

"Squill won't chase after them," said Betony, "because he won't want to mess with the king. Kaflabad law is different from Yergud law; Felix and I fell afoul of it once. The king is completely bonkers, and he wouldn't like Squill trying to tell him what to do one little bit."

"You are as kind as a palm tree, Scoffit," said Goodbody, "and an example of helpfulness beyond compare."

"How touching," said Rhino. "Can we go home now?"

"I think Nimby should take Betony and the humans to the Divide," said Ironclaw. "Grimspite and I will head for Yergud, to see what we can do about Snakeweed."

Fuzzy's eyes narrowed. "Are you sending me straight back to Andria, then?"

"No. I want you to escort Nimby, in case there's any trouble with the jinx box. I think the best course of action would be to drop it down a spitfire fissure when you reach the Divide."

"Good idea," said Grimspite.

Fuzzy perked up. "Smooth."

"And after *that*, I want you to fly straight back to Andria."

"But . . ."

"No buts."

Goodbody climbed onto Scoffit's back, turned to Ironclaw, and offered to call in to the library to speak to Thornbeak.

"Why?" asked Ironclaw.

"To tell her that Fuzzy's fine, of course."

"Oh," said Ironclaw vaguely. "Right."

They prepared to part company. Betony gave Ironclaw a hug, which, as usual, embarrassed him enormously. Just before he took off, he turned to Felix. "Fermat's Last Theorem," he said thoughtfully. "Is that a real puzzle or not?"

Felix laughed. "You can take a stab at solving it yourself, if you like. It's based on Pythagorean triplets. Bronzepinion triplets, to you."

"Oh, yes?" said Ironclaw.

"Prove that there are no whole-number solutions to the equation $x^n + y^n = z^n$, when n is greater than 2."

"Sounds like fun," said Ironclaw.

Scoffit flew the first part of the journey very gently. The spit-fire eruption had stopped almost as suddenly as it had started, and she soon left its effects far behind. Before long, she was descending on the other side of the mountains, and she came to a very pleasant valley with caves at one end. The snow was melting here, and purple flowers were pushing their way through what remained of it, although there were curious wisps of smoke curling up everywhere.

"What's going on down there?" asked Goodbody. "It's as though someone's been lighting dozens of tiny fires."

Outside the largest cave was a wooden board. The name TURPSIK had been crossed out and replaced by CUDWEED'S STUD FARM. FIRE-BREATHERS FOR EVERY OCCASION. Squill's own fire-breather was lying curled up nearby, next to a very handsome female. The female was incubating some eggs. When Scoffit looked more closely, she could see that there were fire-breathers dotted all over the valley, most of them quite young. Squill, Catchfly, Pepperwort, and a japegrin Scoffit didn't recognize were sitting on a log, eating supper. A female japegrin — who bore a strong resemblance to Squill — was ladling something into bowls. It was a nice domestic scene, and no one looked as though they were going anywhere in a hurry.

Scoffit flew in a little closer. No one was looking up at the sky; they were all too busy eating. She wanted to overhear some of the conversation, if at all possible.

"That's Squill," hissed Goodbody. "Do be careful."

"I know," said Scoffit. "But I don't intend to run any unnecessary risks. I'm going to use those trees as cover."

Squill seemed a lot more relaxed than the last time Scoffit had seen him, and it was strange to recall that this was the japegrin who had threatened to pluck her if she didn't deliver the lamp to K'Faddle & Offspring for refurbishing. She dropped a little lower — and then she really *was* hidden behind the trees, but close enough to eavesdrop.

237

"I think it's the right decision, Dad," said the female.

"You haven't met him, Cudweed," said Squill to the unknown japegrin. "I'm not talking about a local dignitary here. If Snakeweed intends to take over, retirement looks like far and away the best option."

"I think you're making a mistake," said Cudweed, who, presumably, was Squill's son-in-law.

"He didn't look awfully well to me," interjected Pepperwort. "Maybe he won't last very long."

"*I* wouldn't just resign," said Cudweed.

"No, you'd fight it out and get turned to stone for your pains," said the female. "Just plain stupid, you are." She turned to Squill. "Move in whenever you like, Dad. We'll get one of the caves refurbished. We're going to be rich when those wild fire-breather eggs hatch."

"Wild fire-breather eggs?" said Squill, alarmed. "Is that female a wild one?"

"Isn't she beautiful?" said Squill's daughter.

Squill choked on his fertle juice.

One of the young fire-breathers suddenly spotted Scoffit. It roared defiantly, then thought better of it and ran to its mother.

Scoffit didn't hang around any longer. She didn't fancy being barbecued in midair.

The weekly meeting of the Yergud town council took place in the old ballroom of the hotel. All the guilds were represented — and all of them, apart from the restaurant group, were now under japegrin control — even the fishing industry, which had once been the sole preserve of the one-eyes.

The door that led directly to Squill's office opened — but instead of Squill's portly personage, a different japegrin emerged. This one was thin and sharp-faced, and he looked confident and clever. "Fellow beings," he said, with a smile.

A couple of guild representatives looked quizzically at each other, and a couple of others scratched their ginger heads and looked as though they were trying very hard to remember something that had just slipped their minds.

"Fellow beings," repeated the stranger. "I bring you news that concerns your thane, Squill."

A murmur ran around the room.

"Certain . . . *irregularities* . . . have come to light. Squill has resigned."

The murmur grew in volume. The japegrin held up his hand for silence. There was something very commanding about him, despite the slenderness of his stature. Silence fell.

"His deputy has appointed me acting thane in his place."

"And just who the gaping gill slits are you?" demanded someone.

"I know who he is!" called out the restaurant rep, who was the only lickit there. "Snakeweed!"

A ripple of laughter ran around the conference room, which rapidly turned to guffaws and near-hysteria.

"You can't reverse a spinning-wheel hex," spluttered a fishmonger, with tears running down his face.

"Trust a lickit to come up with a crazy idea like that!"

"Brains made of sugar!"

The acting thane held up his hand for silence, and the laughter petered out to a few snickers and a giggle. "I grant you there's a resemblance," said the japegrin. "A strong resemblance. And why not? My name is Snakeroot, and I am Snakeweed's brother."

"Snakeweed didn't have a brother!" shouted the lickit. "I know, I read his biography: *Snakeweed, a Study in Selfishness.* He was an only child, doted on by his mother and then abandoned when she decided she'd rather have a pet cutthroat!"

"That book was a pack of lies," said Snakeweed. "Cheap publicity for the Castle of Myths and Legends. Now then. Squill wasn't the best thane ever, was he? Took rather a lot of your profits in taxes. And what improvements have you seen to Yergud as a result?"

The council members looked at one another. Then they looked back at the acting thane.

"I want to know what's been going on," said Snakeweed. "I want to know where your money's been going. And then I want to do something about it."

Someone started to clap, then another and another. A moment later, the place was in an uproar, and the cheering reached ear-shattering proportions.

"He put a super-tax on fish over a certain weight," shouted someone.

"Diverted the geothermal water from my greenhouse to heat his fire-breather stables. Fire-breathers don't *need* heat."

The complaints went on for some considerable time, with Snakeweed asking for the occasional bit of clarification, and the audience only too willing to grant it.

"Spent far too much on trying to find a soft icing," ventured the restaurant rep.

"Spent far too much on kitchen staff *altogether*," sniped someone.

"The soft icing's a good point, actually," said Snakeweed. "Using community funds for personal projects."

"He's spent loads on security for one of his quarries. No one knows why."

"Which quarry?" asked Snakeweed.

"The southwest one."

"Has he struck gold, do you know?"

"He wouldn't tell us if he had, now would he?" laughed an airline rep, who had taken Snakeweed's radical invention of advertising to his heart a couple of years before. He had EASY-FLAP embroidered on his hat in silver letters, on the front of his tunic, and printed all over his stationery. Business had boomed ever since.

"It seems to me," said Snakeweed, "that I need to investigate this first. If it turns out to be a *source* of income, rather than a drain on it, we'll all be better off. Oh, incidentally —

before we break up for drinks and snacks — there was an incident a couple of days ago. Rumor has it that a powerword was used. Anyone know anything about it, or notice anything strange?"

"My wand snapped," said someone. "It was a cheap one, though."

The meeting broke up for fertle juice and mushroom tartlets. This was unusual; Squill never gave anything away, not even a drink of water and a cracker. Snakeweed asked for the export records for all eight of the Yergud quarries, and flicked through them. When he came to the sixth sheet of paper, he stopped. "This quarry ceased production two moons ago," he said. "The others have been sending stone to Tiratattle on a regular — and very profitable — basis. What's been going on?"

The japegrin shrugged. "Don't know. That's the quarry with the high security, though."

"Do you have any decent fire-breathers in the stables?"

"Squill took the best one, but we do have others."

"Get one saddled. I'm going to investigate this matter myself."

The only fire-breather that was fed and rested was a young one. It was a bit skittish, but Snakeweed was clearly an experienced pilot, and the stable hand had no qualms about letting him take it. The southwest quarry was the farthest one from Yergud, but the young fire-breather was fit and lively, and they were there before moonrise.

As it went into its landing glide, a couple of japegrins came running out of the sentry station, wands at the ready. Snakeweed ordered the fire-breather to let out its jets of identification flame — but either it had forgotten the correct code or it wasn't allowed to land there, which was odd. The perimeter barricade was featherproof, but it wasn't scaleproof. One of the japegrins fired his wand, and the fire-breather took some imaginative evasive action.

Snakeweed had to struggle to keep his seat, but he managed it. He leaned right out of the saddle and disarmed both japegrins with a wave of his wand and a hex rhyme. One of them collapsed to the ground immediately. Snakeweed dismounted and faced the other japegrin with a slight smile on his face. "You haven't checked your scrying bowl recently, have you?" he said, polishing his wand on his sleeve. "If you had, you'd know that my name's Snakeroot, and I'm now officially the acting thane. I'm here to find out what's been going on. Why production has stopped. Well?"

"Squill ordered it," said the japegrin.

"And why, exactly, would he do that?"

"Because of what we found."

"And what *did* you find?"

"I don't know. I'm not senior enough. It's top secret."

"Not to me, it isn't," said Snakeweed dangerously.

"It's something they found in the mine."

"Mine? What mine? I thought this was a quarry."

"It was, to begin with. Here." The japegrin took a torch from the wall, ignited it with a wave of his hand, and gave it to Snakeweed. He then took a second one for himself, and lit that as well. Snakeweed sneezed as the smell of burning pitch cleared his sinuses, and he followed the japegrin to what appeared to be an elevator shaft.

"Coming up!" yelled someone from below. It was an odd sort of voice, as penetrating as a skewer, hoarse and high-pitched at the same time with a rising intonation that made everything sound like a rhetorical question, shouted in a high wind.

After a moment or two, a metal cage started to clank its way upward, accompanied by a worrying smell of rust and a tuneful selection of grating sounds and screeches. There were no magic carpets employed as elevators here. They couldn't be trusted to keep quiet about issues they felt should be common knowledge, because they all had an *Integrity* thread in their warp.

The sun set before Nimby reached the Divide, so the party decided to stop for the night at the Pink Harpoon. Fuzzy said she'd perch on the roof. "But before I get my head under my wing, Felix," she said, "you've got a little job to do."

"Job? What job?"

"The jinx box," Betony reminded him. "You've got to drop it down a spitfire fissure."

"Oh," said Felix. He wasn't looking forward to it one bit, which was, perhaps, why he kept forgetting about it. Or maybe the jinx box had a hand in the forgetting — if *hand* was the right word for a receptacle. It certainly had uncanny powers — would it really allow itself to be destroyed without a struggle? And besides that, the jinx box knew so much. . . . It knew things, perhaps, that Felix would like to know, things that, once the box was destroyed, would be gone forever.

"This place is a dump," said Rhino, poking the cross-eyed fish sign with his finger. It swung back and forth, creaking protestingly — then it parted company with its bracket and fell into the snow with a soft plop. He laughed.

"I can't do it tonight, can I?" said Felix. "There isn't one of those fumarole things here."

"There's a geyser around the back, though," Fuzzy pointed out. "The inn does all its laundry in the pool. The water's actually boiling at one end. That should do the trick."

"Sounds kind of chancy. Ironclaw specifically said spitfire *fissure*."

"Oh, just get *on* with it, Felix," said Betony.

Felix took the jinx box out of his pocket. This time its coloring was more subtle: pink-and-gray toadstools. The curve of its lid actually *felt* like a mushroom cap — soft yet resilient, smooth yet slightly sticky, leather pretending to be velvet. He wanted to hold it close and stroke it — and, at the same time, he wanted to throw it as far away from him as he could.

Betony looked at it with distaste. "They're poisonous, those toadstools," she said.

Somehow, Felix wasn't surprised.

"While you're throwing it away, I'll go inside to reserve some rooms and order some food," said Rhino.

"Coward," muttered Felix. But he said it under his breath, so that no one could hear. He walked around to the back of the inn, and Betony, loyal and supportive as ever, followed. Fuzzy watched them from the roof.

The pool steamed like a Turkish bath, blinding them now and then with clouds of vapor and then clearing once more.

246

Felix was aware of a film of moisture on his face, then on his clothes, and on his hands. . . . His fingers became really slippery, and before he knew what was happening, he'd dropped the jinx box and the lid had sprung open.

"Well, hello again," said the box, in its slimy little voice.

"Pick it up and get rid of it *now*, Felix," said Betony.

"Have you forgotten what I offered you, darling?" said the box. "The antidote to the spell that froze your parents? What an ungrateful daughter you are. Imagine how your parents would feel if they knew you'd had the opportunity to bring them back to life, and you'd refused it."

"Stop it," said Betony.

"They fed you, clothed you, played with you, read to you, dried your tears . . ."

"No, they didn't. That was my sister," said Betony.

The box changed tack. "Imagine what it will be like for them, if you leave them petrified for another sixteen years. When they awaken, their friends will all be old people. Their own parents will probably have died. They may have grandchildren by then, and they'll have missed their growing up . . ."

"Shut up," said Betony, covering her ears.

"The potions trade will have moved on. They'll be way behind the times, they'll have to retrain. . . . But you can prevent all that. All Felix has to do is to say *hocus pocus*."

Felix looked at Betony. He remembered how devastated he had felt when Snakeweed turned his own parents to stone, six months earlier. And he remembered how wonderful it had felt when he brought them back to life. Hearing his father's voice again, and giving his mother the hug to end all hugs. It was within his power to give Betony the best present ever.

"Two little words, Felix," said the jinx box. "Just two little words. Think of the *good* you will do."

"Betony?"

"I . . ."

"*Hocus pocus,*" said Felix, thinking, *Nothing ventured, nothing gained.*

"Felix!" Betony sounded absolutely horrified. "What have you *done?*"

Felix suddenly felt shortsighted and naïve. Gullible, even. What *had* he done? It was as if he'd been hypnotized by the box, and now he'd come to his senses again. He looked around. Everything had remained exactly the same. Not one of the party had keeled over, and the sky had stayed where it was.

"So what did it do?" asked Betony.

"What did what do?" The jinx box sounded genuinely perplexed.

"The powerword," said Felix. "What did it achieve?"

"What powerword?"

"You know."

"No, I don't."

"It's forgotten it, Felix," said Nimby. "Same as it forgot the other one, once Grimspite had used it."

248

Felix picked up the box, being careful to hold it in such a way that it couldn't spring shut on his fingers.

"Chuck it in the pool," said Betony.

Felix hesitated. Drowning the box in a pool of boiling water had never seemed as foolproof as hurling it into a spitfire crevasse. He imagined the box sinking to the bottom and lying there in wait, plotting its revenge, so he decided to follow Ironclaw's instructions to the letter, and snapped the box shut. It made a crunching sound, as though it had crushed some tiny bones in the process. The others looked a bit dubious when he told them what he'd decided, but they agreed in the end that a fissure was safest. It took Felix three tries to put the box away — he kept missing his pocket altogether and dropping it in the snow. At one point, he could have sworn it wriggled, but his fingers were now so cold he couldn't really be certain of anything.

"Here, Betony," said Fuzzy, removing something from her leg pouch. "Take this inside and see if you can discover anything of interest." Although she didn't say it in so many words, they all knew what she meant — see if your parents have come back to life.

Betony took the crystal ball from the brazzle. "I don't see what use that's going to be," she grumbled. "It doesn't even work right."

"It hasn't been showing the future," said Fuzzy, "but it *has* been showing things that are happening elsewhere. Go inside, order some supper, and surf it for a while."

"Surf it?"

"I've been telling Fuzzy about the Internet," said Felix. He couldn't understand Betony's reluctance to find out what had happened. If it had been *his* parents, wild horses wouldn't have stopped him. Betony went inside, but she was dragging her feet.

Fuzzy ruffled her feathers. "I know you were trying to do the right thing, Felix, but I think we're still going to get the double effect," she said. "Something good and something bad, in equal measure."

Felix was feeling really miserable. "I never get it right, do I?" he snapped. "I try so hard to do things for the best, but they always seem to have repercussions I never thought of."

"It's not your fault, Felix," said Fuzzy. "Blame the sorcerer who irresponsibly created the jinx boxes all those centuries ago, just to make money. It can be easy to invent something, and surprisingly difficult to get rid of it again." And with that, she put her head under her wing and went to sleep.

Felix rolled up Nimby, and he and Betony joined Rhino inside. The big log fire was blazing away in the fireplace, and there was a welcoming smell of hot spiced drinks and new bread.

"Three of you this time," said the landlord, "and not one of you a japegrin. You'll give this place a bad name."

"Our gold's as good as anyone else's," said Betony furiously.

"What gold?" queried Rhino.

"Ironclaw gave me some, to tide us over," Betony hissed at him.

They made their way to the same booth as before, and sat down. The candle on the table guttered wildly as the family of japegrins at the next table got up and left. Felix insisted that they all look at the menu, although Betony was wriggling with impatience.

"We don't want to antagonize the landlord any more than we have to," he said. "If the waiter tells him you're using a crystal ball, he might think you're a ragamucky in disguise — and then we *would* be out on our ears in the snow."

"On our ears?" said Betony, and she giggled. "You couldn't land on yours — they're not big enough." She giggled again, but the giggle sounded like nerves.

They ordered the fish casserole. As before, it took a long time to arrive, but once the waiter had come and gone, Betony was free to set up the crystal ball. She stood it on a rush place mat, put her hands on it, and blew out the candle so they were in semidarkness. The glass began to glow with a pearly lavender light.

At first, all she saw were swirling gray shapes, like speeded-up clouds. Rhino leaned over her, trying to see into the ball as well, so she elbowed him out of the way. When that had no effect, she kicked him on the shin — and that *did* work. The gray turned to a speckled green — trees, probably.

Gradually, other things came into focus, and she realized she was looking at her own home, the tree house in Geddon. It was dusk, and a few pink clouds lingered overhead. Her sister, Tansy, was busy with the yard rake, and her brother, Ramson, was sitting on a pile of logs, playing a lute. She grinned. Good thing there was no sound. She looked harder at the lute. It wasn't Ramson's; it was a much classier model altogether.

"Move your hands over the glass," said Felix. "You can control the view — see farther to the left, or the right, or higher up. Do you know where you are?"

"Geddon," said Betony. "I can see Tansy, raking the yard. Oh — there's Vetch."

"Who's Vetch?"

"Tansy's boyfriend. Maybe that lute belongs to Vetch, because it's . . . *Blazing feathers.*"

"What?" said Felix, clearly alarmed. "You've gone as white as a sheet."

Betony let go of the ball and turned to him. Her eyes were glistening, and her lower lip wobbled for a moment. "They're not there anymore," she said. She turned back to the crystal ball and ran her hands feverishly over its surface. "Oh, why can't I get the picture back?" she wailed. "I should never have taken my hands off it. . . ."

"Hey," said Felix, putting a hand on her arm, "calm down. *Slow* down. What aren't there anymore?"

"The statues of my parents," said Betony. She moved her hands a little to the right.

"Maybe it's good news."

Betony bit her lip and moved her hands more slowly, although it was an effort. The picture came into focus again.

Tansy had stopped sweeping. Betony watched her go over to the rope ladder and lean the broom against the trunk of the tree. Then she climbed the ladder, disappearing from view for a moment, and reappearing on the lowest balcony, which led to the sitting room. Betony slid her hands up until she could look through the window.

And there was her mother, standing with her hands on the windowsill apparently talking to Socrates, the family's potted plant. Betony rubbed her eyes with the hem of her tunic and looked once more. No, she hadn't been mistaken. And then the emotions crowded in on her so quickly that she felt as though someone had beaten her up and cuddled her — both at once. Her mother was really, truly standing there, no longer made of gray-and-white marble. Her blond hair stuck out in the slightly old-fashioned tangle that Betony knew so well; her cheeks were pink, and she was dressed in that horrible sludge green dress she'd been wearing when the accident happened, four years ago. Only four years? It seemed like a lifetime. Betony wanted to fling her arms around her, smell that musky cologne she always wore, hear her laugh, feel that horrible scratchy dress against her face. The trouble was, all she could hear inside her head was her mother complaining about the way she didn't do her homework, the way she brushed her hair, the way she answered back.

After a moment, her father came into view, carrying a piece of paper covered in green writing. The sitting room candles had all been lit, and the room looked warm and cozy and welcoming. She felt a stab of homesickness. Her father crossed over to the biggest candle and held the paper above it until it caught fire. Then he watched the paper burn until he couldn't hold it any longer, and he had to drop it into a ceramic dish. *It's a spell*, thought Betony. *It has to be if it's in green ink. I bet it's the broken-bone spell, the one that went wrong and turned them to stone.* She felt a powerful urge to hug him and tell him it didn't matter that he got things wrong all the time. Then she remembered his vagueness, the way he never remembered her birthday, the way he sometimes seemed to look right through her. Why was life never straightforward? After a moment or two, Tansy appeared, looking flustered, and started to say something.

"Oh," said Betony out loud, "how I *wish* I could hear what they were saying."

"What who are saying?" queried Felix.

Betony turned to him, her eyes shining. "*My parents.*"

"Your *parents?*" He felt so relieved that his knees went weak, and he had to sit down. "It worked, then?"

"I'd much rather *not* hear mine," said Rhino.

"Well, yours haven't been turned to stone for four years, have they?" snapped Betony.

"I wish."

"Betony, I am so pleased," said Felix, giving Rhino a dirty look and feeling that *pleased* was a woefully inadequate word. What on earth did you say to someone whose parents had just been brought back to life? "Does that mean you want to go home instead of coming over to my world, then?" he said. As soon as the words were out of his mouth, he realized they were the wrong ones.

Betony's mouth narrowed to a thin line. "I don't know what I want," she said. "It's all a little sudden."

"What's going on in here?" said the landlord, striding over. "Why have you blown out the candle?"

Betony hurriedly put the crystal ball under the table, on top of Nimby.

"You want to get a better supplier, you do," said Rhino quickly. "Cheap rubbish." He flicked the wax rim with a fingernail, which rather obligingly came away, allowing the molten wax around the wick to spill onto the table.

The landlord looked annoyed, but he took the candle away and brought another one. Rhino grinned at Betony and Felix. For the first time, they'd all been pulling together. And, for the first time, they actually grinned back.

That night it was feather beds, hot baths, warm spiced milk, and no complaints. Bliss.

Grimspite was going for a job interview. He had applied for kitchen jobs before — as a lickit, naturally — and going for a junior cook's position seemed the best way into Squill's headquarters to find out what Snakeweed was up to. Brazzles were a no-no in Yergud, so he left Ironclaw at the perching rocks, feeling he had to apologize for leaving him out of the action.

"Don't mind me," said Ironclaw cheerfully, smoothing out an area of sand with his wing. "You're never bored with a dirtboard. That carpet has quite a brain for a textile, suggesting that the combination of science and magic isn't thirteen plus thirteen at all. It's thirteen *times* thirteen — or even thirteen *to the power of* thirteen. Thirteen plus thirteen is chickstuff — twenty-six. So is thirteen times thirteen — one hundred and sixty-nine. Thirteen to the power of thirteen is another matter altogether." He ruffled his feathers with glee, and immediately started scratching things in the dirt. "Thirteen times thirteen times thirteen times thirteen times thirteen . . ."

Grimspite left him to it, and went off to Squill's HQ. He announced himself at the reception desk, smoothed down his white robe, checked that his fingernails were clean and that the cut on his hand wasn't too obvious. It was healing nicely; his two-legged form was better for the wound than his four-legged form, because he didn't have to walk on it. He made his way to the kitchen.

The head cook looked him up and down and said, "What do you know about cakes?"

Cakes were Grimspite's weak point. As a sinistrom, he was much more interested in fish and meat; his book hadn't dealt with desserts at all. "I can do a sparkle sorbet," he said, hoping he could remember the method. He'd done one for Betony once, because she really liked them. It was one of the simplest of magical puddings: pureed fruit with a delicate crust of sugar frosting that tinkled like wind chimes as you ate it, and flickered from pink to green and back again.

"Not exotic enough for the acting thane," said the chef. "He's given me this recipe for soft icing, and I need a cake that will do it justice."

"Acting thane?" queried Grimspite.

"Snakeroot. He's much harder to please than Squill. He's come up with all these cakes I've never heard of. I mean — Macaroons, Battenbergs, Madeiras. Have you ever heard the like?"

"Never," lied Grimspite, knowing that only Snakeweed could have asked for cakes that had originated in another world. "Sorry. I'd have to do some research. How long have we got? What I mean is — where's Snakeroot? If we knew where he'd gone, we might have some idea when he'd get back." Grimspite knew this line of questioning was clumsy, but he couldn't think of anything else.

"He's visiting the southwest quarry, the one on the other side of the glacier. He didn't say when he'd be back, but the day after tomorrow is probably a good bet. What do you suppose a Bath bun is?"

"Something you eat in the bath, I suppose," said Grimspite.

"And rock cakes?"

"You've got me there," said Grimspite. "I'm obviously not right for the job. Thanks for interviewing me, anyway." He made his way to the exit, and as he went through the door and out into the courtyard, he saw the chef wrinkle his nose and look mildly puzzled.

Ironclaw was hopping up and down and squawking excitedly when Grimspite got back to the perching rocks. "Thirty trillion, four hundred and ninety-seven billion, five hundred and ninety-eight million, nine hundred and sixty-eight thousand, nine hundred and ninety-three," he said.

Grimspite looked blank.

"Thirteen to the power of thirteen!" squawked Ironclaw.

"It's significant, is it?"

"No," said Ironclaw. "It's just ever so *big*."

I'll never understand him, thought Grimspite. He told Ironclaw what he'd found out, and they took off and reached their destination by sunset.

Ironclaw turned his magnifying vision onto the quarry as they approached, and was surprised to see that the fence surrounding it was, in fact, a hedge — and a very strange hedge, too. Its spiky leaves were completely devoid of snow. He looked more closely. Each leaf was a vicious crescent moon of

258

shiny dark green, as sharp as a sickle, and there were thorns on the branches. "I can't cross this," he said. "It's a predator hedge. It's feather-proof. A fire-breather might be able to get over it, since it's covered with scales, but brazzles and triple-heads and carrionwings would hit an invisible barrier and crash to the ground. Amazingly high security for what is, for all intents and purposes, just a quarry."

"Never mind," said Grimspite. "Wait for me behind that rocky outcrop. You'll be sheltered from the worst of the weather. I can get through the hedge if I revert to my four-legged form."

"What are you going to do once you're on the other side?" asked Ironclaw.

"Finish the job I started six moons ago," replied Grimspite, with steely resolve. "I should never have left Snakeweed alive."

Scoffit and Goodbody arrived in Andria as night fell. Goodbody had never seen the sea before, so Scoffit took a quick flight around the bay to let him see how extraordinarily big and remarkably wet it actually was. Then she flew back into town and landed at the main crossroads. There was no point in going to the library now — it would be closed for the night. There seemed to be a lot of activity in its vicinity, however, and Scoffit saw that the road to the library had been cordoned off. A couple of wise-hoofs were walking around carrying clipboards and looking officious. One of them glanced at Scoffit and said, "No flying over the library after sunset."

"What's going on?" asked Scoffit.

"There's been a major theft," said the wise-hoof.

"What, books from the library?" Goodbody was incensed. "Is there no decency left in the world?"

"Not books," said the wise-hoof. "Statues."

"*Statues?*" Scoffit laughed.

"It's not funny. Five of them vanished, just a little while ago. Big statues, too. It's a complete mystery."

Scoffit and Goodbody parted company, and Scoffit flew out of town to the perching rocks — which were very up-market and not what she was used to at all. Goodbody spent the night at Bedstraw's Lodging House, worked his way through most of the menu, drank too much fermented fertle juice, and threw up. He was cramming in as many bodily experiences as he could. The following morning, he had a headache, which wasn't anything near as much fun. Bedstraw gave him an herbal infusion, which helped enormously, and by the time he'd had breakfast and met up with Scoffit, he felt a lot better. They flew to the library, and landed on the gravel path outside.

Neither Scoffit nor Goodbody had ever visited the library. They stared in amazement at the sprawling one-story building, which was set in extensive grounds. The landscaped gardens were dotted with statues, with little paths weaving between. A team of cuddyaks was grazing the lawns to the consistency of velvet, and the sweet peppery scent of purple peribott was everywhere. Spring had arrived in Andria, and the contrast with the bleak snowy landscape around Yergud was very marked. A lesser spotted tease was singing somewhere in a lace-petal tree, among frothy white blossoms and clouds of coral butterflies.

Brad Goodbody surveyed the building itself with a mixture of disbelief and awe. It seemed to have crept outward from some central point while no one was watching, unplanned and unregulated. "It is magnificent," he declared, admiring the way it was composed of such strange, asymmetrical shapes. "My own library is but a fertle seed compared to this, the fruit itself."

"They've built a new wing since I was here last," said Scoffit. "It looks like a pair of lungs."

"There is beauty in offal," agreed Goodbody.

"That's not exactly what I meant," said Scoffit. "I wonder whose statue used to be on here?" she added, kicking an empty plinth with her foot.

The main door of the library burst open, and an irate brazzle charged out. "What do you think you're doing?" she squawked, her feathers flat with fury. "Isn't it bad enough that the magnificent statue of Flintfeather has disappeared, without you adding insult to injury by kicking his pedestal?"

Scoffit looked at Goodbody, and Goodbody looked at Scoffit.

"Sorry," said Scoffit.

"I haven't seen you around here before," said the female, her voice losing none of its severity. "You'll need a ticket if you want to take out any books. Who are you?"

"Brad Goodbody. And you are?"

"Professor Thornbeak."

"Fuzzy's mother?"

The brazzle's demeanor changed completely. "Fuzzy? You've seen Fuzzy?"

"Indeed," said Goodbody. "She is as smooth and glossy as a fried quaddiump's kidney."

"But not as dead, I hope?"

"She is very well," said Goodbody. "She's escorting some humans back to the Divide, then she's coming straight here."

"I see," said Thornbeak. "Have you seen anything of Ironclaw on your travels? Big brazzle, always looks a mess . . ." She seemed about to add something, but a second glance at Scoffit's less-than-perfect plumage stopped her.

"He's gone to Yergud with Grimspite," said Goodbody. "To straighten things out. It looks as though Squill's decided to retire, now that Snakeweed's back. Though he's calling himself Snakeroot, and pretending to be his own brother."

"*Snakeweed?*" Thornbeak lashed her tail. "I think you'd better tell me everything. Come into my office."

She led the way into the building, and along innumerable book-lined passages until they reached a door with her name emblazoned on it in gold. Once inside, she offered Goodbody a chair, and Scoffit one of the three branches that were affixed to the wall. They were all beautifully carved and, without a doubt, genuine antiques.

"This library is amazing," said Goodbody. "I'm something of a bibliophile myself. . . ."

"Really?" said Thornbeak.

Down on the beach, five figures skipped in and out of the waves.

"Doesn't this feel good?" said a brittlehorn, rolling in the sand.

"Wonderful," agreed a small-tail, kicking a stone into the water with his cloven hoof.

"What do you think turned us back into ourselves?" asked a diggeluck.

"I think it must have been a powerword," said the biggest of the five, a brazzle. "I don't see what else could have done it."

"This is going to rewrite all the history books," said a wise-hoof, whisking his rump with his tail. "I only got turned to stone a couple of decades ago, so I know what's been going on." He looked at the brazzle and grinned. "When you turn up, alive and well, it's going to cause a lot of trouble."

"Why him in particular?" asked the diggeluck.

"Because he's the most famous of all of us. His name's Flintfeather."

"Ah," said the brazzle. "There's something I think you ought to know. . . ."

15

Grimspite had sat on his haunches for some time in the snow, on the wrong side of the predator hedge, thinking about how he was going to reach Snakeweed. He would have to be very careful. The only things that could cross a hedge like this were fire-breathers, because they had scales rather than fur or feathers. He knew that if he broke any of the branches as he pushed his way through, the weeping sap would glue him to the plant — and the more he struggled, the tighter the trap around him would close. He gave himself a good scratch (which always improved his morale) and set off at a trot around the perimeter, looking for a weak spot. Even with Grimspite's exceptional night vision, the task was a difficult one. He peered into the hedge time and time again, looking for a way through, but all he could see were twisted and tangled branches, and a dark mass of interlocking sickle-shaped leaves. This was really a job for Scoffit — she'd have been immune to the sap. On the other hand — or paw — she wouldn't have been able to rip Snakeweed apart the way a sinistrom could.

In the end, it took Grimspite all night.

When he finally found a place where the hedge was thin enough to squeeze through, it didn't actually take him all that long — and when he emerged on the other side, he just stood and stared. The stone being quarried here was pink marble. Closest to him, chipped and irregular chunks of it were piled up, all higgledy-piggledy, covered with a fresh dusting of snow that made them look like lumps of flesh coated with sugar. Farther to his right, there were slabs of it stacked in blocks, presumably waiting for transportation.

The walls of the quarry were sheer, and there were naturally occurring cracks in the rock. Into these, wooden pegs had been driven. There were a lot of empty buckets lying around, and after a moment or two, Grimspite figured out what they were doing — pouring water onto the wooden pegs to make them swell, so that eventually they split the marble of their own accord. It was the sort of thing that was taught in stuff studies at school.

He spotted a little sentry house, made of logs, with smoke issuing from a chimney. A fire-breather was curled up outside, asleep. The snow around it had melted, and the veined pink-and-white marble beneath looked like slices of smoked grunt-beast. Next to the sentry house was a bigger log building — probably an administration center. Was Snakeweed in there, going through the accounts? Grimspite trotted over to the building and peered through the window. There were rows and rows of cabinets, a few chairs, and a couple of desks — but that was all. He turned his attention back to the sentry house.

Two japegrins were sitting by a fire, toasting buns, but neither of them was Snakeweed. Grimspite considered going inside and asking them whether they'd seen him anywhere, but he decided to use that as a last resort. Seeing a sinistrom in the flesh — or smelling one — tended to have an alarming effect on some people. Going rigid with fear and paralysis of the vocal cords were popular reactions. Torture sometimes overcame this, but Grimspite had given up torture some time ago.

He carried on with his inspection of the rest of the quarry, and discovered some tunnels. This looked more promising. The first one he tried didn't go very deep, nor did the second. But the third one had a shaft that went vertically down, deep into the ground. There was some sort of metal contraption as well, and Grimspite suddenly realized he was looking at the pulley of an elevator. How bizarre. Magic carpets were usually used as elevators — you didn't need to go to all this mechanical bother. He peered into the shaft, but he couldn't see anything. He looked around for a bell, but there wasn't one. How did you get the cage to ascend, then? He was pretty sure this was where Snakeweed had gone — there wasn't any other answer, for the fire-breather hadn't left the compound.

He leaned his head over the shaft and listened. Sinistroms had very sharp hearing, and after some concentrated ear work, he reckoned he could hear something breathing. He took a deep breath and shouted, "Oy! Are you in charge of the elevator?"

There was a sudden snort, as though whatever it was had just woken up. Then there was some rustling and grunting, and the sound of something clearing its throat. Then whatever-it-was yelled, "Going up!"

After a moment or two something metal started to clank its way upward, accompanied by a cloud of rust particles and a lot of screeching.

When the cage arrived, it looked as though it had been designed by whoever had dreamed up the library — in other words, it might have designed itself if that were possible. There were no right angles anywhere, and the threads of the mesh sides seemed to cross one another at random. Grimspite stepped into it rather tentatively, and the gate snapped shut behind him like a trap. On closer inspection, the grille did look like teeth — those curved needle-thin spikes that belong to very deep-sea fish. The cage started to descend, and everything became incredibly dark.

The dark didn't usually bother Grimspite. He had very good night vision — as long as there was *some* light. There didn't seem to be any at all down here. He felt the walls closing in on him. It was the way he used to feel when he'd been sent back into his pebble. Crushed. He didn't like this. He didn't like it one bit. Every second was taking a minute, and every minute was taking an hour. The cage didn't descend at an even rate, either — it jerked and wobbled and speeded up and slowed down for no apparent reason. He began to feel a bit seasick.

After an eternity, the absolute black lightened to gray. Gradually, the light increased until the cage shuddered to a halt at the bottom of the shaft. Three flaming torches were fixed to the rock wall, throwing a sickly yellow light partway down two tunnels. The nasty fish-mouth gate opened, and Grimspite jumped out of the cage and onto solid rock, and looked around.

The creature that confronted him was something he'd never actually seen before, although he'd heard about them. It was huge. It was mean. It was a troggle — he'd heard it called a troll in the other world. It sat there and stared at him with its little ice-blue eyes, the chain that worked the elevator looped over its shoulder. It obviously hauled the cage up and down all by itself, for there was a faint sheen of sweat on its skin. It would hate the daylight, so a career as an elevator operator down here was ideal.

"Hello," said Grimspite, unsure how to tackle this.

The troggle grunted. Its lips hardly moved, although its yellowish tusks quivered slightly. It had a square flattish snout, and big pointed ears that stuck out at an angle. Its hair was thick and a dull brownish-gray, like old rope, and it had two knitting needles stuck behind one ear. It had the

most muscular body Grimspite had ever seen on a two-legged being, which may have been why it didn't seem bothered by the sight of a sinistrom.

It really is awfully ugly, thought Grimspite — and then he felt guilty, for he knew he wasn't exactly the epitome of beauty himself. He tried the lightweight approach. "Nice elevator," he said.

"Snot," said the troggle.

"I suppose it *is* a little rusty," conceded Grimspite. "But you handle it very well."

"My *name's* Snot," said the troggle. "Or Mr. Snot, if I don't like you. What's yours?"

"Grimspite," said Grimspite.

"Bad luck," said Snot.

"Sorry?"

"Having a horrid name like Grimspite."

Grimspite decided not to pursue the matter. "Had many visitors today?" he asked.

Snot held up two fingers.

"And which way did they go?"

The troggle pointed to the right-hand tunnel.

"Thanks." Grimspite seized one of the torches in his mouth, and headed off into the gloom.

He came to the end of that tunnel fairly quickly, which was depressing, so he went back. The troggle was leaning against the elevator shaft, knitting. Grimspite had intended to slip into the other tunnel as surreptitiously as possible, but Snot looked up and saw him.

"That's nice," said Grimspite, pointing to whatever it was the creature was making.

The troggle held it up. It was a gauntlet. He wasn't knitting with wool at all — he was using a ball of wire.

"Is it for you?" asked Grimspite, edging around so he could get to the second tunnel.

The troggle shook its head.

"Who's it for, then?" asked Grimspite. Nearly there.

"Squill's daughter. For training fire-breathers."

"Fire-breathers don't bite."

"The females do."

Grimspite couldn't think of anything further to say, but he was in the right place now, so he said good-bye and trotted off down the second tunnel. At one point the tunnel forked, but the new passageway looked like a natural feature of a cave system, and Grimspite wondered if it came out somewhere else entirely. He continued along in his original direction.

He saw the flickering of the other torch as he rounded a bend. It occurred to him that the owner of the torch would be able to see *his* torch as well, which kind of lost him the element of surprise. He felt like a complete idiot. He should have known better, he really should. He stopped, wondering what to do.

"You may as well keep on coming, now that you're here," said Snakeweed's voice. "I've got you covered with my wand, whoever you are. Turn tail and flee, and I won't answer for the consequences."

Grimspite had no option. If Snakeweed used his wand in this confined space, there really would be an avalanche. He was surprised Snakeweed hadn't realized this. He turned the corner and stepped into the light. The tunnel widened out into a cave here, but it was a dead end. The cave was full of wooden boxes, all labeled, and the walls were decorated with pictures painted directly onto the rock.

"Grimspite," said Snakeweed. "Well, well."

"Hello, Snakeweed," said Grimspite, laying down his torch. "The spinning-wheel hex didn't last, then."

"Someone used a powerword," said Snakeweed.

Grimspite felt depressed all over again. "Me," he said.

"*You?* That was remarkably irresponsible of you, and remarkably lucky for me."

Grimspite decided to change the subject as quickly as possible. He glanced around. "So what's all the secrecy about?" he said.

Snakeweed smiled. "This," he said, and opened one of the boxes.

At first, Grimspite didn't understand. The box was full of artifacts — knives, crossbows, cooking pots, belts, jewelry, jackets, hats. It took him a moment to notice that the clothing was multicolored. Then it took another moment or two for him to register how strange this was. Grimspite had spent a whole year in the other world, so he'd grown used to people wearing all the colors of the rainbow if they wanted to. But in this world, the tangle-folk wore only green, the ragamuckies brown, the japegrins purple, the lickits white, the diggelucks gray. . . . He sat back on his haunches, thinking.

"Curious, isn't it?" said Snakeweed. "Now look at the paintings."

Grimspite turned his attention to the rock walls. There

272

were scenes of everyday life, depicted in bright lively colors —
hunting scenes, gathering scenes, dancing scenes. But the
subjects weren't japegrins or lickits or tangle-folk — they
were a mixture of all of them. Some had red hair, some blond,
brown, black . . . and they all had pointed ears.

"I don't understand," said Grimspite.

"Neither did I, at first," said Snakeweed. "I've spent the
whole night down here, thinking about it. At least, I assume
I have — is it day yet?"

"Midmorning," said Grimspite. "So what was your
conclusion?"

"That this cave system was home to a people who existed
a long, long time ago. There's another tunnel, but it's fallen
in. This cave would have been much easier to get to, in the
past. All these boxes contain the things this society left
behind. I think there must have been a big spitfire eruption,
and they decided to leave — as quickly as they could."

"I don't understand the necessity for all of Squill's
secrecy."

Snakeweed laughed. "These people were the common
ancestors of all of us — well, not you, you're a shadow-beast.
I mean the japegrins, the tangle-folk, the diggelucks —
we're all related."

And suddenly, Grimspite understood. "Wipes out japegrin superiority in one fell swoop, doesn't it?" he said. "If
a ragamucky had the same great-great-whatever grand-
father . . ." He laughed. "How do you justify treating your

273

distant cousin like trash? Oh, yes, I can see why Squill wanted to keep *this* secret. But what about you, Snakeweed? How are *you* going to use it? Are you going to bury it as well, so that japegrin dominance continues to get worse and worse until you — well, you rule the world?"

Snakeweed coughed, took a handkerchief from his pocket, and blew his nose one-handed. He kept the wand pointing at Grimspite with the other. "Some rather interesting things have happened to me since I came out of my enchanted sleep," he said. "But I wouldn't expect a sinistrom to understand."

"Try me."

"I think I should probably just kill you."

"Funnily enough, I was thinking exactly the same thing."

"I'm the one with the wand," said Snakeweed.

"And I'm the one with the teeth," said Grimspite.

"And I'm the one with the pair of very sharp knitting needles," said Snot, appearing behind them. "I'm not having someone firing a wand down here — whatever next? I'm going to send you both straight back up to the surface, where you belong, and the guard can deal with you. You don't have the faintest idea how to behave yourselves underground. I bet neither of you can even knit."

And before either Grimspite or Snakeweed could really take this in, the troggle had picked them both up, one under either arm, and was carrying them back toward the elevator shaft.

"More than my job's worth to have you two kill each

other," said Snot. "Squill would have me tortured. He'd send me up to the surface and tie me up in the open air on a horrible sunny day, when there wasn't a cloud in the sky. Probably in the spring, when the gorsit's in flower. Ugh."

"Squill's resigned, Snot," said Snakeweed, twisting himself around and trying to reach his wand.

"Well, you would say that, wouldn't you?" said Snot, shifting Snakeweed slightly and flicking the wand away with his thumb. "And it's *Mr.* Snot to you now. Can't abide the spring. All that birdsong. All I want is a nice dark hole and a lot of gray. Lovely color, gray."

Grimspite was feeling very pleased with the way things had turned out. Once in the elevator cage, he would still have his teeth, but Snakeweed didn't have his wand anymore. The odds were definitely in his favor.

When they got to the bottom of the shaft, things didn't work out quite like that. Snot threw Snakeweed into the cage and shut the door. Then he dumped Grimspite on the floor, held him in place with his foot, got out his knitting needles, and proceeded to knit a muzzle with his ball of wire. He cast off with a sigh of satisfaction, severed the end of the wire with his tusk, pushed it onto Grimspite's snout, and twisted the trailing ends into a knot. Then he hobbled his legs together. After that, he opened the cage door again and dumped Grimspite inside. "That should take care of both of you," he said, looking pleased with himself. He looped the elevator cable over his shoulder and started to pull.

Things got dark once more very quickly. Grimspite was feeling irritated with himself — immobilized by a troggle. It was so demeaning. He dare not change into lickit form, because he would be the wrong shape for the muzzle and the hobbles, and they would cut into him.

"The last time we met," said Snakeweed, out of the gloom, "you told me you'd come to rip me apart. And then you didn't. Why?"

"I don't really like extreme violence anymore," said Grimspite. "On second thought, though, I'm prepared to make an exception in your case."

"And I don't like being ruthless anymore," said Snakeweed. "However, I'm prepared to make an exception in *your* case."

"You don't like being ruthless anymore?" said Grimspite sarcastically. "That's about as likely as a sinistrom losing its stink!"

"Or its interest in disemboweling things."

"There was a reason for that," said Grimspite. "I was separated from my pebble, and I got free will. I really am not the person I was."

"I'm not the same person, either," said Snakeweed. "And there's a reason for that, too. I'll give you the benefit of the doubt on the disemboweling, Grimspite — based on the fact that you put me into an enchanted sleep in that castle, when you could have ripped me to shreds and hung my intestines from the curtain rod. Now I want you to listen to *me*. I may not have my wand, but I think I could just about strangle you if I put my mind to it. You're fairly securely trussed-up."

He had a point. "OK," said Grimspite. "I'm listening."

"When you jerked me out of my coma with that power-word," said Snakeweed, "I felt absolutely ghastly. It was the middle of the night, and I was completely alone. After a while I managed to crawl out of the four-poster bed and look around. They'd turned me into an *exhibit*." He looked disgusted.

"I know," said Grimspite.

"Posters on the walls, a glass case full of Global Panaceas' products, some imitation sinistrom stones, and a very good painting of you."

"I never visited."

"Wouldn't have expected you to. Anyway, I tottered downstairs, intending to look at the fire-breather timetable and see when the next one left for Tiratattle. That's when I started to cough — coughed so much I threw up — and I knew I was really sick."

The cage shuddered and clanked, and Grimspite felt queasy enough to empathize more strongly than he might otherwise have done.

"This tangle-person came over," Snakeweed continued. "Fully qualified wisewoman, examined me there and then. Told me she was sorry, but I didn't have long to live."

"Ah," said Grimspite. News like that could be just as life-changing as losing your pebble.

"There was nothing she could prescribe, either. I sat there for a long time, until the sun rose, thinking. There wasn't a direct fire-breather to Tiratattle, but there was one to Andria, so I caught that, intending to change and get the express. But when I read the in-flight magazine, I realized that the true seat of power had shifted to Yergud, so I switched flights. Imagine my surprise when you turned out to be one of the passengers."

"You had the chance to kill me when we crash-landed. Why didn't you?"

"Because I'm not the same person anymore. It wasn't a you-or-me situation, either, the way it was down in the cave. You see, I started to see things differently. When you don't have a future, power becomes rather pointless — and you look at what you're going to leave behind instead. In my case, it was a pile of misery. I started to wonder whether it would be possible to do something about it."

"That's the way I felt," said Grimspite. "I decided to write a book to show that not all sinistroms were monsters."

There was a moment of silence.

Then Snakeweed said, "I'd better untie you," and he removed the wire muzzle. The hobbles were a bit trickier because of the dark, but Grimspite could now help things along with his teeth. Any lingering doubts he had about Snakeweed's intentions toward himself had now gone — although Snakeweed's intentions toward the rest of the world might be more questionable. Presumably, any doubts

Snakeweed had about Grimspite would go the same way when Grimspite didn't disembowel him.

There was a pause, during which no one disemboweled anyone.

"Someone recited another powerword yesterday," said Snakeweed.

Oh, dear. "That'd be Felix."

"He's over here again?"

"Yes. He's got a jinx box — the one that was used to store the Common Language. He was supposed to destroy it, though."

"Good intentions, but *so* naïve when it comes to magic," said Snakeweed. "There is something useful *we* could do, though."

"What?" asked Grimspite. He thought he could see a faint glimmer of gray above. He was desperate to get out of the elevator; he hated it.

"Make those rock paintings public knowledge. Turn the caves into a major attraction. Show everyone that japegrins and tangle-folk and diggelucks and lickits are related."

"And ragamuckies." It was definitely getting lighter. Grimspite felt his spirits lift slightly.

"Are you with me?" asked Snakeweed. "I imagine you're going straight back to the library. You could publicize it. The library has the right sort of prestige."

Grimspite could see Snakeweed's face now. He didn't look very well. "Yes, all right," said Grimspite, and he transformed himself back into a lickit — and just in time, too, for daylight flooded the cage and they found themselves aboveground.

The guard was standing at the pit head, accompanied by another japegrin, wands at the ready.

"You don't need those," said Snakeweed.

"That's a sinistrom," said the guard, aiming his wand at Grimspite.

"No, it's not," said Snakeweed. "There's another entrance. The sinistrom escaped. This is a famous cookbook author. *Dining Out on Mythical Beasts?*"

The japegrins looked at each other.

"That pomegranate sauce recipe?" queried the guard.

"First, disembowel your cluck-bird," said Grimspite, quoting his most famous dish, "and hack it into four pieces . . ."

"That's the one," said the guard. "Substituted a lesser spotted tease for the cluck-bird, but it was still delicious." He gave a tentative sniff, but the wind was blowing the wrong way, and Grimspite's shadow-reek didn't reach him.

"What was he doing down in the mine, then?" asked the second japegrin.

"He's going to be my restaurant adviser," said Snakeweed. "You see, we're going to turn this place into a theme park, just like the castle in the forest."

Not just *like the castle in the forest*, thought Grimspite. *This is going to be educational, not profit-oriented.*

The japegrins looked at each other again.

"There are some wonderful rock paintings down there," enthused Snakeweed. "Everyone should be able to see them. And there's this other opening, farther down the mountain, that would make access a lot easier. It needs a proper entrance. I'm on my way to Yergud now, to get hold of some diggelucks to get things moving. Wand," he added, snapping his fingers at the guard. "I lost mine down below. Thanks. Fire-breather saddled and ready to go?"

The japegrins nodded.

"You can drop me off on the other side of the hedge," said Grimspite to Snakeweed, as they climbed aboard. "Ironclaw's waiting for me. Nice idea, by the way. The theme-park thingy."

"I thought so," said Snakeweed.

"You ought to find yourself a fish supplier for the restaurant while you're in the area. Vattan's world famous for it."

Snakeweed nodded, and coughed again.

"I don't quite know how to put this," said Grimspite. "But . . . er . . . how long do you have?"

"No idea," said Snakeweed. "That's why I want to get on with the theme-park idea as fast as possible."

16

Scoffit landed in the main square in Kaflabad, outside Ziggurat Three, and looked around in astonishment. The buildings were totally different from anything she'd ever seen before. Tier after tier, placed on top of one another in descending size. Then a balcony, or a ledge — wide enough to accommodate fruit trees and flowering shrubs and the occasional restaurant — until you reached the main building, which was perched at the top, like a nest.

"It's nice here," said Scoffit. She breathed in the scent of the waxy orange flowers that tumbled down in extravagant clusters from the first balcony. Underlying this was a faint reek of decay, which pleased her to no end. It was so hot here that waste disposal would be a well-respected profession.

"It's a long way up," said Goodbody, clutching his lamp in one hand and shading his eyes with the other as he looked up at the headquarters of K'Faddle & Offspring, eight stories above him.

There was a notice at the foot of the first set of stairs that read: NO TRIPLE-HEADS, MAGIC CARPETS, BRAZZLES, OR CAR-RIONWINGS BEYOND THIS POINT.

"I'll wait for you," said Scoffit. There was a fountain a little way off that had a drinking trough at its base, in some nice dappled shade beneath a stand of palm trees.

By the time Brad Goodbody had climbed the steps to the first story, he could see that Scoffit had her head under her wing. By the time he climbed to the second level, he could swear that he could hear her snoring. He carried on toward the third set of stairs, passed the time of day with a couple of fruit trees, and shared a rather good joke about turning over a new leaf with a succulent that bore a strong resemblance to one in his greenhouse.

When he reached the third level, he passed a nomad, coming down the other way. The nomad was holding a crystal ball, and he looked absolutely furious. He glanced at Goodbody's magic lamp and said, "If you think they'll give you a refund, you've got another think coming."

Goodbody pointed to the crystal ball and said, "Problems?"

"Shows what's happening on the other side of the world instead of the future," said the nomad. "What's the use of that? I wanted to place a bet on next week's Textile Trophy. There's a couple of magic carpets that have caught my eye, but they're not sure things." And he stalked off.

Something that showed what was happening elsewhere would be extremely useful, you fool, thought Goodbody, remembering the television news broadcasts Rhino had boasted about in the other world. Television had a lot in common with crystal balls, now that he thought about it. Television predicted the weather and told people whether to take their raincoats with them.

He continued climbing but, to his horror, he found himself out of breath. He stood there, his ribs heaving, absolutely terrified. Just how long was this body going to last? It wasn't until someone else stopped from a similar cause and smiled at him that he realized panting was a normal reaction.

Another level up and another dissatisfied customer, carrying a cracked scrying bowl. He glanced at Goodbody's lamp. "Brandee been giving you trouble, has he?" he inquired.

"He's disappeared," said Goodbody uncomfortably, unable to think of anything else to say on the spur of the moment.

"There's been a lot of that the last couple of days. There's a rumor that someone somewhere used a powerword, though that bunch . . ." He jerked his thumb at the building at the top of the ziggurat. "That bunch is denying it. Naturally." He then called K'Faddle & Offspring something unprintable, and went on his way.

Goodbody continued up the staircase. Two more people passed him, both carrying lamps not dissimilar to his own. By the time he reached the top, he had encountered no fewer than nine angry customers.

The building that was the company's headquarters looked as though it was made of the same material as a jinx box —

the watered-silk effect was impressive, and the colors changed as you approached it. Goodbody pulled the tail of the alarm-bell-bird, and was surprised to hear his favorite bangithard soloist executing a complicated but catchy riff. *Of course*, he thought, *you hear what you want to hear*. The place is a showcase for magic of every sort.

The silken wall split open like a ripe fruit, and he entered the building. A creature with an orange carapace and five sets of pincers turned its stalked eyes toward him and said, "Welcome to K'Faddle and Offspring. How can I help you?"

The brandee-that-was suddenly realized that telling the truth would be most unwise: He had developed free will, so he would be instantly fumigated. He noticed a state-of-the-art wand stuck in the creature's belt, and a couple of feelers of uncertain function on its forehead. He told the receptionist that he had bought the lamp at an auction and been cheated. The brandee had vanished, but the paperwork that had come with the lamp spoke of a library and a greenhouse. Could these, at least, be redeemed?

The receptionist nodded, and agreed to have the lamp gutted as long as the shell remained with the makers for refurbishment afterward and Goodbody gave up all claim to it.

Goodbody agreed. The whole procedure would take several days, during which time he needed to buy a house with sufficient space for all his books and plants — not to mention a nice hollow tree trunk, suitable for a carrionwing. Feeling pleased with the outcome, he left the building and went back to Scoffit. "We're going house hunting," he said.

After a few disappointments, they found a courtyard house built around just the right kind of garden for Goodbody's plants. The hollow tree would have to be imported, but that wasn't a problem — there was quite a wide choice in the catalogue. There was space for a large library, and a first-class restaurant was a short stroll away. Goodbody intended to make up for lost time as far as food and drink were concerned.

"It's all turned out rather well, hasn't it?" he said to the carrionwing.

"I think we should drink a toast," said Scoffit.

"I thought you ate toast?"

"Not this toast," said Scoffit, pouring two large fermented fertle juices.

When Felix woke up the next morning, he forgot where he was for a moment. He was warm and comfortable, and the Pink Harpoon's feather mattress was surprisingly soft — so soft he felt as though he were floating. He could have stayed in bed for a lot longer, but he knew there was something important he had to do. . . . He opened his eyes.

"Morning, Felix," said Nimby, sounding far too bright and lively. "Fuzzy's gone off on an early morning hunt, but she shouldn't be too long. I'm just about to pop out for a quick flight myself, since it's a nice day and I need to twisty-strip some sunlight. I've cleared it with Betony."

"Fine," said Felix sleepily. When the carpet had gone, he dozed for a bit longer. Then he got up and fished in his backpack for his toothbrush. There was a real bathroom here, which would be a luxury after the recent hardships. His fingers closed around the cataloguing quill. *Drat!* he thought, *I didn't give it back to Ironclaw*. He took out his notebook and

scribbled a reminder to himself to hand it over to Betony when they got home, so she could bring it back with her. Then he laid the pen on the notebook and went into the bathroom for a shower. When he came back, he noticed that the quill had been busy on its own. He glanced briefly at what it had written, but it didn't make immediate sense. It was getting late, so he put both the quill and the notebook away and went downstairs. Betony and Rhino were already there, eating smoked roe on pepper bread and drinking hot honeyed milk.

"Are you ready, then?" asked Rhino.

"Ready for what?" Felix sat down. He dug his knife into the big yellow pat of cuddyak butter and smeared it over his bread.

"Dropping the jinx box into molten rock, of course," said Rhino. "I wonder if it'll explode."

"Oh," said Felix. Trust Rhino to bring him down. "Can we do it after breakfast?"

"You're just chicken," said Rhino cheerfully. "I don't see why, though. The box may have tricked you into saying one of those powerwords, but nothing much happened."

"Nothing much?" squealed Betony. "*Nothing much?* My parents only came back to life, that's what. Not to mention a lot of other things."

Felix stopped with a forkful of food halfway to his mouth. "A lot of other things? What do you mean?"

"Some other statues."

"What other statues? How do you know?"

Betony looked shamefaced. "I wanted to see some more of my parents, so I used the crystal ball again when I went up to my room. It didn't show them to me, as it happens, but it showed me a lot of other things. You know that statue of Flintfeather, outside the library?"

Felix nodded.

"It's not there anymore."

"Maybe someone stole it."

"Don't be silly, it's huge."

"I thought that was a real statue."

"So did I. But Quillfinger the small-tail's gone as well, and so has . . ."

"Hang on," said Felix, as something occurred to him. "What's Thornbeak going to do if Flintfeather turns up alive and well? Her book was a biography of him."

"Oh, I'm sure Thornbeak's perfectly capable of getting around that," said Betony airily.

"So you don't think that was actually the *bad* effect of the powerword, then?" snapped Felix. "I was kind of hoping it was. I was kind of hoping that was the end of it. I was kind of hoping we hadn't unfrozen something ghastly that has yet to make itself known to us."

"Why are you so touchy?"

"Because I want to eat my breakfast."

"Well, get on with it, then," said Betony.

Felix glared at her, but he seemed to have lost his appetite. He was scared of the effect the jinx box had on him. Even just talking about it. That was it. He was *scared*. And it wasn't just the jinx box he was frightened of, and whatever self-defense mechanisms it had — what about the picture the box had shown him of Betony, standing on the Divide, tears running down her face? What was that all about?

He suddenly realized he'd been drifting, a hunk of pepper bread halfway to his mouth. Rhino was deep in conversation with Betony. The pair of them were laughing as though they'd known each other for years, and Felix felt a stab of jealousy.

Rhino said something under his breath, and Betony had a fit of the giggles.

"What's the joke?" asked Felix, pushing his plate away.

"There isn't one," said Betony. "That's why it's funny. What's a pachyderm, Rhino? The jinx box called you a pachyderm, ages ago."

"Someone who's handsome and brave and . . ."

"And as strong as a cuddyak," said Betony, and the two of them went into hysterics.

"It means to be like a rhinoceros," said Felix coldly. "Thick-skinned."

Suddenly, the door slammed open with a bang. An icy draft blew through the opening, accompanied by a flurry of snow. The beautiful start to the morning had vanished in a cloud of snowflakes. Felix could hear a faint jingling of bells outside, and the snort of a cuddyak. The figure that marched in was almost completely submerged beneath layers of fur, although some of his ginger hair was barely visible beneath his hat. He had a pair of the local-style feathered earmuffs hanging around his neck like two dead chickens. After a moment's pause, he kicked the door shut, stomped over to the bar, and thumped his fist on it. The pewter mugs jumped on the spot, clinking as they landed, and a cheese rolled across the counter, tipped over the edge, and fell to the ground. The landlord came rushing out of the kitchen, looking worried.

"I've got a very important person in my sleigh," said the

japegrin, "and he wants lodging for the night." He glanced across at Felix, Betony, and Rhino and said, "And you can tell them to get lost. This is a japegrin inn."

The landlord opened his mouth to say something, and then shut it again.

The sleigh driver opened his greasy fur coat and pulled out the crossbow he'd been carrying beneath it. It was like watching a magician pull a rabbit out of a hat — the weapon seemed far too big to have been hidden there. He slammed it down on the bar and said, "Either you get rid of them or I will." His gaze flitted over Felix and Betony and came to rest on Rhino. "Got to be a half-and-half, he has, with his red hair and his muddy eyes."

"At least I wash," said Rhino.

There was a stunned silence.

After a moment the landlord said, "He was just leaving."

And then, out of the blue, the eerie wail of snagglefangs started up — distant, but unmistakable. The driver looked sharply at the landlord. "Since when have snagglefangs hunted by day?"

The landlord became defensive. "They don't. Ever. No one's even *seen* a live one by daylight. They turn to stone at sunrise."

"Really?" said the driver sarcastically. "Doesn't sound like it to me."

The landlord looked at Felix. "Can you hear them?"

Felix nodded.

The landlord turned to Betony. "You?"

Betony nodded.

"So can I," said Rhino.

The landlord looked horrified. The howls got a little louder.

"I've got the thane of Yergud in my sleigh," said the japegrin. "I'd better go and bring him inside."

"I thought the thane had resigned," said Rhino.

"This is the new one, half-trash," said the driver, heading for the door. "His name's Snakeroot."

Felix and Betony looked at each other, aghast.

"Snakeweed," said Betony.

"Grimspite and Ironclaw can't have found him, then," said Felix gloomily.

"Or . . ." Betony didn't finish her sentence.

"Grimspite can take care of himself, surely?" said Rhino. "He's got jaws like an industrial vice and fangs like carving knives."

"He can still be killed with a wand," said Betony.

"Ssshh — listen," said Felix. "The snagglefangs have gone quiet."

"That's bad," said the landlord. "That's really bad. They always go quiet when they're creeping up on something. Makes sense."

The driver reappeared in the doorway and bundled someone through. Then he went out again, presumably to get the cuddyaks to safety in the barn.

"This is an honor, Your Excellency," said the landlord, with a hurried bow to the new arrival. "Did you see any . . . er . . ."

"Snagglefangs? No." The figure unwound his purple scarf, shook off his hood, and looked around the room. "Well, if it isn't Felix," he said. "How are you?"

The landlord's mouth dropped open at such familiarity.

"A lot worse than I was five minutes ago," said Felix.

"Not on my account, I hope," said Snakeweed. "Grimspite said you were over here."

Before Felix could react to this, there was a lot of bellowing and bell tinkling from outside, followed by the twang of a crossbow, some swearing, and a yelp.

"Where *is* Grimspite?" asked Felix, trying not to think about what was going on outdoors.

"On his way to Andria. He's going to publicize my new venture for me."

Felix shook his head. "Grimspite working in partnership with you? Never."

Snakeweed shrugged. "We came to an understanding. And talking of understandings, I understand you're in possession of a certain jinx box?"

Felix stiffened.

"Oh, don't worry, I'm not about to relieve you of it," said Snakeweed, and to Felix's surprise he shuddered. "No, thank you. But you do realize it was the last powerword you used that released the snagglefangs from their stone prisons so that they could hunt by day?"

"No," said Felix, with a sinking feeling. "I hadn't realized." It was so obvious, now that he thought about it.

Flintfeather coming back to life hadn't been nearly horrible enough to be the downside of *hocus pocus*. This was. Once again, he'd tried to do the right thing, and had caused a lot of misery instead.

"Unpredictable stuff, magic," said Snakeweed. "Sort of like science, really."

The door slammed open again. The japegrin driver staggered through and barred the door behind him. "They're out there," he said. "At least twenty of them. We're surrounded. I did get one, though. And the cuddyaks are safe."

"There's plenty of salted meat and pickled fruit in the cellar," said the landlord. "Not to mention three whole barrels of fertle juice. We can hold out."

Rhino looked dubious.

"It won't come to that," said Betony quietly. "When Fuzzy comes back from her hunt, she'll scare them away."

"Hot drinks all around, then," said Snakeweed. "On me." He dumped a handful of coins onto the counter.

The landlord went out the back to heat up some milk. After a moment there was a clattering sound, as though something had been knocked over — then silence. They all looked at one another, and Snakeweed drew his wand. The driver picked up his harpoon and fitted another bolt. After that, the only sound was of people breathing and the occasional crackle from the fire at the far end of the room.

The white shape slipped into the room so smoothly that

Felix almost didn't see it. Then, quite suddenly, and directly opposite him, was the grizzled face he remembered so well. The last time he'd seen it, it had been pressed against the window of the rescue hut. This time, the body beneath it was tensed to spring.

Betony made a funny little noise in her throat, and Rhino shouted, "*Run!*"

The snagglefang leaped. It seemed to hang in the air, defying gravity — then it crashed into the wall next to him, and there was a shower of purple sparks.

Snakeweed wiped his wand against his cloak, a faint smile on his face.

Felix stood up, feeling a bit wobbly. "You saved my life," he said.

"Makes a change from trying to take it," said Snakeweed. "The landlord must have left the back door open. Let's get it shut. Grab one of those torches off the wall, and light it from the fire."

Felix did as instructed. The pitch sparked and spluttered, and he felt a lot better with a weapon in his hands. The two of them headed for the kitchen. To Felix's horror, there were two more snagglefangs in there, and the landlord was sprawled across the floor, quite dead. Felix didn't look too closely.

There was something about the frozen immobility of the person who had been alive and talking a few moments before that chilled him to the bone.

He lifted his torch. The flame caught the draft from the open back door and flared up, and the snagglefangs turned tail and ran. Felix slammed the door shut behind them and went to the window. The snow was clearing. As he watched, a shadow crossed the road outside — and suddenly, the snagglefangs were streaking away into the distance, exactly the way they had done at the rescue huts.

Fuzzy had returned from her hunt.

17

"I think there's something you ought to know," said Fetlock the wise-hoof, standing in the doorway to Thornbeak's office in the library.

"You've found the statues?" said Thornbeak, glancing up at the librarian from the manuscript she was studying.

"Not exactly." Fetlock looked uncomfortable.

"Not exactly? They've been broken up for building rubble or something?"

"Not exactly."

Thornbeak closed her book. "What, exactly?"

"I think you should fly down to the beach."

"Why?"

The wise-hoof looked even more uncomfortable.

"Fetlock, you're being very annoying."

"I know," said the wise-hoof. "Sorry. But I really think you should go."

Thornbeak cleared away her papers, left the building, and flew down to the sea.

For a moment she thought Ironclaw had returned, for there was a large male brazzle scratching around in the sand. It looked as though there had been a celebration of some sort — a small-tail and a wise-hoof were dancing in and out of the waves, a diggeluck was sitting with his back against a rock, swigging from a gourd, and an elderly brittlehorn was rolling around like a foal. Thornbeak turned her magnifying vision on to the brazzle and realized immediately that it wasn't Ironclaw. This one was far too handsome. Nor was it Stonetalon, their son. Nevertheless, there was something familiar about him. The hooked beak, the noble brow, the athletic build.

She turned her attention to the small-tail. There was something familiar about him, too. The slant of his eyes, the curl of his horns; he looked just like the statue of Quillfinger, the scribe who had written down the first Tangle-Commonspeak dictionary. . . .

She moved on to the brittlehorn. The brittlehorn was a dead ringer for Ivorynose, the philosopher. The diggeluck looked like Delveditch, the moat designer, and the wise-hoof appeared to be a reincarnation of Pastern, a librarian who had vanished under mysterious circumstances twenty years ago. She'd known him quite well.

She studied the brazzle once again — and then he looked up, saw her, and squawked a greeting.

And that was the moment when Thornbeak realized every single one of the revelers on the beach had once been a statue on the grounds of the library. *Well, pull my tail and run*, she thought, *it's Flintfeather*. She felt a surge of delight — she knew so much about him, she'd spent fifty years researching him and writing about him. He was extremely good-looking. She wondered who had turned him to stone, all those centuries ago, and why. And then she thought — my book. It's completely irrelevant now. And it was doing so *well*.

Betony and Rhino crept along the passageway at the top of the stairs. The Pink Harpoon was a really old inn — it was big and rambling with twists and turns and dark little corners that could easily have concealed a snagglefang.

"I hope Felix is OK," said Betony, her voice squeaky with anxiety. "I thought he was following us. He must have stayed behind with Snakeweed. How are we going to know if it's safe to go back downstairs?"

"We go back to the landing and listen, I suppose."

"We don't have any weapons, Rhino. Oh, how I wish Fuzzy would come back."

"We probably couldn't see her even if she already has," Rhino pointed out. "The windows up here don't give much of a view."

"I wish you hadn't dragged me up here."

"I'm sorry," said Rhino. "I thought I was doing it for the best. We probably *would* have been better off staying with the others. The driver had a crossbow, and Snakeweed had a wand."

"You can only use a wand a certain number of times before it needs recharging."

Rhino smiled. "Science and magic aren't really all that different, are they?"

They came to the end of the passageway and tackled the corner in true blockbuster-movie style, pressing themselves against the mossy wall and poking only their noses around the corner.

The white shape at the end of the next corridor turned to look.

Betony froze. Rhino grabbed her by the hand and pulled her back the way they'd come. Before they were halfway to the stairs, the snagglefang rounded the corner. If it hadn't stopped to have a celebratory snarl, it would have been curtains for both of them — but the beast clearly thought the hunt was over and he could pick them off at his leisure.

Rhino let go of Betony's hand and forced open one of the windows with his elbow.

"What are you *doing?*" screamed Betony. "We're on the second floor. It's too far to jump!"

Rhino simply pushed her toward the window. Then he grabbed her around the waist and lifted her right up, so that she had to kneel on the sill.

"Rhino!" cried Betony. "What are you *playing* at? I'll fall!"

"I'd rather you jumped!" called a silky little voice.

All of a sudden, it was clear that Rhino had spotted Nimby hovering just below the window, and seized the chance to save Betony. She glanced back over her shoulder at him. The snagglefang had stopped snarling and was walking toward him in a horribly deliberate way, with a businesslike expression on its scarred white face. "What about you?" she said.

"I'm too big to squeeze through there. Go *on*, Betony, jump!"

Still she hesitated, so Rhino pushed her. There was a moment when she was falling, her gasp frozen in her throat, and then Nimby cupped her fall.

Rhino took a deep breath and prepared to die fighting. He'd never done anything heroic before, and the adrenaline was pumping through his body, making his heart beat faster and the tips of his fingers tingle as though he'd had an electric shock. He was thinking faster, too. He could see that the snagglefang knew it had him cornered, for it treated itself to a protracted growl. How effective would his bare hands be against a wolf-thing the size of a small bear?

And then he remembered. He still had a couple of firecrackers left. He moved his hands to his pockets, slowly, slowly. The creature was just watching him at the moment, and licking its black lips. To his relief, the firecrackers were in one pocket and the cigarette lighter was in the other. He pulled out a little cardboard cylinder — slowly, slowly — then the lighter, and moved his hands behind his back. He was going to have to light it blind.

The snagglefang took a pace forward.

There was a dry rasping click as the cigarette lighter failed to light.

The snagglefang took another pace forward.

I'm going to die, thought Rhino. He tried a second time. The lighter flared up, burned his finger, and went out again. Trying not to fumble, he flicked it once more with the ball of his thumb. This time, he managed to ignite the little blue fuse without burning himself, and he hurled the firecracker straight at the snagglefang.

There was a bang — a muffled bang, not the sort of explosion that had razed the ragamucky shack. A real damp squib. But it was enough to send the snagglefang yelping back downstairs. Rhino stuck his head out of the window. He could see Nimby hovering a little way off, with Betony on board — and then he saw the snagglefang race out of the building with its tail on fire, and run off down the road. Fuzzy appeared from nowhere and chased it.

When they all met up again outside the inn, Felix was relieved to see Betony in one piece. But when she leaped off Nimby, it was Rhino she ran to. And if that wasn't bad enough, she then proceeded to give him the most enormous hug.

"You're a hero, Rhino," she said, and she told everyone what he had done.

Rhino felt a sort of warmth replace the hyped-up feeling he'd had upstairs. Despite her elfin beauty, Betony was as tough as they came. The urge to make fun of her had gone. She was all right.

The japegrin driver led his cuddyaks out of the barn and harnessed them to the sleigh. Then he turned to Snakeweed and said, "Shall we go, Your Excellency?"

Snakeweed smiled. "Time to say good-bye again, Felix. Though not as acrimoniously as before, I hope." He held out his hand.

Felix shook it, although it didn't feel quite right. "Those caves," he said. "Are you going to charge admission?"

There was a faint flicker of something behind Snakeweed's eyes. "It's got to be self-supporting, Felix. There's the publicity to pay for, and the upkeep, and that predator hedge will have to go. It needs a decent landing strip for firebreathers as well."

They watched Snakeweed climb aboard the sleigh. The japegrin shouted at the cuddyaks, and with a snort and a bellow, they were off. Felix, Betony, and Rhino could still hear Snakeweed coughing when the sleigh was just a tiny speck in the distance.

"Come on, then," said Betony. "Let's go."

Rhino suddenly seemed reluctant to move.

"What's up?" asked Fuzzy.

"I thought you were desperate to get home," said Felix.

"I was desperate to get *away*, when there was a price on my head," said Rhino. "That's not quite the same thing."

"Don't you want to go back now, then?" asked Betony.

"I got my wish, didn't I?" said Rhino. "Respect."

"What about your parents?" asked Nimby.

"What about them?"

"They'll be worried."

"No, they won't."

"Are you sure?" said the carpet. "I only had a weaver, you see, so maybe I don't understand."

"They've got five other sons. Gary — that's my oldest brother — my mom hasn't heard from him for years. Good riddance, was what she said. He was always in trouble, see. I liked Gary a lot, actually. He was always OK with me, took me fishing and stuff. Moved up to the Midlands somewhere — Birmingham, I think. I could say I went to live with him, that I'd been in contact all the time. That I had his cell number all along."

"And how are you going to say that, if you stay over here?" asked Felix.

Rhino turned to look at him. "You could do it," he said.

"No way," said Felix.

"Why not?"

"I'd be lying."

Rhino just looked at him.

304

"If they're not bothered, Felix, I don't see that it matters," said Betony.

Oh, it matters, thought Felix. *This was* my *place, my own private world. It gave me adventure, it gave me friends, it gave me a* life. *And now Rhino wants to live here. Rhino, the person from my own world who I hated above all others.*

"We need to talk about this," said Fuzzy, with a sharp glance in Felix's direction. "Let's head up to the Divide, and have lunch up there. Then, when you've dumped the jinx box down the fissure and Rhino's decided what he's going to do, we can go our separate ways."

"Sounds good to me," said Rhino.

Felix was trying really hard not to be a wet blanket, but the horrible feeling of impending doom wouldn't go away. Every time he managed to think about something else, it would creep back, souring everything and making the hairs on the back of his neck stand on end. Something was going to happen when he jettisoned the jinx box, he was sure of it, and it involved Betony getting really upset. Why did everything have to have a downside? The downside of Rhino's wish being granted was one he hadn't anticipated at all. Rhino was happy here now, and he no longer wanted to go home. If Felix was honest about it, he was dead jealous. Staying in this world with no strings attached would be wonderful. But he had parents who loved him, he had responsibilities. He had to go home.

Perhaps a look into the crystal ball might prepare him for

305

what was to come. He managed to pull his face into a smile, and then he climbed onto the carpet with the others.

Thornbeak landed in the sand, and found herself tongue-tied for the first time in her life. Flintfeather, mathematician and apothecary to the king, author of the book *Strength in Feathers*, inventor of the spell that had cured Felix's heart complaint. Flintfeather, whose biography she had spent fifty years writing, whose statue she had admired every day on her way to work, whose fame stretched as far as Kaflabad and beyond. Flintfeather, whose intellect had been beyond compare. Flintfeather, her hero.

"Hi there," said the brazzle. "You're a good-looking bit of fluff."

Thornbeak's beak dropped open. When she realized it, she shut her beak with a loud clack.

"I've been a statue for a long time," said the brazzle, stretching out one of his wings — lazy, athletic, overtly masculine. He ruffled his feathers and flattened them again. He was a very good-looking brazzle indeed — broad-chested and muscular, and his plumage was glossy and bright. He cocked his head to one side. "What's your name, silky-rump?"

"Thornbeak," said Thornbeak. The conversation wasn't going quite the way she'd anticipated.

"Hold on a moment, velvet-paws, while I give myself a preen. Can't chat to a hen looking like this." He had an earthy voice, well used, slightly sardonic. He started to preen himself, taking great care with every feather. Thornbeak didn't quite know where to look.

Ivorynose the brittlehorn came over. He nodded politely to Thornbeak and said, "We live in interesting times, Professor."

Thornbeak wondered how he knew she was a professor when he'd been stone for the past three hundred years, but he was pretty intimidating, the way senior brittlehorns frequently were, so she didn't ask.

"Two powerwords have been used in the past few days," the brittlehorn continued gravely, looking into the middle distance. "I have meditated on this, and I can tell you that the first gave free will to every brandee, and the second gave all stone-enchanted beings their bodies again."

"*Abracadabra* and *hocus pocus?*" queried Quillfinger.

"The very same," said Ivorynose. "How did you know?"

"They're some of the powerwords that were stored in the jinx box that was used to collect the Common Language," said Quillfinger. "We were colleagues for a while — absolutely the most unpleasant receptacle it has ever been my misfortune to encounter. The third command of that particular trio is *open sesame*. It creates unity where once there was division. If *that* gets spoken by a mythical being, we ought to take advantage of the harmony it could bring, while being on our guard for the downside that must, inevitably, accompany it. We should have the biggest conference the world has ever seen. Tangle-folk, nomads, one-eyes — even the japegrins. Unity from disunity."

"Sounds like a good idea," said Thornbeak.

"But not as good an idea as having lunch with Flintfeather," said an earthy voice. "Go on, you know you want to."

"Take no notice of him," said Pastern, the wise-hoof. "He's the reason *I* got turned to stone twenty years ago. I had my suspicions, you see."

"Suspicions?"

"That he wasn't really a statue."

"Not only was he not a statue, he's not even Flintfeather," said Ivorynose.

"Spoilsport," said the brazzle. "I was doing really well with the hen, too."

Thornbeak drew herself up to her full height. Her eyes narrowed, and her tail flicked dangerously back and forth. "So who *are* you, exactly?"

The brazzle had the grace to look a bit sheepish. "Topaztoe."

"Go on."

"After Flintfeather died of old age, the chief librarian commissioned a statue of him. The trouble was, Flintfeather wasn't the most beautiful brazzle you've ever seen. He had one leg shorter than the other, a dragging wing, a scar on his beak, and a bald patch on his rump. . . . By the time the statue was completed — a good likeness, by all accounts — the chief librarian had died as well. The new chief hated the statue on sight. He was trying to turn the library into a thing of beauty. He told the sculptor to do another, and use as much artistic license as he liked — but he wouldn't pay the full price for the first statue. The sculptor was so annoyed that he decided to cheat. He hired a sorcerer to develop a freezing spell and find a willing subject who looked like every hen's dream."

"You."

"That's right, golden-eyes. I was short of cash at the time, and it was easy money. It was supposed to wear off after fifty years, but it took more than four hundred. That's cut-rate spells for you."

"But all male brazzles are mathematicians. Didn't you check out the spell?"

"Not my strong point, math. I'm a wow at reverse plummets, though."

"There's something we all ought to be aware of," said Quillfinger. "The third powerword of that trio is the most powerful of the bunch, a level thirteen spell."

Topaztoe moved a little closer to Thornbeak.

Thornbeak moved away a little.

"Science or magic, it doesn't matter which you use, it's *how* you use it that counts," said the brittlehorn. "It's a good thing science is only a legend. Flintfeather calculated that if science really existed, the combination of a scientifically powered object and a level thirteen spell would be catastrophic."

"But science *isn't* a legend," said Thornbeak.

"Are you sure?"

"Yes."

"Ah," said Ivorynose, closing his eyes. "I'll need to contemplate that for a while."

"We've got a very good lunch," said Rhino, spearing the steaks he'd discovered in the kitchen of the Pink Harpoon, and placing them across a fiery fissure.

"I found some of that peppery bread, and some pickled fish, and some seedcake," added Betony.

"All I used to eat were hamburgers and chips," said Rhino. "Do you know, I actually *prefer* all this stuff now?" He laughed.

"Fuzzy," said Felix, "could I take a look in the crystal ball?"

"Sure," said Fuzzy, passing it over. "It's a little too bright out here, though." The sky was a deep cobalt-blue, and there was a lot of glare from the snow.

"Why don't I turn myself into a tent?" said Nimby. "I've done it before, last summer in the desert, remember?"

"Great idea," said Felix, trying to sound normal. He didn't feel normal. He was dreading the moment when he had to take the jinx box out of his pocket and throw it down the fissure. The sense of foreboding was getting stronger all the time, he could almost hear a clock somewhere, ticking away the last minutes of . . . of what? His time in this world? His childhood? His *life*?

He found himself a nice warm patch near the fissure and draped the carpet over his head. Then he placed his hands on the crystal ball, and waited. The ball started to glow with its faintly mauve light, and the usual swirling gray clouds appeared. This time, however, something different happened. The light faded, and intensified, faded and intensified, until it was flicking on and off like a strobe. After twenty seconds or so, it slowed down, then stopped. The scene that gradually came into focus was a place Felix recognized immediately — the grassy stage outside the palace in Andria, where the dance festivals were held.

It looked like a fine summer evening, and the place was packed. He couldn't hear anything, but he could see that people were clapping and cheering. The queen was standing center-stage, dressed in a gorgeous green velvet gown that was covered with emeralds. She raised her hand for silence, and presumably silence fell. In her other hand, she was holding a many-faceted silver orb, fastened to some sort of stand. Every so often, it glinted with rainbow colors, like a dewdrop caught in the sunlight.

"I know what that is," said Nimby, sounding really excited.

"Can you see what's happening as well, then?" asked Felix.

"Yes, I can. It's the summer dance festival, and the queen's handing out the . . . the . . ." The carpet suddenly sounded too full of emotion to speak.

"It's the Magical Objects Bravery Award, isn't it?" said Felix. "Are we actually looking into the future this time, Nimby?"

"Yes. I think that's what all the ebbing and flowing of the

311

light was about — the ball was flicking forward through night and day. If we'd counted, we'd know exactly how far into the future we were."

"It didn't go on all that long," said Felix. "I think we're still in the same year."

A wise-hoof trotted across the stage, carrying a crystal ball. Nimby groaned.

"What?" said Felix.

"Don't tell me he's won it again," said the carpet. "I couldn't bear it."

"In my world," said Felix, "the previous year's winner often presents the trophy to the new winner."

"That crystal ball's won it three years in a row."

"Stop being so pessimistic. Just shut up and watch."

They watched as the queen made some sort of speech.

And then a magic carpet flew onto the stage and curtsied by laying itself down on the grass before the queen. Its coloring was unmistakable — a beautiful cherry-red, with a blue-and-cream design in the middle.

"*That's me!*" said Nimby.

"That's amazing," said Betony, when a hugely excited Nimby told her the news. "You actually got the ball to work right? To show you the future? Let me try. . . . Nimby, keep *still*, will you? I can't see if I don't have you as a tent."

"I don't think I want to see the future," said Rhino, watching Betony disappear beneath her cherry-red canopy.

Felix turned to him. "Why? Scared you'll lose some of that *respect* that's so precious to you?"

"Felix, can't you just drop it?" said Rhino. "I'm not the same person anymore. I kind of stopped feeling angry. Back at school, I hated anyone who was cleverer than me, richer than me, had halfway decent parents. And then — like that's not enough? — I watched you change from a skinny little wimp into someone who was OK. I'm sorry I made your life miserable, all *right*?"

Felix knew he'd taken a cheap shot, and suddenly he wanted to make amends. Fear was making him far too testy. "I've got a confession as well," he said. "I'm scared. Scared that the jinx box will defend itself by trying to make me say another powerword. And that the bad effect will be *really* bad this time."

"Don't open it."

"I don't intend to."

"Well, then . . ."

"I just have this feeling . . . I can't explain it."

Rhino looked thoughtful. "Crossing the Divide — it's like going up in a space rocket, or down in a deep-sea submarine. It's risky. You don't know for sure that you'll ever get back again — and you've done it of your own free will. You're no coward, Felix, whatever you say about being scared at the moment. I'd be terrified, too."

Felix didn't quite know what to say. A compliment from Rhino was a rare and wonderful thing.

"I'm scared of flying." Rhino was clearly in the mood to reveal all his weaknesses. "I'm not technical. I don't understand how airplanes work, I don't understand how brazzles fly, and I have no idea how the crossover thing works. And neither have you."

"Actually," said Felix, "I do understand it. Well, some of it. It's all to do with the indivisible self. The fact that you can't split yourself in two."

"An amoeba can."

"An amoeba's not self-aware."

"It's alive, though. Why is being self-aware such a big

deal? And when does it happen? There's a whole range of creatures from amoeba to human. Where's the cutoff point? A worm? A dung beetle? A rat? A chimp?"

"You're getting off the point," said Felix, who didn't have an answer.

"What *is* the point?"

"That if you're equally split into two on a Divide, the gravity tries to pull you apart, can't, and sends you off somewhere else instead."

"Here?"

"Yes."

"*That's* scary," said Rhino. "How come throwing a stupid silk box down a hole scares you even more?"

Felix hesitated. He was surprised to find himself having a conversation like this with Rhino. He suddenly realized they'd never actually — honestly — talked before. "You remember when the jinx box told us all the things it could give us?"

Rhino nodded. "Yeah . . . '*There's something else you want now, above all else. And I'll tell you how to get it if you say hokey cokey for me.*'"

Felix smiled at Rhino's neat evasion of the powerword as he quoted the jinx box.

Rhino looked thoughtful. "Did it have something to do with Betony? She has to be the prettiest girl I've ever met, even if she does have slightly odd ears."

Felix nodded, slightly annoyed that Rhino had guessed.

315

"It showed me a picture of her, looking really upset, standing . . . right here."

"And you think she was upset because — somehow — the box had killed you?"

Felix shrugged, trying to look more nonchalant than he felt.

"That's why you wanted the crystal ball, to find out what happens. But it showed you something else instead."

"Yeah. Made Nimby's day."

"What's that?" said the carpet. He was hunched over Betony, who was still looking into the crystal ball.

"Made your day. The Magical Objects Bravery Award."

"Oh. Yes." The carpet lifted off Betony, and landed back on the ground.

Betony stood up and gave the ball back to Fuzzy to stash in her leg pouch. "It just showed me Snakeweed haggling with someone in Vattan's fish market," she said. "Waste of time."

"Felix," Nimby continued, "I've been thinking. You know my theory? The one that Ironclaw said was groundbreaking?"

"The magic and science combination factor?"

"Yes. Well, the thing that gave me the idea was seeing what happened to your flashlight when it was hit by the plummeting hex. It melted."

"So?"

"I think you ought to make absolutely certain you don't

316

have anything scientific on your person when you destroy the jinx box. Just in case. It is, after all, a magical object."

"Good point," said Felix. "I don't have the flashlight any longer, but I've got a watch . . . and a compass. I'll take them off."

"I don't have my cell phone anymore," said Rhino. "Squill never gave it back."

"It doesn't matter about *you*," said Felix. "You're not the one doing it."

"There's no need to be so rude," said Betony.

Felix clenched his fist and dug his nails into the palm of his hand. He'd snapped at Rhino again, and he really hadn't meant to. "I'm sorry," he said. "I've got a headache." He could feel a pulse beating in his neck, and a tightness in his throat. Something nasty was waiting for him, he was sure of it, nasty enough to make Betony cry — and Betony hardly ever cried. He took the eyeglass case out of his pocket. Today it was decorated with teeth. A couple of them had cavities, one of them was completely black, and the four canines were bloodstained.

Rhino leaned over the fissure and peered into its depths. "I can see molten lava from here," he said. "The steak's ready, too."

"I brought some platters," said Betony, always the practical one. She passed them around. "Not to mention two whole gourds of the very best fertle juice."

Felix decided to eat first. The food was really good, and he had a horrible feeling that the jinx box would scream or have

317

hysterics or something. He didn't think it would go quietly, anyway. It would be like killing something — in cold blood, too. He might not feel like eating afterward, and this was his last meal in Betony's world. The last meal of the condemned man. He tried to stop thinking about it, and concentrated on his lunch.

"If I didn't go back," said Rhino, thinking aloud, "I'd have to find somewhere to live, and I'd have to get a job."

"Easy," said Betony.

"What could I do?"

"Loads of things. You're a mythical being — they'd have a job for you at the Castle of Myths and Legends, no problem. You'd get a room and all your food, too. People *dress up* as human beings there. You're the real thing. You wouldn't even have to have a molding spell done on your ears."

"I didn't know about those," said Felix, managing a smile.

"Actually," said Betony, "*I'd* forgotten about them until now. Maybe I should do one on myself, so that I fit into your world a little better. I can recite the *undo* when I get back."

"Good idea," said Felix.

Betony thought for a moment. Then she rubbed her ears with snow, stood on her head, and recited a little rhyme. When she turned herself the right way up again, she looked almost human.

"How would I get to this castle place?" asked Rhino.

"I'll take you," said Fuzzy.

"That's settled, then," said Rhino. "I'm staying. No more double physics. Smooth!"

"Hey!" said Fuzzy, doing a high five with her wing. "Smooth!"

Felix felt annoyed all over again. When Betony had finished her vacation in his world, she'd come back here. She and Rhino would meet up from time to time, have picnics on the beach, talk about old times, visit Ironclaw, go to dance festivals. He stood up, in exactly the right frame of mind to commit murder, and took out the eyeglass case. The opening edge had suddenly and inexplicably become razor-sharp, and he cut himself. It hurt. He dropped the box, and the lid sprang open. A drop of blood landed in the snow.

"Hello there," said the box. "What can I do for you today? A little entertainment? How about a natural disaster? No? An execution, maybe? A massacre, perhaps?"

Felix didn't reply.

"I know," said the box. "Why don't you say *open sesame* and see what happens? *Open sesame* would benefit the whole world, Felix. Bring people together. Get rid of divisions. How can you say no to that?"

"Quite easily, when I know there's a downside." His finger was bleeding heavily now. He found a tissue and bound it tightly around the cut.

"Not much of a downside. Oh, it'll bring some people together who I'm sure you'd rather *didn't* get together . . .

But that's nothing compared to a whole community in harmony — japegrins, ragamuckies . . ."

"Which people will it *bring together*?"

The box just laughed.

"Betony and Rhino," said Felix.

"You said it, not me," said the box.

"Did someone mention my name?" said Rhino. He glanced over Felix's shoulder at the jinx box. "Oh, stop worrying, Felix. All you need to do is *not* say the powerword." He grinned. "It's a bit like not thinking about pink elephants, isn't it?"

The box waited until Rhino was out of earshot again. "*Open sesame* is a level thirteen spell," it said. "Very, very powerful. Oh, well. If you're not going to say it, let's hope for the sake of this world's future that Rhino has a pink-elephant moment."

"I think we ought to let this world decide its own destiny," said Felix. "If Rhino and Betony getting together were *really* the only bad side to saying that word, what would be in it for you? I thought your speciality was chaos?" And with that he stooped down, scooped up the box, snapped it shut, and stepped over to the fissure.

A blast of hot air hit his face. Whether it was that, or the fact that the eyeglass case suddenly developed a shiny satin exterior, he didn't know. He felt it slip through his fingers and drop down onto the rock, neatly avoiding the crack itself. He thought he saw it do a half-twist in the air, which surely couldn't be possible — but it did land on its edge, and the case opened again. He made a grab for it, but, as before, it slid away from him.

"I know what you've got planned for me," hissed the jinx box in its oily little voice, all pretense at joviality gone. "You're going to kill me, roast me alive, burn me to a crisp . . ."

Felix lunged at it again, but once more it evaded him, sliding a little farther down the slope. In a moment, it would reach the steep bit and start to ski all the way back to Vattan.

". . . cremate me, carbonize me, turn me to ash . . ."

"Stop it," said Felix, spooked by the unbroken stream of synonyms.

"Stop what?" said Fuzzy, turning around to look at him, perplexed. "Why are you talking to an icicle?"

". . . toast me, incinerate me, bake me . . ."

It was changing its appearance as it spewed out its vocabulary. It had become a laptop again, and there were flames on the screen. It slid farther away from him, and he scrambled after it.

". . . pyromaniac, arsonist, fire raiser . . ."

"Where are you going, Felix?" asked Betony, her voice growing fainter.

"Where do you think?" said Rhino. "He's just drunk half a gourd of fertle juice. Nature calls . . ." His voice faded away.

It was like following a dog that didn't want its leash put back on. A few steps closer, almost there — and then it would slide a little farther and be just as out of reach as ever. Felix knew he was getting angry and when he got angry, he got reckless. He needed to keep a cool head. He sped up, rounded a promontory — and found himself teetering on the edge of a crevasse. It wasn't very wide (too far to jump across, though), but it was deep. The jinx box was trying to kill *him* before he exterminated *it*. He backed away carefully, his heart in his mouth. A section of ice broke off and tumbled downward, turning in the air like a diver.

"Oh, well," said the jinx box. "Better luck next time."

"There won't be a next time," said Felix, trying to catch it off guard and kick it over the edge. He just missed.

"I think you ought to stop acting like a child, and watch my screen for a moment," said the jinx box, slipping a little farther along the edge of the precipice. It obviously wasn't going to move too far away and lose the chance of tipping Felix over. "I'm going to show you what will happen to you when you try to destroy me."

A picture of Felix appeared on its screen. Felix knew he shouldn't watch, but he couldn't help himself. He saw his body turn completely transparent, so that he looked like an ice sculpture, shiny, with a very faint blue tinge. Then he shattered into thousands of pieces, like a broken windshield.

"I like that way of bumping someone off," said the box cheerfully. "It's got a really arty feel to it. Fire and ice. Love them both."

The screen tilted toward him, and he saw a raging inferno — the library, in flames. He could see thick wads of pages turning to stacks of white ash. Touch one of them with a fingertip and it would disintegrate. The picture switched to the Ziggurat Gardens of Kaflabad. Every single plant was dying, as though someone had sprayed the fruit trees and the flowers with Agent Orange.

"That was the Andrian library burning, wasn't it?" said Felix. "And after that it was the King's Gardens at Kaflabad."

"No. It was the *Hanging Gardens of Babylon*, Felix. And it wasn't the Andrian library, it was the *Alexandrian* library. Where all the books in your known world were stored, including all the spell books. I invented the Divide spell a long time ago, you see, and I've been owned by many different sorcerers. And what fun we've had. Where do you think Andria got its name? From me, that's where. A corruption of Alexandria. I corrupt everything; it's in my nature. Even powerwords. Speaking of which, I've got some more for you. I'd love you to try *open sesame*."

"Not interested."

"I'm astonished that you've never asked me about the words from *this* world that became powerwords in *yours*. Harmless little words over here, just for fun. *Zizzipadoo. Boggaliood.* But over there they can get you anything you want."

The laptop screen flicked to a picture of Felix, older, but still recognizably Felix, in a mortarboard and gown. He was standing outside what could have been an Oxford college. "Don't you want to make your parents proud of you, Felix?" cajoled the box. "Don't you want to know what the words are?"

"No, thanks," said Felix. "And I'll get to college on my own merit, thank you, not by magic."

"Really? How scrupulous of you. Oh, well. How about your own laboratory? The Nobel Prize for physics? A knighthood? Sir Felix Sanders . . ."

Felix inched closer.

The box didn't seem to have noticed; it was in lecture mode. "You could have power beyond your wildest dreams. You could do so much good, Felix. Anyway, I've shown you the past. Now I'll show you the future." This time it *was* the Andrian library. "Such a shame," chortled the box. "All that learning. And once it's lost, this world will be no different from yours, Felix. The magic will go, and the steam engine will arrive — followed by the internal combustion engine, the jet engine, telephones, televisions, computers, pollution. . . . You could stop all that, of course. Just by saying *open sesame*. Say *open sesame*, just once, and you save both the King's Gardens and the library. And after *open sesame* there's *mumbo jumbo* and *shazam* and *ali kazam*, and all the wonderful things they will achieve."

"I don't believe you," interrupted Felix, finally getting close enough to kick and connect.

The box flew up in the air — and as it did so, it turned end over end and mutated from a laptop to an eyeglass case, a jewelry box, an urn, a tea caddy, a sea chest, a wickerwork basket, an amphora . . .

Felix took a couple of steps closer to the crevasse, so that he could continue to watch it fall . . . a barrel, a satchel, a sarcophagus, a handbag, a coffin. . . . He watched for as long as he could, until his angle of vision made the box disappear from view. He thought he heard a plop, like something landing in red-hot lava, but he couldn't be sure. It was a long way down.

Nothing else happened. He didn't turn to ice and shatter into a thousand pieces. He didn't burst into flames. He heaved a huge sigh of relief, and some of the weight seemed to lift from his shoulders. The box had been the mother and father of all liars. He went back to the others.

"You must have been desperate." Rhino smirked. "You've been gone ages."

"I kicked the jinx box over a precipice into some molten lava," said Felix.

"Oh, well done," said Betony.

"It tried to kill me first," said Felix. "That made my job a lot easier."

"Time to go, then," said Nimby. "Emptied your pockets? Nothing scientific anywhere?"

"No." Suddenly, he knew what it was that he had wanted so much. He closed his eyes. *Betony*. He wanted a way of staying with Betony. Forever. And it just wasn't possible. Or was there a way? What if he spoke *those words*? A leap of faith — or a surrender to temptation? *What should he do?*

"What's the matter, Felix?" asked Betony.

He opened his eyes. Everyone was staring at him. But when he tried to speak, he found that he couldn't. He shook his head.

"Are you still thinking about the *open sesame* thing?" asked Rhino. Then he went chalk-white, swore, and said, "Pink elephants."

There was a sound like a thunderclap, although it wasn't a thunderclap. The sound reverberated for far too long.

A split appeared in the fabric of the mountain itself, although no molten rock or ash spewed out. Rhino gave out a piercing scream. Then he lay down in the snow and started to roll around in it. Before Felix could really take in this odd behavior a wind sprang up, and within seconds it was whistling around them, slapping their hair against their cheeks and shrieking in their ears. A moment later they were all struggling to stay upright — Fuzzy most of all, for she was the biggest. Nimby had rolled himself up so that he wouldn't get swept away. The sky darkened with ludicrous speed, and flurries of snow started to whirl around them.

"What's happening?" yelled Betony, her blond hair whipping out around her head in a halo. "Is it another eruption? What's wrong with Rhino?"

"The crack in the mountain!" shouted Felix. "It's right over the Divide!"

"What?" yelled Betony.

"The crack's right over the Divide!"

"You'd better be quick, then!" shrieked Fuzzy, her spiky head feathers flattened against her skull. "Go and stand across it, before it splits too far! I'll look after Rhino!"

"Come on!" Felix grabbed Betony by the hand and dragged her over to the fissure.

"No, Felix!" screamed Betony. "It's too dangerous!"

"What?" yelled Felix.

"It's too dangerous!"

"It's too dangerous!" boomed a voice from the depths of the chasm that had opened up.

Felix and Betony looked at each other, hand in hand, aghast. Although the voice seemed to bounce off the rock itself, like an echo, there was something horribly familiar about it. Something smarmy. The wind dropped a bit, and they could hear each other more easily.

"It can't be," said Felix.

"It can't be . . ." came the reply.

"It's the jinx box," said Betony.

"It's the jinx box . . ." echoed the voice.

The wind abated even further, but the sky stayed eclipse-dark and the snow continued to fall. The fissure remained just a couple of feet wide, but there were ominous creaks and groans from the rock below. Out of the corner of his eye, Felix saw Fuzzy help Rhino stand up, then pluck a feather from her breast and give it to him.

"You don't get rid of me as easily as all that," said the voice from the chasm. "Neither fire nor ice can annihilate me."

"I thought you said you'd destroyed the box, Felix!" shouted Nimby.

"I thought I had!" Felix called back.

"Aren't you wondering why the powerword had such a dramatic effect?" asked the box.

Felix didn't reply. The feeling of doom had receded a little; he felt more on top of the situation. The word had been spoken — not by him, true, but they had all survived it.

"Look at Rhino," said the box.

Felix turned and stared. Rhino was standing there, looking very shaken — minus his trousers. Felix blinked, and looked again. No, he hadn't been mistaken, despite the veil of snowflakes. Rhino bent down, picked up his cloak, and wrapped it around himself.

The ground shuddered, and the chasm widened a little more.

"Guess what Rhino had in his pocket, Felix," said the jinx box.

Felix glanced across. Rhino's eyes stared whitely at him from a soot-blackened face.

"Another firecracker," said Nimby faintly.

"And that equals . . . disaster!" crowed the jinx box. "The Divide will split wide open, Felix — and then it will close forever. No more traffic between your world and this. No more jolly little visits. Severance, Felix. Complete severance."

"This isn't the only Divide," said Felix stoutly.

"It will close *every* Divide, the same way the first powerword released every brandee, and the second one released every prisoner of stone. You've got to choose, Felix. This world or the other? And so do Betony and Rhino."

"I've chosen," said Rhino. "I'm staying here." He sounded a little better. Felix suddenly realized why Fuzzy had given him one of her feathers — to heal his burns.

The mountain groaned again, and the chasm opened a little more.

"Act quickly, Felix, while you can still straddle it, for shortly it will open too far, and then it will slam shut for good." The jinx box was sounding more and more manic — in its excitement, it seemed to have forgotten that when the rocks crashed together again, it really would be destroyed. Withstanding extremes of temperature was one thing — the crushing force of a mountain was something else.

Felix looked at Betony. "Your world or mine? Which is it to be?"

Betony stood there, the tears streaming down her face, exactly the way she had appeared to Felix on the laptop screen. Felix felt as though he'd been kicked in the stomach. Was everything else true, then? Would the library burn to the ground and the Ziggurat Gardens turn to dust? Would this world become just like the other?

"I can't, Felix," said Betony. "I want to see my parents."

And I can't stay, either, thought Felix, *much as I'd like to. I can't disappear again. I can't do it to my parents. It would destroy them.*

The chasm creaked open a little farther.

"The box is a liar, Betony," said Felix, desperately wanting to believe it. "Come *on*." He dragged her across the snow, and pushed her so hard that she had to straddle the crevasse or fall into it. He held her in place with one arm and pulled the notebook from his pocket. More by luck than judgment, he opened it at the right page and read out the spell.

Just before he lost consciousness, the ground jerked beneath him with a force that made his teeth shake. A blood-curdling scream rose from the depths of the chasm, cut short as the two rock faces slammed shut.

19

When Felix came to, he knew immediately that he must be on the Pennine Divide, for he could feel something cold and wet landing on his face. The snow had gone, replaced by English winter drizzle; he'd have known it anywhere. He opened his eyes. Betony was lying there next to him, looking strangely human with her magically rounded ears, and Nimby was spread-eagled by her side. *Good*, thought Felix, sitting up, *I'm glad she didn't let go of him. We've got our transport back to Wimbledon. Everything's OK. I knew it. The jinx box was just a nasty, spiteful troublemaker.*

He stood up and stretched. Changing dimensions always made him feel a bit odd, as though he'd just gotten over the flu. He went over to Nimby. It wasn't good for a magic carpet to be lying flat out like that in the rain. "Hey, Nimby," he said. "I'd get up if I were you."

There was no response.

I suppose I'd better roll him up, thought Felix, *pile side in, until he's back with us*. He lifted the carpet's fringed end and tucked it under. It felt surprisingly limp. How odd. When they'd crossed over before, Nimby had been up and hovering around before he and Betony had even gotten to their feet.

Felix peered at the leaden sky, but the cloud cover was too heavy for him to guess the time of day. He'd left his watch on the other side of the Divide, along with his compass. He still had his backpack, of course — that had been strapped to his back. Betony stirred slightly, so he went over to her. She sat up and glared at him.

"What?" he said, taken aback by her expression.

"You've got a short memory. You dragged me over to a spitfire crevasse, forced me to straddle it, and held me prisoner while you read out the Divide spell. What gave you the right to make that decision for me?"

"We're all right, though, aren't we?"

Betony looked at him as though he'd just crawled out from under a particularly unsavory stone. "Where's Nimby?" she asked.

"There," said Felix, pointing to him.

Betony walked over to the carpet and unrolled him. There was a slackness to him that hadn't been there before. She stroked his pile with the palm of her hand and called his name. Still no response. She shook him gently. Nothing. She shook him much harder.

"He's taking a long time to come around, isn't he?" said Felix.

Betony looked up. There were new tears glistening in her eyes. "He's not coming around," she said. "He's dead."

"*What?*"

"He's not magic anymore," said Betony. "He's just a carpet. That's dead, isn't it? When you've been aware of everything, and able to communicate, and to reason things out, and then you can't. I'd call that dead."

"How can you be sure? Maybe it's just taking him a long time to recover."

"Aren't you going to say something like, '*Oh, dear*, how are we going to get back to Wombledon *now?*'"

"Wimbledon," said Felix automatically.

Betony's look of scorn could have scorched a hole through asbestos.

"I'm sorry, I'm sorry," he said. "Look, let's cross back over again. Maybe there's somewhere we can take him. K'Faddle and Offspring — they do magical repairs."

"Weren't you listening? We can't *get* back. The Divide has closed for good."

"No, it hasn't. I don't believe it, I *won't* believe it. The jinx box was a liar." Felix opened his notebook and started to flick through it, looking for the Divide spell. Instead of a lot of blank pages and a few vocabulary notes, the book was now filled with writing — not his own writing, either. It was far too neat, and it was in violet ink, not black ballpoint. His flicking became more and more feverish. "What's all this stuff?" he said, his voice getting shrill and agitated. "I don't remember all this . . ."

"We'd better start walking," said Betony coldly, rolling Nimby up again and tucking him under her arm.

"No, hang on, I've got it."

Betony sighed heavily, but she straddled the Divide and waited as Felix read out the spell.

Nothing happened.

"I told you," said Betony. She took a candle stub from her pocket, waved her hand over it, and recited the ignition spell. Nothing. "Magic doesn't work over here anymore, Felix."

"I must have left something out," said Felix. "I'll try again."

He tried again. Still nothing.

"It's no use," said Betony, but Felix wouldn't listen. He made her stand there while he tried again and again.

After the thirteenth time, Betony lost her temper, and he finally gave up. They started to walk, taking turns carrying the carpet, which got heavier and heavier the wetter it became. By the time they reached the village, they, too, were soaked through, and utterly dejected.

"At least Nimby knew he'd won the Magical Objects Bravery Award," said Felix, in an attempt to cheer Betony up.

"Crystal balls are notoriously inaccurate," said Betony. "He saw himself accepting the award, didn't he? How likely is that now?"

"Don't you see, it doesn't matter," said Felix. "The important thing was the pleasure Nimby gained from having *thought* he'd won it. Whether it's true or not is neither here nor there."

Betony shrugged.

Felix knew he didn't have enough money to get both himself and Betony back to Wimbledon. He would have to phone home, but he didn't have the right change, either, so he went into the first shop he came to. He could have called collect, of course, but it didn't seem like the most diplomatic way to start this particular conversation. The shop was a general store, which brought back vivid memories of the one between Vattan and Yergud, with its magical feel-good cloaks hanging on a rack. He could have used one of those to lift his mood. Betony would never forgive him for stranding her over here. He knew only too well what being trapped in another dimension felt like.

To his surprise, the shop was about to close. He looked at the clock on the wall — it was only two-thirty. Without thinking he said, "Closing early? Got here just in time, didn't I?"

"What do you expect on Christmas Eve?" said the shopkeeper.

Christmas Eve? Felix was shocked — he'd forgotten all about Christmas. Then he realized he must have looked it, which would appear very odd. "We're tree worshippers at home," he said. "We don't celebrate Christmas."

"My oh my," said the shopkeeper. "Some parents really have no idea how to bring up kids. Here, have a chocolate bar. And one for your sister outside. You look as though you could use them. Do you want some plastic to protect your carpet?"

"Thanks," said Felix. It was a timely reminder that there were nice people in his own world. He accepted a black trash bag, and went back out to Betony. "It's Christmas Eve," he said, wrapping Nimby up in the plastic. It felt like putting him in a body bag. "My father will be back. He'll know we did an illusion spell on Mom and he'll be furious, because he'll guess where we went."

"That's your problem," said Betony.

"It's yours as well," said Felix. "Look, I'm sorry. I'm very, very sorry. If we *really* can't ever get back to your dimension, we're going to have to get my dad to help us. People don't just come from nowhere in my world. They have birth certificates and passports and medical records and . . ."

A white van drove past and splashed dirty water all over them.

"Was this the thing you wanted above all else?" asked Betony suddenly. "Did you wish for a way of staying with me forever?"

"Yes," said Felix, his voice barely audible. "I'm sorry."

There was a long silence, when all he could hear was the rain.

"I suppose it was a compliment, really," said Betony eventually. She managed a faint smile. "I'll miss Thornbeak more than my parents, to be honest about it. I feel sorry for them,

336

though, coming back to life and finding me gone. Missing me by a whisker. Although Tansy was always the favorite." She wiped a strand of wet blond hair out of her eyes. "If I can't go back, I'll have to find somewhere to live, and get a job."

"That's where this world does have some advantages," said Felix, thinking, *At last there's something positive I can offer her.*

A motorcycle roared out of nowhere, making both of them jump, and disappeared just as rapidly. Betony looked shaken; the noise had been very sudden and very loud.

"I'm sure you'll be able to live at my house," Felix went on. "It's huge. The reason my parents never had more children was because they might have been born with the same heart condition I had. But my mom would love a daughter, I know she would."

Betony stiffened slightly. "I don't want someone bossing me around. I haven't had that for four and a half years."

Felix glossed over it. There were some things that really weren't worth going into just yet. "You wouldn't have to get a job, though. To begin with, you'd go to school. Then you'd choose your favorite subject . . ."

"History."

". . . and you'd go to college and study just that. And then, maybe, you'd work in a museum, or go on expeditions to dig things up."

Betony looked impressed. "I'd have to help your mom gather toadstools, though, and stuff like that."

Felix laughed. There were a lot of problems ahead, he

337

could see that, but maybe . . . just maybe . . . things would be OK. "I'd better make that phone call," he said.

Felix's father shouted for quite a long time. Then he calmed down, told them to find a hotel, have some dinner, and wait for him there. Some hours later, he arrived in his car, paid the bill, and put Nimby in the trunk. He'd met the carpet before, the previous summer. He went tight-lipped when he realized what had happened. Felix wanted to hug him for caring, but things were still a bit tense. Then he drove them back to Wimbledon, and on the way, Felix told him everything that had happened and that there was no way back to Betony's world ever again.

"Well, I can't say I'm sorry, Felix," said his father. "I just got back from Edinburgh, but when your mother told me you were at a sleepover, and she wasn't the least bit worried that you hadn't come back . . . Well, I just knew."

"Can Betony stay with us?"

"Yes. Although how we're going to manage the paperwork, I'm not quite sure. I'll think of something. But no more illusion spells on Felix's mother, Betony, all right?"

"I don't think they'll work anymore, Mr. Sanders," said Betony. "The two worlds have been severed for good. I'll have to make do with science from now on."

"You must be very upset about being separated from your parents."

"I think I'm more upset for *them*, if you know what I mean. They got turned to stone four and a half years ago, but it'll seem like yesterday to them. It seems like ages ago to *me*. I've gotten used to not having them around, but they're not used to me not being there."

When they got back, Felix's mom was delighted to see them. She asked them if they'd had a good time, made them some hot chocolate, and heated up some mince pies. Then she sent them off to bed.

The following morning, Felix bumped his head on something when he woke up. He turned to look. It was a Christmas stocking. Once again, he'd forgotten what day it was, despite the previous night's festive snack — it just didn't seem important. He jumped out of bed, seized the stocking, ran into Betony's room, and woke her up. She, too, had a stocking.

Opening them was hilarious. Felix's mom had always filled a stocking with small presents — something to keep him busy when he was small, when he woke up at the crack of dawn; something to keep him quiet before he went downstairs to open the gifts from relatives. She had filled Betony's stocking with all the things she'd have expected a fourteen-year-old girl to want — makeup and hair clips and pretty stationery. Felix had to explain what everything was — and he didn't know what some of them were himself! Girl stuff. Weird.

"Chocolate brazzles?" said Betony, holding up a box she'd just opened. "They're the wrong shape."

"Brazils," corrected Felix, laughing. "They're nuts."

"Oh," said Betony, popping one in her mouth. "What's this?" She pulled the cap off a sparkly gold pen. "Eye paint?"

Felix laughed again. "It's a pen," he said.

"Find me some paper," said Betony. "I want to give it a try."

Felix went back to his room, and the first thing his eye fell on was his notebook. He grabbed it, and then he remembered Thornbeak's cataloguing pen, which he would now never be able to return to her. He felt a wave of sadness. She would miss Betony more than Betony's parents would, in all likelihood. Betony had been a really good history apprentice; Fuzzy was more interested in travel. And what about all the other friends he would never see again? Ironclaw, Grimspite . . . even Rhino. Better not to dwell on it. He took the notebook back to Betony and opened it for her to write in.

"What's all this?" said Betony. "It's not your writing. Your writing's nearly as bad as mine."

Felix peered at it. The writing had been executed in an immaculate copperplate script. "I think the brazzle quill wrote this," he said. "All on its own. Remember the book titles it gave us in the brandee's study? It's in that same purple ink, too."

Betony popped another chocolate Brazil into her mouth. "What does it say?" she asked, her cheek bulging.

Felix read a couple of paragraphs, and stiffened. "I'll begin at the beginning," he said, flicking back. "I think it's pretty important."

I, Dewfeather, quill of quills, cannot deny my nature. My nature is to write, and write I must. My quest is to create order from chaos, wherever I find it. At the moment, I am incarcerated in a backpack with a jinx box that is as crazy as a cactus. However, I do have a notebook at my disposal, and writing in it may well preserve my sanity.

Betony laughed. Felix smiled, and continued.

Most of the words stored in the box have already been arranged in alphabetical order and reproduced in Quillfinger's dictionary. However, some of them were too dangerous for general consumption, thus have never seen the light of day. I have no idea how long I shall remain in my present location, so I shall amuse myself by defining each of these powerwords, and I shall place a spell over them so that only a brazzle may read them. In my experience, only brazzles have the integrity to be in charge of information such as this.

"Sounds just as pompous as Ironclaw," said Betony affectionately. "It was his feather, after all."

There was a moment of silence as both of them had their own thoughts, which was broken by the sound of movement downstairs. Felix's mother was doing things in the kitchen. The smell of baking bread drifted up the stairs.

"Hang on," said Felix. "How come we can read this, if it's only meant for brazzles?"

"The spell won't complete, will it?" said Betony. "Magic doesn't work over here anymore."

"Oh, right," said Felix, moving on hastily.

There was a sudden aroma of sage and onion stuffing, and Felix felt the first rumblings of hunger. But breakfast could wait. This was more important. "The quill has put the words in alphabetical order. So we'll start with *abracadabra*." He smiled. He could say it with impunity. *Abracadabra* had no effect over here.

The word abracadabra was originally written out on a piece of parchment in a triangular formation, and hung around the neck of someone with a fever or a toothache or the ague in order to cure it ~ like an amulet. It looked like this.

Felix held up his notebook so that Betony could see.

```
A B R A C A D A B R A
A B R A C A D A B R
A B R A C A D A B
A B R A C A D A
A B R A C A D
A B R A C A
A B R A C
A B R A
A B R
A B
A
```

"Like all powerwords," he continued, *"it came from another dimension. Over there, it was a Cabalistic charm, and its aim was to unite the finite and the infinite."*

"That makes sense," said Betony. "The brandee became finite when he turned into a nomad — he can now eat and sleep and all those things, but he will also die, just like anyone else. Before, he could only be killed by accident."

When spoken by the appropriate agent, this power-word will release a brandee from bondage, and render his lamp inert. The brandee will attain free will.

Free will, of course, is merely an illusion, for a creature's behavior is governed by its determination to survive. Other magical conditions may also be affected. If a scientific object is present when abracadabra is declaimed, however, the effects are much greater.

"And that's it for that entry."

"How about *hocus pocus*?" said Betony.

The sage-and-onion smell was superseded by one of coffee and freshly squeezed oranges.

"Breakfast, you two!" called Felix's mother.

"We'll come back to it after we've eaten," said Felix, and they went downstairs.

Breakfast was his mother's wonderful walnut bread — with butter, smoked ham, and honey or marmalade. There was fruit juice and coffee to drink, and it was Betony's first experience of coffee. She didn't like it, but she struggled through it because it would have looked a little odd to confess she'd never tried it before. After breakfast, there were the big presents to open.

They went into the living room. A stately Christmas tree stood in the corner, scenting the room with pine. It was festooned with sparkling little string lights and silver tinsel. Paper decorations hung from the ceiling, and more lights winked from the walls. Betony gaped in amazement.

Once again, Felix's mother had made a real effort to include Betony in the celebration, and she'd bought her some very fashionable and rather expensive clothes. Betony had never worn anything but green — except for a brief episode in Felix's world last summer — and she held the clothes up against herself and looked in the mirror. Then she went and put them on.

"I know what she likes," said Felix's mother, with a smile. "She borrowed some of my clothes last summer, didn't she, after she got caught in a downpour?"

Felix tried to disguise his disappointment when Betony returned. She'd tied back her hair to reveal her rounded ears, and apart from her eyes — just a little too slanted and a little too green — she looked just like anyone else from school. A lot prettier, admittedly, but no longer an elf. He gave her the present he'd bought for her a couple of weeks before. A history of the world, in lots and lots of chapters.

"That's just so smooth," said Betony, flicking through it. "I'm really going to enjoy that."

By the time Felix had opened all his own presents — he had lots of uncles and aunts and cousins, as well as the full complement of grandparents — it was time to feast. Betony's face lit up when she saw the meal, and she tried everything, from turkey to gravy to sprouts with chestnuts. The Christmas pudding, with its crown of flames, was the biggest hit of all. After that, it was slumping in front of the television. Although Felix had seen *Jurassic Park* several times before, it was all new to Betony and he had to keep explaining things. She was more impressed with the helicopter than the dinosaurs. The dinosaurs simply reminded her of fire-breathers.

It was late in the afternoon before they were able to get back to Felix's notebook.

"Hocus pocus is an otherworld conjurer's command," read Felix, *"used to bring about some sort of change."*

"That makes sense, too," said Betony. "From stone back to flesh. What's a conjurer?"

"A pretend magician," said Felix.

"Do *open sesame* now."

Open sesame was the command used to open the robbers' den in "Ali Baba and the Forty Thieves," from The Tales of the Arabian Nights.

"So once upon a time it really worked?"

Felix smiled. "I'm afraid not. *Arabian Nights* is a book."

"Oh, well. Go on."

Open sesame is a negative powerword ~ it unlocks that which was locked. However, mathematical spells such as the Divide spell have a negative result, and two negatives make a positive. A positive will work in the opposite way, and close the Divide for good. If a scientific object is present when open sesame is declaimed, however, and something attempts to cross the Divide before it closes completely, the result is catastrophic. When the tug on the organism reaches the point at which it can stand it no longer ~ the moment when the indivisible self usually escapes into another dimension ~ the escape route is no longer there. Therefore, the self will do the seemingly impossible, and actually divide.

"What does *that* mean?" asked Betony.
"Dunno," said Felix. "I'll keep reading, OK?"
Betony nodded.

As self is only an illusion, anyway ~ a convenient method of transporting half-twists . . .

"What's a half-twist?" asked Betony.
"Ironclaw explained it to me once," said Felix. "It's like DNA in my world — the part of you that carries the you, in every tiny building block of your body."

"Oh," said Betony.

"Oh!" said Felix.

"What?"

"Listen to this! . . . It's unbelievable. . . . *The end result is two identical organisms on either side of the Divide, both of whom think they are the true image.*"

They looked at each other.

Betony shook her head in wonderment. "There's another you and me, back in my world?"

"Apparently."

"And do they know about us?"

"I have no idea," said Felix.

Betony suddenly clapped her hands, and her eyes lit up. "Do you realize what this means, Felix? In my world, Nimby may still be alive. And Thornbeak will still have me as an assistant — Fuzzy's useless — and my parents will get to meet me again, and . . . What?"

Felix had gone as white as a sheet. "I've just thought of something else," he said.

"What?"

"If magic doesn't work over here anymore, does that mean my illness will come back?"

When Felix came to, he was aware that he was shivering before he was aware of anything else. He opened his eyes and sat up. He realized he was sitting on snow, so he got to his feet. Everything was pearly gray and misty, as though he'd found himself in the middle of a cloud.

He stood up and stretched. Changing dimensions always made him feel a bit odd, as though he'd just gotten over the flu. He went over to Nimby. It wasn't good for a magic carpet to be lying flat out like that in the snow. "Hey, Nimby," he said. "I'd get up if I were you."

There was no response.

Betony stirred slightly, so he went over to her. She sat up and glared at him.

"What?" he said.

"You've got a short memory. You dragged me over to a spitfire crevasse, forced me to straddle it, and held me prisoner while you read out the Divide spell. What gave you the right to make that decision for me?"

"We're all right, though, aren't we?"

Betony looked at him as though he'd just crawled out from under a particularly unsavory stone. "Where's Nimby?" she asked.

"There," said Felix, pointing to him.

Betony went over to him and stroked him with the palm of her hand.

"What happened?" said Nimby, fluttering to life. "Why are we still here?"

"What do you mean, still here?" said Felix.

A big shape loomed out of the mist, followed by a smaller one.

"Fuzzy?" said Felix. "Rhino? You've come across, too?"

"You haven't gone anywhere," said Rhino. "Look, here's your watch and your compass . . ."

Felix stood there, looking from one to the other. "That's crazy," he said.

"How weird," said Rhino, holding Felix's watch to his ear. "It's stopped." He looked at the compass, and then he shook it. "That's not working anymore, either."

After a moment or two Betony said, "You mean, I'm not stuck in Felix's world for the rest of my life?"

"No," said Fuzzy. "You're still in your own world, and the Divide has closed for good."

Felix turned to look, but the red-hot gash in the mountain

wasn't there anymore. The place where the Divide had been was just a ridge of gray rock, poking through the snow. "*No.*" He shook his head. "I don't believe it, I *won't* believe it. The jinx box was a liar." Felix opened his notebook and started to flick through it, looking for the Divide spell. The others glanced at one another. His flicking became more and more feverish. "What's all this stuff?" he said, his voice getting shrill and agitated. "I don't remember all this . . ."

"Let's go back to the Pink Harpoon," said Rhino. "We'll freeze out here."

"No, hang on, I've got it."

"It won't work, Felix."

"I've got to try."

He straddled the ridge and read out the spell. Nothing. He tried again. Still nothing.

"Pink Harpoon, then?" said Nimby.

Felix sighed heavily, nodded, and climbed aboard.

By the time they reached the inn, the mist had gone, the sun had come out, and Felix had realized that Ironclaw's quill had been busy on its own. They sat down outside, on the veranda, and read what it had written. The double negative had done irreparable harm — it had created a positive, which had worked the opposite way and closed the Divide forever.

"I'm really sorry, Betony," said Felix, looking up from the notebook. "You never did get your vacation in my world. Subways and escalators aren't that great, though, honest."

"You're being very fully fledged about all this, Felix," said

351

Fuzzy. "You do understand that you're stranded over here for good now, don't you?"

For some reason, it hadn't sunk in. He knew it, on a practical level, but the implications just hadn't hit home. They did now: He doubled over, put his head on his knees, and groaned. He'd been through all this before, the first time he'd visited Betony's world. He'd agonized over his parents' grieving for him, imagined living without them, wondered how much he would miss them. After a moment or two, he realized that this time, it didn't cut quite as deeply. He was older, for one thing, and healthier. More independent. He didn't need them as much as he had. And his father would *know* where he'd gone, would know he hadn't died. He'd miss both of them, certainly, but he wouldn't miss his own world all that much. Exhaust fumes and prepackaged food and the crush of the rush hour? This world was nicer, fresher, unspoiled. Perhaps it might even stay that way, now that the jinx box had really and truly been destroyed. And he wasn't the only human anymore, either. There was Rhino to reminisce with, if that was what he wanted — and Rhino was OK these days. Nevertheless, Rhino had remained with Betony after all, the downside the box had predicted. . . . Would she prefer his company in the end?

"I'm the idiot," said Rhino. "I'm the one who said the word by mistake. I'm sorry, Felix."

"You had that firecracker in your pocket as well," said Nimby. "Science and magic. I *knew* it. I bet that's why you couldn't cross back."

"Shouldn't we finish reading the rest of the quill's entry and find out?" said Betony.

"OK," said Felix dully. What difference did it make how it had happened? It had happened. He found the right part and ran a finger along the text:

If a scientific object is present when open sesame is declaimed, and something attempts to cross the Divide before it closes completely, the result is catastrophic . . . the self will do the seemingly impossible, and actually divide.

"Turn sideways, Felix," joked Rhino. "Nope, you're still all there."

"Oh, wow," said Felix. "Listen to this! It's unbelievable."

The end result is two identical organisms on either side of the Divide, both of whom think they are the true image.

Betony gasped. "There's another you and me, back in your world?"

"Apparently."

"And do they know about us?"

"I have no idea," said Felix. "But I won't have to worry about my parents never seeing me again."

"And what about you?"

Felix smiled. "I've got you. And Ironclaw. And . . ."

"Hang on," said Betony. "Was this the thing you wanted above all else? Did you wish for a way of staying with me forever?"

Felix felt his face go red.

"Idiot," said Betony, punching him on the arm. "But I'm glad you're here."

"What are you going to do for a job, Felix?" asked Rhino. "Are you going to come to the castle with me?"

"I need to think about it," said Felix. "I was getting interested in magic as . . . well, physics with a half-twist. I'd like to study magical theory, really."

"I think we all need to get back to Andria and have a massive squawk party," said Fuzzy. "The craggy little details can wait."

The best party ever was held in the palace at Andria a couple of moons later, courtesy of the king and queen. It marked the close of the first interbeing equality conference, the opening of Snakeweed's cave painting center, the summer dance festival, Turpsik's poetry extravaganza, and the end of brittlehorn meditation week.

At first, everyone had viewed Snakeweed's presence at the conference with extreme suspicion — especially when he confessed his true identity and dispensed with his Snakeroot alias. A couple of small-tails had thrown rotten fertle fruits at him, a wise-hoof had tried to pass a motion barring him altogether, and a triple-head had advocated barbecuing his liver and serving it with pukeberry sauce. Then a brittlehorn had suggested that actions spoke louder than words. After all, Snakeweed had organized new perching rocks and refurbished the caves at Yergud, thereby starting up a whole new tourist industry, which seemed like very good news for the whole region. The admission fees weren't too exorbitant, either. He was good at organization; it was what he did best. A party of important people had traveled to the caves yesterday, for a private viewing, and were due to arrive back in Andria in time for the party.

Betony's friend Agrimony had borrowed the family firebreather, Sulfur, who was now big enough to carry six people. The fortunate six were Agrimony, Betony's brother, Ramson, her sister, Tansy, and Tansy's boyfriend, Vetch — plus Betony's mother and father. They were due to land at the airstrip in the late afternoon.

Betony was nervous and excited by turns. She couldn't decide what to wear; she wanted to make a good impression on her parents, who'd never seemed to have all that much time for her, and she wanted to look grown-up as well. She'd made her own way in the world for the last four and a half years — and now she was apprenticed to the most celebrated historian of modern times. In the end, she opted for a milky-green dress with an undulating hem, decorated with tiny beads. She wore the emerald pendant that Felix had given her last summer, which warded off vampreys, and a pair of matching green suede dancing shoes.

"You look gorgeous, Betony," said Thornbeak, who'd come to pick her up. She herself looked exactly the same as usual — immaculate.

They arrived at sunset. It was a beautiful evening, and most people were outside. There was a wailing ensemble on the raised grassy section outside the palace, and a squawk band at the other end of the green for the youngsters. One lickit after another was arriving with trays of delicacies, and some small-tails were dispensing drinks. The smells were delectable — roasting nuts, sugary pastries, mulled fertle juice, spiced milk shakes. There was a separate area set aside for carcasses, because quite a few brazzles and a carrionwing were coming. Scoffit had flown over from Kaflabad.

Ironclaw was busy mingling with the other guests. "Quillfinger, I'd like you to meet . . . what's your name again?"

"Stonetalon."

"Quillfinger, this is my son, Stonetalon."

Stonetalon was a very handsome young brazzle who was deeply involved in optimization and scheduling — working out the shortest flight routes, while also taking in lots of different destinations. He was very ambitious and had produced the latest timetables for *Easy-Flap*.

"Solved a tricky little problem the other day," Ironclaw said, fluffing out his chest feathers. "Fermat's Last Theorem."

"Oh, that," said Stonetalon. "Yes. There are two different ways of doing it, did you realize?"

"No," said Ironclaw, rather taken aback.

Quillfinger laughed.

"The second method involves elliptic equations . . ." Stonetalon began.

Thornbeak landed beside them. "Haven't seen you for a while, son," she said.

"Busy, busy, busy," said Stonetalon. "Is my sister here?" He spotted someone on the other side of the green and angled his head to see better.

Thornbeak looked around.

Fuzzy had dyed one wing black and the other one red, and she was dancing to some squawk music with a big athletic-looking brazzle.

"Topaztoe," said Thornbeak in a strangled voice. "I'll peck his eyes out," and she launched herself into the air.

Scoffit had brought Goodbody with her. Goodbody was now employed by K'Faddle & Offspring, who had had another triumph of marketing with their crystal balls. Goodbody had pointed out that although K'Faddle crystal balls were pretty useless at predicting the future, they weren't bad at showing what was happening somewhere else.

As a means of long-distance communication, they *were* the future. He was elaborating on the advantages of this to Pepperwort, who had taken early retirement and was now keeping purebred waggle-ears. He was looking forward to the first shearing. Once he'd spun and dyed the wool, he could start thinking about knitting patterns.

Felix was feeling on top of the world. Although he did miss his parents, he'd enrolled in a brittlehorn magical theory course in Andria, and he was loving it. He was living at Bedstraw's boardinghouse, on the same floor as Betony, and Ironclaw was paying him an allowance until he graduated. He spent a lot of time in the library — which had nearly finished its reorganization now that they had the cataloguing pen again — and he often met up with Betony for lunch.

"How are you feeling?" he asked her.

"Nervous."

"It's strange. For so long, I've been the one with the parents — and you've been the one without. And now it's the other way around."

"They're here," said Betony.

A group of tangle-folk were walking across the grass. Felix recognized Betony's parents immediately — he'd seen them as statues. Agrimony was wearing something skimpy and expensive, and Tansy didn't look quite as plain as she used to. Vetch and Ramson strolled along behind, their lutes slung over their shoulders, trashing the squawk band.

"Betony, darling," said Betony's mother, giving her the sort of hug you give people if you think they've got something contagious. "How you've grown. And you must be Felix." She glanced toward the stage. "They're good, aren't they, that wailing ensemble. I think I cured the lead singer of ear rot a few years back. I'd better go and say hello." She drifted off.

"Ought to go with her, I guess," said Betony's father, and he followed suit.

Betony watched them walk away, an expression of sheer disbelief on her face.

"They're working on this new potion," said Tansy. "Cures spindle lung. Snakeweed's agreed to test it for them — on *himself*. How generous is that? There could be side effects, but he says he doesn't care, he owes everyone a bit of personal risk. And he thinks it's working already."

Betony didn't reply.

"Come on," said Felix, deciding that she needed distracting, "let's go and mingle."

"Felix, aren't you going to introduce me to your human friend?" asked Agrimony, tossing back her forest of blond hair. "He looks really interesting."

Rhino was talking to Snakeweed about setting up visual displays and getting the right balance of showmanship and education. "And I'm using the moat," he said. "I've got a pair of shreddermouths living there — Gulp and Gobble. They pop their heads up every so often and snap their jaws. The kids love it."

"Rhino, this is Agrimony," said Felix.

"Hello," said Rhino, taking in Agrimony's glittery clinging dress and her sparkly green face paint.

"Touch base again soon, then," said Snakeweed, giving Rhino a wink. "Like your idea about getting the troggle to knit souvenirs. Snot can't bear daylight, of course, which is why he isn't here in person — although he has given me some knitting patterns for Pepperwort." He patted Rhino on the shoulder and headed off in Pepperwort's direction. On the way, he got sidetracked by the group of important people who had just arrived by fire-breather, raving about the caves and how wonderful the paintings were. Snakeweed started to tell them about something called gunpowder, and the way explosives could be used instead of drilling spells to construct useful things like canals and tunnels. It was just a matter of time before he got the recipe.

"Felix tells me you've been promoted and that you're managing the castle," said Agrimony, fluttering her eyelashes.

"That's right," said Rhino.

"Smooth," said Agrimony.

Felix smiled. Rhino had confessed to him earlier that evening that he used to see himself leaning on the hood of a Ferrari, wearing a sharp suit and shades and chatting on his cell phone. These days, he leaned against his personal fire-breather, wearing handmade tangle-tunics and communicating with someone on the other side of the world via a K'Faddle crystal ball.

"You must pay us a visit," said Rhino.

"When?" said Agrimony.

Felix and Betony grinned at each other and moved on.

Grimspite was enjoying himself. Ironclaw had looked at the Big Bang figures, and Fuzzy had helped him calculate a spell that neutralized the sinistrom reek. She'd kept this quiet from her mother, of course, for hens didn't mess with math as a rule. The anti-stink spell hadn't done anything for Grimspite's appearance, however, so he had diplomatically opted for lickit form. He was discussing his new book, *The History of the Sinistrom*, with the owner of the world-famous Yergud bookshop.

"Like the sound of it. I'll do a special promotion," said the bookseller. "I'm going to expand the shop, anyway — there's going to be a lot more tourism in the area, with Snakeweed's Cave Experience opening next moon."

"Is that what it's called?" said Grimspite, alarm bells starting to ring in his head.

"Yes. The admission isn't too expensive, either. Although a family of thirteen might find it fairly pricey."

"Excuse me," said Grimspite, and he elbowed his way through the crowd to where Snakeweed was graciously accepting some corporate invitation to a wailing concert. "I want a word with you," he hissed.

"Can't it wait? I'm a busy being again these days."

"No, it can't." Grimspite noticed that not only had Snakeweed's pallor gone but he'd put on some weight, and he wasn't coughing. "You're not at death's door anymore, are you?" he said.

"I'm testing a potion for Betony's parents. Least I could do. Too soon to tell, though, too soon to tell."

Grimspite had a sudden urge to transform himself back to his four-legged form, but he fought it. "Don't spin me a line, Snakeweed; you're completely better. You've got a future again, just like Felix. Only when he was given his life back, he didn't start planning an empire. Listen, if you don't make admission to those caves free, I'll come looking for you one dark night. And I won't be in lickit form, either."

Snakeweed's hand made an involuntary movement toward his wand, and stopped.

Grimspite sighed. "Forget I said that. Knee-jerk reaction, as they say in the other world. Violence isn't the answer to anything. Look — if you waive that admission fee, you'll get ten times the number of people visiting. The whole *point* of opening up the caves is to show everyone that they're related to one another. You'll be hailed as a social visionary, not a profiteer."

For a moment Snakeweed didn't reply. Then he smiled and said, "You're right. OK. Admission will be free." It was only when Grimspite was out of earshot that he added, "And the merchandising possibilities would increase tenfold as well . . . particularly if we can build an access road by tunneling through the mountain."

Turpsik the one-eye was arguing about subtexts with Pewtermane the brittlehorn, and they both seemed to be greatly enjoying themselves. It had taken Pewtermane half a moon to walk there from Geddon, but he had done it. Turpsik was going to read some of her poetry a little later, and Pewtermane was really looking forward to the one about starvation and hypothermia. Turpsik's ode to an iceberg was now a classic.

Felix looked around at the company, and at the enormous number of friends that he'd made. Yes, he would miss his parents — but they still had him. He wondered how differently the two versions of himself would turn out. How much would the two divergent worlds mold his essential self? If he really could be reproduced like this — cloned, almost — what was identity, anyway? An illusion that depended on sheer chance for the form it took? Nothing was set in stone, not even Betony's parents. And what *had* appeared to be set in stone wasn't necessarily genuine — Flintfeather had turned out to be a schemer called Topaztoe. It was strange that Betony was so stuck on history, because how did you ever really know what *had* happened, and what *hadn't*?

There was a stir at one end of the grounds; people were looking up into the sky. Felix searched for the identification jets of flame from a fire-breather, but he couldn't see any.

There was a shape, though, dark against the bloodred sky. It was gliding in, quite slowly, reminding him of an albatross coming in to land.

The fact that the area below cleared very quickly suggested that whatever was arriving was viewed with considerable respect — or fear, even. There was a most unorthodox mix of beings at this party, creatures that never normally had time for one another. Triple-heads and lickits were discussing recipes; carrionwings and diggelucks were talking about landscape gardening; tangle-folk and japegrins were dancing together.

When Leona the riddle-paw landed, somehow Felix wasn't surprised. It must have been quite an arduous flight for her, for her wings weren't all that powerful. But she was just as dangerous and cunning as the sphinxes of his own world were said to have been, which was why she quickly had a space around her. Sheathing her claws with the flick-knife sound he remembered so well, she lashed her dragon tail and surveyed the scene with her beautiful sloe-black eyes.

"Hello, Leona," said Felix, stepping forward.

"Hello, human child," replied the riddle-paw, in her low, menacing purr.

"You're just the person I wanted to see," said Felix.

"I'm never the person anyone wants to see," said Leona. "Apart from Ironclaw, and that's purely a mathematical relationship. So prrrecisely *why* would you want to see me?"

"Because you're a sorceress of the first order."

"Go on."

"Well . . . I've been split in two."

"I know," said Leona. "What is your question?"

"Is there any way I'll ever be able to find out what's happened to the me in my old world?"

"Why would you want to?"

"Well . . . he's me, isn't he?"

"Not anymore," said Leona. "That's like saying twins remain exactly the same. They don't. They have different experiences from the moment they become aware. You may well have reacted identically to begin with, on both sides of the Divide, but as what you experience diverges, the people you become will diverge, too."

"So the me over there is already different from the me over here?"

"Of course."

A sudden explosion of applause from the direction of the stage made them turn to look. "Hello, everyone!" trilled the queen, clearly audible even at that distance. "Isn't this just *so* much fun? The dancing will start in a moment, and the king's found a new one that you're all going to love — it's got a few twirls with . . ."

The wise-hoof emcee stepped over to her and whispered something in her ear.

"Oh, yes," said the queen brightly. "The Magical Objects Bravery Awards." She was wearing a gorgeous green velvet gown that was covered with emeralds. The wise-hoof handed

her a many-faceted silver orb that glinted with rainbow colors, like a dewdrop caught in sunlight. The queen held up her hand for silence.

"That's your magic carpet at the side of the stage, isn't it?" said Leona, ignoring the queen's order.

"Betony's," said Felix. "We'd better go and watch." The two of them moved forward and found a place very near the front, since people seemed remarkably willing to get out of their way.

"This year's award goes to Nimblenap . . ."

Felix watched Nimby fly onstage and bow, and a lump came to his throat. "The Nimby in my world never got to experience this," he said. "I hope the other Felix finds a way of making it up to him."

"He'd have a hard job," purred Leona. "In your world, Nimby's dead."

Felix looked at her, horrified. "What?"

"When the Divide closed," said the riddle-paw, "the half-twist straightened out. No magic can operate in your world anymore."

"So Nimby's *dead?*"

"Yes."

"And I wouldn't be able to do the ignition spell anymore?"

"No."

"And Betony wouldn't be able to perform any illusion spells?"

"No."

"And the reverse is true over here," said Felix, remembering the way his compass had stopped working and his watch had stopped ticking.

"That is correct."

So the other me is going to have a scientific future after all, thought Felix. *I feel sort of sorry for him. Magic's more fun. I guess Betony will still become a historian — she'd love all the museums. Life, eh. There are good and bad parts wherever you are — pluses and minuses in both worlds. But without the bad parts, the good ones would be meaningless. At least I got to stay with Betony. I wonder if her ears will stay rounded over there, though? Things might get tricky if . . .*

And then the most terrible thought occurred to him.

"Leona," he said, hardly daring to speak it out loud, but knowing that he must. "If magic no longer works in my world, does that mean that my cure has been reversed as well?"

"Why do you want to know?"

Felix had to dig his fingernails into the palms of his hands to stop himself from shouting out, *Isn't it obvious? I don't want to think of my parents watching me die within the next few weeks. I don't want to think of Betony stranded in my world, alone.* But, of course, it wasn't obvious. Leona was a sphinx — she'd probably eaten her own parents; she wouldn't understand at all. Or was she giving him a chance *not* to know? What did he want, ignorance or the truth, however bad it was? In the end, all he said was, "It's important to me."

"There's a difference between live magic and dead magic," said Leona. "The twisty-strip DNA thing. A new illusion spell would be live magic, the same as lighting a candle with a wave of your hand. Dead magic is something that's been magically achieved but is no longer actually working. Betony's ears will stay rounded — I assume you did that before you went, because she'd be awfully conspicuous otherwise. And you'll live, Felix, for quite a long time in all prrrobability. In both worlds."

Blazing feathers. That was the best of *all* possible worlds.

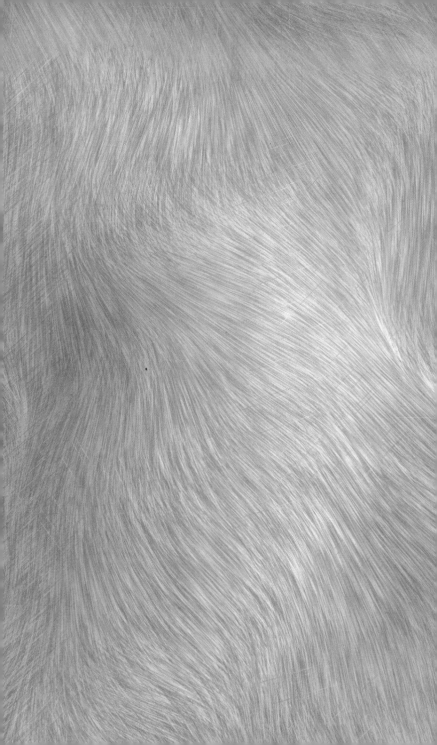